MW00943970

PAPAL JUSTICE

PAPAL

JUSTICE

A CORP JUSTICE NOVEL
BOOK 10 OF THE CORPS JUSTICE SERIES

C. G. COOPER

Copyright © 2015 Corps Justice. All Rights Reserved
Author: C. G. Cooper
Editor: Karen Rought

ISBN: 1514791064
ISBN-13: 9781514791066

**Get a FREE copy of any *Corps Justice* novel just for subscribing at
>> http://CorpsJustice.com <<**

This is a work of fiction. Characters, names, locations and events are all products
of the author's imagination. Any similarities to actual events or real persons are
completely coincidental.
Any unauthorized reproduction of this work is strictly prohibited.

Warning: This story is intended for mature audiences and contains profanity and
violence.

For Kathy Anday-Fallenius, one of the first Corps Justice beta readers. Your generosity and team spirit will not be forgotten. Thank you for the kind words and tireless effort to make me a better author. I know you're still with us, quietly telling me to dot every "i" and cross every "t". God Bless.

To my loyal group of Novels Live warriors, thanks for your help in crafting this novel. Much fun was had by all.

To our amazing troops serving all over the world, thank you for your bravery and service.

And especially to the United States Marine Corps. Keep taking the fight to the enemy. Semper Fidelis

CHAPTER 1

Father Pietro wiped a bead of sweat on the sleeve of his black cassock and leaned against the crumbling concrete wall. The muggy blanket of Mexican steam felt even more intense despite the late hour. Maybe it was the booze. As he stopped to catch his breath, he heard singing in the distance, capped by the distinctive tenor of Father Josef, the head of their small church.

Father Pietro pulled the small bottle of rum out of his pocket and took a burning gulp. He relished the heat moving down his throat as he listened to the hymns signaling the start of the midnight mass. He said a silent prayer of gratitude for the bartender who'd given him the bottle, on the house of course. No doubt the man thought it would usher him into heaven when the time came. If that was the man's wish, who was Father Pietro to disagree? He'd seen all manner of wonders since arriving in Mexico, but none of them of the miraculous nature.

1

Five-year-old drug runners. Nine-year-old prostitutes. Thirteen-year-old cartel enforcers. They were supposed to be his flock, but his gifts had done little to bring them into the fold. Instead, it was Father Josef's love of music that had persuaded a trickle, then a steady flow of new parishioners to join their young community. "Music," Father Josef had said, "has the power to touch the hearts of even the most lost of God's flock."

When Pietro thought of Father Josef, he hiccuped a giggle. Josef had admonished him on more than one occasion for being late or missing an event completely. But what could Father Pietro do? He knew his weaknesses, had admitted them to Father Josef, and although he tried his best to improve, to wipe away his sins, he knew in his soul that it would take a momentous occasion to turn him away from the bottle. It was, after all, the least of his many sins.

Father Pietro was a good man. The poor of Acapulco loved to hear his stories, and they even stopped by to say hello when they were passing through. He'd found a home of sorts, but he missed his home in Italy every minute of every day.

He sighed and took another drink before tossing the empty bottle onto a pile of trash overflowing from the curb and onto the street. The Catholic priest moved on down the dusty sidewalk before the flies he'd disturbed took their wrath out on him. Dealing with Father Josef would be bad enough, but at least now he would have some liquid courage. Thank the Lord for the smallest blessings.

Father Pietro was just rounding the last corner a block before the squat church building came into view, when the squealing of old brakes filled the street. He'd been caught in more than his share of shootings and thought that this could be another. He hid behind a dented blue dumpster and watched as men poured out of three cars as well as a pair of oversized delivery vans. His chest tightened when he saw where they were going, straight into the midnight mass at La Iglesia De La Virgen Bendecida, The Church of The Blessed Virgin.

Screams followed, but were silenced by two gunshots. Father Pietro trembled, mouthing a prayer, his drunken haze gone in a burst of fear. Two more shots sounded, snatching the prayer from his lips. There was shouting, and he could just barely make out a few words, "No one move," and, "Quiet that baby."

He had to do something, but what? Thankfully, whoever was in charge of replacing streetlights in the neighborhood had never done so. Cloaked in black he would be difficult to see. It would be easy to turn and run. No one could fault him if he went to find help, but who would he seek? The police would be of little help at this time of night. They knew the risks of roaming the streets at this late hour as much as common citizens.

Despite his other flaws, Father Pietro was no coward. He'd served in the Italian Army before finding God and The Church. He'd killed other men and nearly lost his own life on more than one occasion. Dying wasn't something he feared. He'd faced it before and somehow he came out unscathed. Some days he prayed for death, yet another item on his growing list of sins.

Swallowing what was left of his apprehension, Pietro picked a point across the street, sprinting there as quickly and as quietly as he could. After finding another hiding spot at the corner, his heart in his throat, his breath coming in gulps,

Father Pietro looked down the block. The sentries were still standing in the same spot, one looking down the road and the other watching the front door of the church.

Thank you, Lord.

Now that he was on the same side of the street as the church, he had more options. One of the benefits of his late night binges was that he knew the area well. He'd slipped into the rented apartments he and his fellow priests lived in next door to their humble church on more than one occasion. Without waiting until fear got the best of him, Pietro took his familiar path around the building and down the back alley.

Either the attackers didn't know the back entrance was there or they didn't care. Luckily, the rear avenue was empty. With his right arm grazing the wall, he moved to the back door. He slipped his key out of his pocket and inserted it into the lock. The door opened with a muted click. Slowly, he pushed the door open and slid into the darkness.

He could hear more shouting now, the thin walls separating the chapel from the living quarters doing little to muffle the sounds. Father Pietro hurried to the small shared bathroom and the discovery he'd made only days before when looking for a place to hided his assortment of after-hours beverages. Whether a product of bad construction or due to the needs of a past tenant, the priest had found a loose ceiling tile. It allowed anyone who knew of its presence to slide the tile aside and peek into the modest chapel.

The sounds of children crying and women pleading made him move as fast as he dared. He stepped onto the edge of the bathtub, getting his hand on the faded panel overhead. He had to place his other foot on the soap holder across the tub in order to lift himself up. He then pushed the ceiling tile aside and pulled his head up through the space.

He almost fell when he saw the scene next door. Two small bodies lay sprawled on the floor, each head lying in a pool of crimson blood. They were only children. Thankfully, he couldn't see their faces because he would have lost his footing; he knew every person in the congregation.

Other than the masked men, Father Josef was the only person standing. The rest of his flock was on their knees, cowering from the intruders. After a quick scan of the space, Pietro counted at least thirty worshippers on the ground, including the two boys, already dead.

"The younger priests and the children under thirteen, stand up now," came the order from one of the masked men. Then to his men he said, "Take them to the vans." The voice was accented, but not in any Mexican dialect Pietro had ever heard. The man was speaking proper Spanish, but there were hints of something that tingled the edges of the priest's brain.

"Please, take me instead," pleaded Father Josef.

"We don't need you, old man," said the man with the AK-47. "I said get up!" He swiveled his weapon at the huddled figures for effect, a handful of young boys finally standing. "You too, boy," he said, pointing at a small child named Francisco.

"He's only a baby!" wailed his mother, her arms wrapped protectively around her other child, a newborn swaddled in a baby blue blanket.

The man's weapon shifted and a burst of machine-gun fire sent bullets slicing into both mother and child.

Father Pietro clapped his free hand over his mouth. He knew the mother well; he had baptized her baby a week before. In that moment, the Catholic priest wished he had a rifle back in his hands. At least then he could have done something. He felt hot angry tears streaming down his face.

"Now, who else wants to die?" asked the masked man.

"Please, no more," pleaded Father Josef, bending down to comfort the boy who'd just become an orphan.

Just then, Father Pietro's foot slipped and he barely caught himself from falling, banging his knee against the wall with a dull thud. Every weapon turned his way. Luckily his head had slipped from view.

"What was that?" Pietro heard the man say.

Father Josef answered quickly. "Bad pipes. They make sounds all night."

Father Pietro tried to calm his breathing as he waited for an extended moment, fully expecting a combined spray of bullets to pierce the wall and his body at any second. The blinding pain never came.

"Get up, all of you. The priests and the children to the door."

Pietro heard shuffling and the murmuring of his people. He had to know what was happening, so he retook his position overlooking the scene, this time making sure he was more stable on his precarious perch.

The parishioners were doing as ordered, and even the two newest priests were over by the front door. Four masked men herded the group by the door onto the street. Father Josef and the others gathered near the makeshift altar.

The leader of the disguised men, joined by two of his compatriots, stepped closer. As soon as the front door slammed closed, he lifted off his mask, glaring at Father Josef.

"Say your last prayers, priest, because tonight you will face Allah's judgment."

If the threat frightened the devout priest, he didn't show it. Instead, he nodded, and turned to his people.

"Please kneel, and pray with me."

Father Pietro watched as they all obeyed, whimpering at the danger just feet away, all kneeling with the priest whose magnificent voice had gathered them together for the celebratory mass.

Father Josef, joined by what remained of his congregation, bowed his head and began praying, "Our Father, who art in Heaven, hallowed be Thy name…"

The rest of the words were drowned out by the thundering rattle of machine gun fire, rounds assaulting the bodies of the assembled innocents, blood spraying and bodies slumping into piles. All Father Pietro could do was watch in horror, fists clenched, hoping that their murders would one day be avenged.

CHAPTER 2

Father Pietro stepped down into the tub so he wouldn't have to see the carnage, his hands cupped over his ears as soon as he hit the ground. His heart ached for the children, for the mothers and for Father Josef. When the gunfire stopped, he sat and waited. The familiar voice of the leader still spoke in Spanish for some reason, even though Pietro's mind had already deduced that the man was some sort of Islamic fanatic. But when he'd gotten a glance at the man's face, he was sure it wasn't Arabic, maybe Spanish or even Italian, but not Arabic.

"You two, go next door and make sure the old man was telling the truth. Meet us back at the warehouse after you're done."

There were grunts from the men and the sound of doors opening and closing. Father Pietro knew he had to go, but where? Surely they would come in from the front and the back entrances. That's what he would have done. That's what he and his men had done.

The back door was the closest, so he decided to close the gap, his senses heightened by the thought of getting his hands on the murderers. It wasn't what a proper Catholic priest should do, but in that moment, Pietro slipped back into his former role, his training taking over.

Doing a quick scan as he crept forward, nothing that could be used in his defense came to mind. He'd have to do it the hard way since there was no time to go to the tiny kitchen for anything that resembled a weapon.

He said a prayer as he settled in next to the rear entrance, his back soaked in stale sweat as he leaned against the wall. The light switch was on the other side, but the intruder wouldn't know that.

Father Pietro heard the front door slam open just as the back door did the same. He caught sight of the tip of a muzzle, its owner scanning the entryway.

Stupid, thought Pietro. You never gave your enemy a glimpse. He knew what was coming.

The man with the gun rushed in, looking right, then moving to look left. That was when Father Pietro's clasped hands crashed down on the man's hand, making him bobble the rifle.

The priest bowled the man over. There was a brief struggle for the weapon, and thankfully he never pulled the trigger, but he did call out for his friend. "Help!"

Father Pietro almost panicked, grabbing the man's head with both hands. But then his anger drove him, all thoughts of forgiveness flew from his mind. He slammed the man's head into the tiled floor, once, then again, and again. After the third thud, the man was no longer moving.

The priest didn't hesitate. He grabbed the man's weapon and moved into the next room, padding quietly as the dead man's accomplice called from the front.

"Where are you?"

Pietro kept moving. A light flicked on in the front hall, then another in the kitchen.

Another stupid move. If it had been Pietro, he would have left the lights off. Better to stalk his prey. But as he'd found in countless operations against the Mafiosi, most human beings were scared of the dark. The only shadows Father Pietro feared were the demons in his dreams.

Weapon scanning, lungs and heart settling, Pietro kept his eyes over the front sight post, a small part of him relishing the feel of a gun in his hands. He wasn't helpless anymore.

No more calls from the front, only the noisy whirr from the ancient refrigerator in the kitchen. As Pietro peered from the darkness, ready to slip around the final corner, machine gun spat lead into the hallway, taking out chunks of cheap drywall and shattering a mirror to the priest's right.

Instead of falling back, Father Pietro rolled into the next room, well below the stream of bullets. It was almost always the same. Enemies rarely aimed low.

The barrel of his automatic weapon came up, his muscle memory taking over. Eyes aligned and finger poised, the head of his attacker came into view for a split second. It was all Pietro needed. He depressed the trigger as he got to his feet, every fiber in his still muscular frame working in harmony, tracking his target to the right and through the thin wall. The intruder was no match for his bullets.

Burst after controlled burst rattled from left, then down and right; the exact trajectory of the falling man. Father Pietro knew before he rushed around the corner what he would find.

The submachine gun had fallen from the masked man's hands and was a few feet away. He was still moving, and writhed even more when Father Pietro stomped a foot on the man's chest, pinning him in place.

Pietro ripped the black balaclava from the man's head and two wide eyes looked up at him. Blood ran from his mouth and it opened and closed like a fish that'd been dropped out of water. Father Pietro knew what was coming. There was no saving this man. So he said a silent prayer for the man's soul, and shot him in the face.

By the time he got to the bar, the owner was closing shop.

"Oh, hello, Father."

"Hello, Ignacio. Don't tell me it's already closing time," Father Pietro said, his voice strained from the fifteen-minute sprint away from the massacre.

"Slow night, Father." He paused and looked closer at priest. "Are you well?"

Pietro gave him a quick nod. "Yes, yes. I was just hoping to catch you before you went home." He knew it was a risk. Soon the entire neighborhood would know what had happened. It wasn't that wholesale slaughter was new to the coastal city. Acapulco had gone from a luxury resort town that hosted international celebrities on its beaches for decades, to the most dangerous city in Mexico. Not only had tourism disappeared, but the per capita murder rate had skyrocketed. There was talk of a renewed push by the Mexican government and several rich benefactors to kick out the narco-traffickers, but so far the lost city was still firmly in the hands of Mexico's ruthless drug lords.

The bar owner glanced at his watch, then back at the priest.

"I do have some paperwork to do before tomorrow. Twenty minutes?"

"Thank you, Ignacio."

Father Pietro sat at the sticky bar and stared at the bottle of vodka sitting next to his half-full glass. He'd heard the sirens in the distance, but resisted turning on the television. He didn't want to disturb the owner, who sat at the end of the bar, no doubt keeping tabs on how much his late night patron was drinking.

The sullen priest's mind wandered back to Italy, to his days on the soccer fields around Naples, along the Amalfi Coast and then finally in Rome. He'd been a gifted athlete. His parents hoped and prayed he would become a professional footballer, maybe even playing for their native Società Sportiva Calcio Napoli. Back then he'd been Gabriel Fusconi, the treasured oldest son. But the Fusconi dreams of soccer stardom came to an end when sixteen year old Gabriel came out of a routine knee operation with unexpected complications. Apparently the surgeon, Gabriel would later find out, had obtained his so-called license through the help of a certain powerful Mafiosi. Such practice was common in Italy. Why work hard in school when you can do a few favors and get a law or medical degree in the process just for having the right connections?

Recuperation from the complications took over two years, and by that time Gabriel's window to play his favorite sport had passed. Those were dark days for the entire Fusconi clan. His parents didn't have much, but they worked long hours to see their beloved son through painful physical therapy, all in the hope that he might strap on his cleats again and take his rightful place on the field.

That never happened. The teams that had once been so anxious to sign him now saw him as a liability. Soon phone calls were not returned, and Gabriel was struggling to complete his final year of school. It was on one of those dark days that he happened to pass by a local coffee shop. There were a handful of Carabinieri cruisers and a military troop transport outside, along with a growing crowd of onlookers.

It didn't take long until two men, obviously Mafiosi, were escorted out not by the police, but by six grim faced soldiers in all black military gear. Gabriel couldn't take his eyes off of the scene as the two men were placed into the back of the troop transport by five of the soldiers.

The final soldier, who Gabriel now saw was an officer (although he didn't understand the rank), went back to talk to the head Carabinieri. Something inside Gabriel stirred. Thoughts of the crooked doctor, images of his mother going to mass every night to pray for his healing, the sound of his father beating his hand on the kitchen table as he tried to figure out how they'd pay all their monthly bills…Gabriel pushed his way through the crowd, somehow slipping through the rest of the gawkers. He waited for the burly soldier to finish, and then cut him off before he reached the gray transport.

"Excuse me, sir. How can I do what you do?"

The soldier stopped and looked at Gabriel.

"What makes you think you could do what I do?"

Gabriel didn't back down. He was almost as tall as the man, just over six feet according to his last doctor's visit.

"I used to play soccer. I'm a good athlete. I work hard."

The soldier's eyes narrowed. "It takes more than hard work to do what I do. Go home and play soccer, boy." The soldier continued on his way.

Gabriel felt his world slipping away again.

"I can't play anymore, sir! A Mafiosi doctor messed up my knee in surgery. But I'm better now. See!"

Gabriel squatted down to the ground and jumped as high as he could. The solder turned around again. There was something in his eyes. Compassion, maybe?

"If you really want to do what I do, enlist in the army, and prove yourself."

"But how do I—"

The soldier cut him off with the shake of his head.

"You'll have to figure the rest out on your own. If you want it, you'll figure it out."

And the soldier had been right. With a renewed sense of purpose, Gabriel edged by with his grades and managed to graduate. The same day he went to the local army recruiting station and enlisted. It would be three long years of trials and training before he would get to the elite special forces unit of the 9th Parachute Assault Regiment (also known as Col. Moschin, or "Moschin Hill"), and their recently formed anti-terror squad. It was a natural fit for the young Italian, and soon he was leading his own secret raids across Italy.

But he didn't want to think about those now. He'd lost himself in that world, and was afraid that he'd somehow get sucked back in. The hate and violence were no longer who he was, except in his nightmares.

Father Pietro shook his head, bringing himself back to the present. What he needed was time. Time to think. Time to come up with a plan. Time to somehow get out of Mexico. Then an idea came to him.

"Ignacio, may I use your phone?"

"Yes, Father."

Ignacio set his cell phone on the bar and slid it down to the priest. Father Pietro scooped it up and said, "Do you mind if I take it outside? Just for a moment."

The owner waved him to the door and went back to his work.

Father Pietro dialed the number from memory, a long ago promise for aid giving him hope for the first time that night. He waited through two rings, then a third. Maybe he'd dialed wrong? Maybe his old friend was no longer alive? Maybe...

Just when his hope seemed as if it would fade into the night, someone answered.

"Yes?"

Despite the one word answer, Father Pietro recognized the raspy voice immediately.

"My friend, I need your help," Pietro whispered.

"Gabriel?"

The priest almost didn't answer.

"Yes, it's me."

A grunt and a chain smoker's wet cough came through the phone before the voice replied, "Tell me how I can help."

CHAPTER 3

The Pope stepped into the private waiting room without his normal retinue. His snow white cassock swept over the threshold, and all five robed men in the room went to their knees.

"Rise, my most cherished brothers. Please."

One by one they rose, taking their cues from the smallest form in front, a hunched man in a brown monk's robe. His eyes glistened when he looked up.

"Holy Father," the monk said, punctuated by a wet cough.

The pontiff embraced the old man and whispered into his ear, "I see time is catching up with you as well, old friend. We are a long way from our running days in Argentina."

The man nodded and stifled another cough. "I apologize for disturbing you, Holy Father."

The Pope smiled and waved the apology away. "Who better than a beloved friend to excuse me from the babbling of Vatican accountants?" He chuckled but his eyes were searching the old man's face. He waved the five visitors into seats at a simple round wooden table. "Now, why was it you wanted to see me?"

The head of the Brotherhood of St. Longinus clasped his hands in his lap, his eyes hard, like he'd just remembered who he was.

"Holy Father, word has reached me that there was an attack against one of our parishes in Mexico."

"I hadn't heard." The Pope's face scrunched in concern. He leaned closer, putting both hands on the table.

"The news will most likely come to your attention soon."

"And how do you know of this attack?"

The hunched form shrugged. "I received a call from an old friend, someone who helped me in the past."

"Is he trustworthy, this man? Who is he?"

"When I knew him, his name was Gabriel. Now he goes by Father Pietro."

"He's a priest?"

"He is, Holy Father."

"Why did he contact you, why not his diocese, or his bishop?"

"I think he believed I could help."

The Pope sat back and digested the news. It was a moment before he replied.

"Does he know about your brotherhood?"

"He does not, Holy Father."

The Pope nodded. "Good. Now, tell me what happened."

The robed man retold Father Pietro's story, along with the priest's description of his attackers, and what he'd done in the apartment next to the church.

The Pope's eyes went just perceptibly wide.

"Let us say a prayer for our brothers and sisters," the Pope said, bowing his head. The others did the same. After a short blessing for those lost and those gone missing, the head of the Roman Catholic Church looked up again. "This is grave, my friend. Do you believe this Father Pietro? How was it that he was able to do what he did?"

There was no accusation in the Pope's tone, just curiosity.

"Father Pietro was a special forces soldier in the Italian army. He saved my life on one of his operations. I owe him a great debt."

"This Father Pietro sounds like more of a man who should be part of your order, no?"

The old man nodded. "He would have made a good brother, but he wanted a break from his old life. There was an…incident that brought him to The Church."

"Ah. God's plans."

Both men nodded as if they'd had this same conversation many times in the past, the mysteries of God's plan and what it meant for humankind.

"He has a good heart, but his past still weighs heavily on his conscience. Even after almost a decade, I could hear the remorse in his voice."

"And you would like to go to him?" the Pope asked.

"As much as it pains me to say it, Your Holiness, my health now keeps me from such a journey. My brothers are more than capable of handling the situation."

"Very well. You know my trust resides with you. You have my blessing to investigate this further. I will do what I can to get you any help you need."

The Pope rose from his seat, the others rising with him.

"Now, if you'll excuse me, I must inform my advisors of our loss."

———

As soon as the Pope closed the door, Brother Luca eased himself back down into his chair. His face was slick with sweat.

"Can we assist you, Brother?" asked another monk, this one a full head taller than Luca.

"I'm fine. Just let me catch my breath."

Brother Luca knew his time was coming. The doctors had given him six months to live, but that was eight months ago. So far he'd done what he'd always done, defied the odds. He hadn't expected the well of emotion to hit him when he saw the pontiff, but the sight of his old friend, the holiest man he'd ever met, filled his weakened body with a relief so profound that he'd almost forgotten why they'd come.

His mind was clearing, and now that he had the blessing of the only man who could put the brotherhood in action, he went back to analyzing what the jihadi's motives might be. The first thing that had come to mind when Father Pietro had told him about the massacre was that this wouldn't be the last. That issue worried the old warrior. If there was one thing he'd learned about this new breed of terror, it was that random acts rarely occurred. No, there was something more insidious happening. He could feel it in his crumbling bones.

With more than a little effort, he stood again and said, "Come, brothers, we have preparations to make."

———

The Pope thumbed his rosary as he walked. It was an old habit from his days in Buenos Aires, when he'd walk the barrios and talk with the poor children as they played in the hot Argentine sun. Seeing Brother Luca brought those memories back in a flood of color.

When he'd first met Luca, the Pope had been a young priest, a child really. His heart was full and his mind constantly thought of ways to help the people of Buenos Aires. It was on one of those long walks that he'd encountered a policeman roughly his age. Back then Luca was a strapping young man, a favorite with the ladies in the neighborhood. He had a penchant for being more than a little full of himself, but the instant they met, they both saw the goodness in each other.

But while Luca might have been a kind and generous man, he was conversely a misguided public servant. He had no problem looking the other way in exchange for crisp bills slipped into his pocket.

He'd asked Luca about it one day, and the policeman had said, "It's no big deal. Part of the job." With a shrug and a smile he'd continued the patrol, his carefree spirit trailing behind him like a superhero's cloak.

But the good times did not last. As both men ascended the steps of their chosen professions, they went their separate ways. The future pope spent time in faraway lands like Israel, Ireland, and Germany. It was only when he returned as the new Archbishop of Buenos Aires that the two men met again.

By that time, Luca was head of the special operations branch of the Buenos Aires police force. He'd made quite a name for himself since his friend had left, taking down a fair share of thugs, counterfeiters and had even made a dent in the growing number of fledgling drug organizations.

But the Archbishop knew as soon as he embraced his friend in Luca's lavish penthouse apartment that Luca was still living his old life, dipping his beak in countless wells to afford such luxury.

They spent the occasional dinner together, the Archbishop always slipping a subtle warning to his friend, but Luca chuckled it away, obviously enjoying his duplicitous life.

Then, eighteen months after arriving back in his home town, he'd received a hurried call from Luca.

"I think I'm in trouble. They're outside and they've brought many men."

There was a banging sound in the background that made it hard to hear what the policeman was saying.

"Who's there, Luca? What's happening?"

Suddenly, a loud crash erupted through the receiver and he heard a scream followed by gunshots. The phone went dead. He called the police and told them what happened. They promised to check on the situation.

Two hours later, he got a call from a policeman who'd been tasked with informing the popular Archbishop about the situation.

"The lieutenant is in critical condition, Your Excellency."

"Please, tell me where he is."

He could tell that the lowly messenger had been told not to say, but he was the Archbishop after all. The policeman told him where to find Luca, and after saying his thanks, he rushed to find his driver, and made the journey to see his friend.

Luca remained in a medically-induced coma for almost a month. During that time, the Archbishop made daily visits to the hospital, always smiling at the grim-faced policemen that stood guard outside the patient's room. Word had spread. Luca was a dirty cop. That was fine when it was kept out of the papers and when he took care of the citizens of Buenos Aires, but now he'd gotten his due. His nefarious business dealings had finally caught up with him.

When he awoke, Luca would only speak with his old friend. So while the Argentine police commissioner wanted Luca's neck, the Archbishop pleaded for mercy.

It was finally decided that the substantial wealth Luca had amassed, including a villa, a penthouse and several businesses, would be sold and the proceeds would be given to the underfunded police force. Luca would be out of a job, but the future Pope had faith that a solution would present itself. And it did.

Only days after Luca signed away his rights to his property, the Archbishop's office got a call from Rome. They wouldn't say why, but the Vatican was searching for former elite military who might consider a new life in Rome.

It didn't take much to convince Luca, whose normally cheerful countenance had turned into a dour shell. When he'd last seen Luca all those years ago, it was on the tarmac saying farewell to his friend, bidding him Godspeed in his new life.

It wasn't until the day he'd been anointed Pope and was given the secrets that so many pontiffs before him had kept sacred that he found out about the Brotherhood of St. Longinus, and its current head, Brother Luca, his old friend from Buenos Aires.

This was the first time he'd had occasion to use the secret brotherhood, but he knew they were well up to the task. Named for the Roman Centurion who'd thrust his lance into Jesus's side upon crucifixion and later converted to Christianity and a life of service, the Brothers of St. Longinus came from elite organizations all over the world, most broken until the brotherhood rebuilt them.

A thought came to the Pope as he neared where his Secretariat of State stood waiting. They were due to meet with the American president within the hour. There was much to discuss, including the spread of radical Islam. The Pope wondered what the president would think if he knew that a new group of radicals was operating south of his own porous border.

He said a silent prayer of thanks for the revelation, and carefully thought about how he could orchestrate a quiet moment alone with the increasingly popular President Brandon Zimmer.

CHAPTER 4

President Brandon Zimmer offered the flashing cameras a smile as the Pope shifted in the chair next to him. The initial meeting between the Vatican staff and his own administration had gone well. This being his first trip to Rome as president, Zimmer's intent was to not make waves. While he didn't necessarily agree with everything the Catholics did, he did respect the man sitting in the chair next to him. His public persona seemed accurate, humble, honest, and straight to the point.

Zimmer's life had always revolved around politics. From the time he was in diapers, he'd been on one campaign trail or another, first for his father, the late Senator Richard Zimmer (D-Massachusettes), and then for himself. His first year as president had been anything but smooth-sailing. There wasn't much he hadn't seen, from dark negotiating rooms to international crises. It was like getting a PhD in human psychology through a fire hose. He often joked with his chief of staff, former SEAL Travis Haden, that their days were divided between *The Good*, *The Bad*, and *The Ugly*.

And through it all, the good-looking American president had honed his skills as an observer, always taking in his opponents and his friends alike. His father had always said, "If anyone ever wanted to hone their bullshit detector, I'd tell them to go into politics." It was true. The actors on the political stage were exceptional in their craft. Zimmer had learned to look past the facade, to see the truth of what lay beneath.

But more than uncovering an unsavory character or pinpointing the true motives of a career politico, Zimmer enjoyed meeting a person who was absolutely genuine in his positive outlook of the world and his place in it. The president knew that the pontiff was such a man. The whole world knew of the man's history, knew of his life of giving, his quest to help the impoverished and persecuted. Zimmer and Haden had agreed: say what you want about the institution, but the heart of the man was what you could really respect.

Zimmer watched as the Pope joked with the cameramen and even poked fun at an Italian journalist. They laughed back, and their response wasn't forced. They loved this man. And why shouldn't they? There was something otherworldly about him, like a glowing orb of pure love surrounded him. Zimmer felt drawn to it. He wanted to step inside and see what it felt like.

A bell rang somewhere in the distance and the Pope raised a finger.

"Gentlemen, I believe that is our cue to adjourn."

The reporters looked disappointed, like they wanted to stay with the man who'd captured the attention of Catholics around the world. As the camera crews packed up their things, the joint contingent of Secret Service and plainclothes Swiss Guard escorted the two heads of state from the room. The president and the Pope walked side by side, the latter chatting away about the reporter he'd joked with, apparently a former critic who had for some reason come around.

"I was hoping to speak with you alone, if you have the time," the Pope said, still following the security.

Zimmer tried not to let his surprise show. The Vatican had been very specific about their timeline. Whoever was in charge of scheduling had the strict discipline of a drill instructor. They'd told their American guests that the Pope was to have lunch with the Sultan of Brunei, or was it Oman?

"I would be honored," Zimmer replied. He didn't have much left on his schedule other than what little sightseeing the leader of the free world could take in. What he wouldn't give for a quiet day of strolling along the streets of Rome like a common tourist.

The Pope touched one of the Swiss Guards on the sleeve and said, "Please take us to my garden."

The man nodded and spoke into his sleeve mike.

It was a simple garden, well-tended, but far from the extravagance of the others he'd seen since entering the Papal Palace. The Pope made his way to a plain wooden bench and sat down. Zimmer did the same, breathing in the fresh March air mingled with the smell of freshly cut grass and damp earth.

"I assume this isn't on the public tour," Zimmer said, marveling at the way the emerald ivy made its way up the steep stone walls.

"No. This is my private garden. Soon I will plant tomatoes, some flowers and peppers that a friend from Argentina has promised to send."

Zimmer nodded. He could see the Pope as a gardener, as content on his hands and knees in the dirt as he was amongst the poorest of the poor.

"Was there something you wanted to speak to me about?"

The Pope's eyes drifted from his visitor to the mounds of dirt waiting for springtime planting.

"I am told that you are a man of your word, Mr. President, that you are someone to be trusted."

For some reason, those words seemed foreign coming from the Pope's mouth, like he'd shifted into another role, into a negotiator.

Zimmer nodded. "And I have heard the same thing about you."

Where is he going with this? Zimmer thought.

"I do not know how much you know about our history, but were you aware that, centuries ago, popes were conquerors, warriors of the Catholic faith?"

"I am. Don't they call Julius the Second the Warrior Pope?"

The Pope chuckled. "Ah, yes. Some days I wish I could know him, see him both in his armor and in the Sistine Chapel yelling up at Michelangelo."

Zimmer laughed. "That would be something to see."

"Yes, yes it would." The Pope went silent, and then folded his hands together. "I was wondering, do you have men at your disposal, men that you absolutely trust, who help you in times of crisis?"

Alarms bells clanged in Zimmer's head. "I'm happy to say that I do. Our military has proven itself on numerous occasions, even during my short time in office."

A slow nod from the Pope. "Perhaps I should have asked the question differently. Are there men at your disposal who possibly only you know about? I believe they call them operatives in the modern world, silent warriors who do your bidding?"

Zimmer resisted the urge to frown. He'd been sucked in like a rookie councilman. It was time to cut this off. "Is there something I can help you with? Has something happened?"

The Pope took a moment to respond. When he did, his eyes had lost a little bit of their luster. "Just before you arrived, I received word that a small Catholic parish was attacked. Half of them were murdered, the other half have been kidnapped."

"I'm sorry to hear that. Where did it happen?"

"In Acapulco, Mexico."

"Do you know who did it?"

"I have been led to believe that it may be jihadists."

Zimmer's throat tightened. He'd been receiving reports of increased terrorist activity in Mexico. So far they'd kept to the shadows, only playing an occasional hand. Zimmer always had the feeling they were being tested, like an enemy probing the defensive perimeter to find weaknesses. Nobody had to tell the president about his country's weaknesses. He'd been to the border. He'd flown over the hundreds of miles of separation between the U.S. and Mexico. So far, no one had come up with a good solution for the problem, and that was something that concerned Zimmer every single day.

"Have you confirmed this?" Zimmer asked, now understanding a bit more why the Pope had brought up the attack.

"I have not, but a trusted advisor gave me the information."

"Are you planning on letting the media know?"

"I had hoped you could give me the answer to that question, Mr. President."

So there it was. The Pope was telling him about the snake slithering in America's backyard, and without the means to do anything about it directly, he was asking Zimmer if he could do something. It wasn't the first time a foreign entity had asked for covert assistance, but it was the last thing he'd expected coming to Rome.

"I would recommend keeping any mention of terrorists out of the media, at least for the time being."

"I thought the same. But the next question would be how do we deal with the situation at hand?"

"I'm sure my people can help. Off the top of my head, I can think of a number of units that can—"

"I am not asking you to do it alone, Mr. President. I am not without my own resources."

At least that was something.

"You mean like contacts in Mexico?"

The Pope shook his head, a smile reappearing.

"You mentioned the warrior pope a moment ago. What if I told you that although I do not have the ability to strap on a suit of armor or jump from a helicopter, I too have a group of men specifically suited for this task?"

The first thing that came to Zimmer's mind was the Swiss Guard. They were one helluva fighting force, but they were far from elite Special Forces.

"Who are they?" Zimmer asked.

"Have you ever heard of Saint Longinus?"

Zimmer's mind searched through the creaky cupboard of childhood Sunday school memories.

"He was Roman." After another second to think, he added, "He was at the crucifixion."

The Pope nodded. "Yes. He drove his spear into Jesus's side. From there, the story is different depending on who is telling the tale. According to official Papal records, Saint Longinus left the Roman military and started his own order. He recruited fellow warriors who had converted to the Christian faith. Eventually they found St. Peter, the first Pope of what was to become the Catholic Church. They swore loyalty to the papacy, and thus, the Brotherhood of Saint Longinus was born. Saint Longinus would die soon after, murdered for his beliefs, but the brotherhood lived on, as it still does today. Every member of the brotherhood was once part of one of the world's elite paramilitary organizations. They are carefully selected, and it takes years before a new member is given the opportunity to serve. For many, this was their last resort. But they are unquestioning in their loyalty, and boundless in their faith."

This was all news to Zimmer. For a man who could find out almost anything about almost anybody, it surprised the American that there were secrets still left in the world.

"And what does this brotherhood do?"

The Pope shrugged. "They are loyal to the Pope, and the Pope alone. I only learned of their existence when I came to Rome. I'm sure that at times they have been put to ill use. I won't pretend that we Catholics have a perfect reputation. I can assure you that this will not happen as long as I live within these walls. But I understand the wisdom of having such warriors on hand. There is only so much that prayer and loving words can do. Am I wrong in saying that where evil men lurk, only the shining glint of the sword can light the way?"

President Zimmer nodded, his mind spinning.

"What do you plan to do?"

"I will send these warriors to Mexico. They are, after all, Catholic monks. They know how to blend in, in their own way. We have contacts in Mexico who can help them in their search. We could use your assistance, should you be able to do so."

Zimmer didn't have to think long. He had just the outfit that could not only deal with the terrorist threat, but could blend in as well as the Pope's secret brotherhood. Probably better.

"Your Holiness, I think I have just the men who can help."

CHAPTER 5

It was the perfect day. The midday sun cast down a welcome warmth, elevating the spring air to a gracious seventy-two degrees. Children threw footballs and sprinted up and down the green grass of the outdoor amphitheater in the middle of the small Florida panhandle town. Lines of patrons snaked past each of the silver bullet food trucks that crafted everything from gourmet grilled cheese sandwiches to organic smoothies. The murmur of walkers and the rumble of passing motorcycles blended together to make what Cal Stokes thought of as the ideal spring break cacophony.

The former Marine looked up at the sky and wondered what life would be like if he could stay on vacation permanently. Unlike most men his age, the ruggedly handsome warrior could afford it. His father had started Stokes Security International (SSI), and the company had grown into a security and consulting powerhouse. Cal was no longer working with his deceased father's corporation, but he was still the official owner.

But the Marine in Cal didn't really care about the money. It afforded him the ability to come and go as he pleased, but he'd also ensured that the majority of SSI's profits were either reinvested or distributed to its hard-working employees.

Besides, Cal was having too much fun in his new gig. As founder of The Jefferson Group, Cal Stokes was beholden to only one man: his good friend Brandon Zimmer, the President of the United States of America. The two still kidded each other about what an unlikely pairing they'd once been. But time and bloodshed have a way of bringing men like them together. Once polar opposites, Cal now considered the president to be one of his best friends.

So when the president had called on his friend to become his back pocket asset, Cal hadn't hesitated. Well, at least not much. He didn't give anyone the satisfaction of saying yes right away. It wasn't how his Marine colonel father had brought him up, and it certainly wasn't part of his, at times, stubborn personality.

A content smile made its way onto his face as he closed his eyes and enjoyed the sun's soothing rays, a nap coming on before long.

"Get up, sleepy head, it's time for lunch."

Cal rolled over and looked up at Diane Mayer, his girlfriend, and one of the best things he had going. She was wearing a teal knee-length cover-up over her bathing suit, and he couldn't see her eyes through her oversized sunglasses. That didn't matter. The same thought came flashing to his mind as quick as her playful smile. *She is beautiful.*

"Do we have to? It's so nice down here."

Cal reached up and grabbed her hand, trying to pull her down to the ground.

"I'm serious, Cal, I got a table."

He groaned and got to his feet. If there was anything he didn't need right now, it was more food. The CEO of The Jefferson Group (TJG), Jonas Layton, who also happened to be a billionaire, had rented a beachfront home for all of TJG's employees to stay in. The ten bedroom house was perched on the edge of the Gulf. The view of the emerald and aqua water was amazing, and the food was right on par with the best restaurants on the coast. Their secret? TJG's resident professionally trained chef and former Marine, Master Sergeant Willy Trent. From shrimp boils on the beach to oyster po'boys on the deck, the nearly seven foot tall former Marine stuffed his friends the only way he knew how, first class.

Cal and Diane were almost to the popular *Shrimp Shack*, where Diane had already declared that they would be ordering a dozen raw oysters and one of their famous lobster rolls, when the phone in Cal's pocket buzzed. He pulled it out and Diane nudged him with her elbow.

"I thought you left that at the house," she said.

"You know I can't do that, babe." He looked down at the caller ID. "I have to take this. Put in our order, okay? This should only take a minute."

Diane sighed, but she nodded and stepped into the tiny restaurant to place their order. Cal walked toward the beach and answered his phone.

"Yes, your highness?"

"Cal, I told you only to call me that when we're in the presence of ladies," President Zimmer answered immediately, completely serious.

Cal chuckled. "I apologize. I'll have to remember to grovel a little more when we go out clubbing next time."

The president returned the laugh. "I'm sorry to call. I know it's the first vacation you've had in a while."

"No problem. What's up?"

"I'm at Eglin, paying my respects. I was wondering if you might have time to drive over."

An Army Blackhawk helicopter had gone down two days earlier in a training accident near Santa Rosa Beach. Seven Marine Raiders and four National Guardsmen were killed. Cal and his TJG team had hoisted more than a few drinks to their memory.

"How long will you be there?"

"We're leaving tonight."

Cal did the math in his head. Eglin Air Force Base was just over an hour from Seaside, but with spring break traffic it might take longer.

"How about I leave right after lunch? See you just after two o'clock?"

"Perfect. I'll see you then."

Cal ended the call and went to find Diane. She was sitting under a white pavilion gazing out over the beach, her blond hair dancing in the breeze. Despite his recent disinterest in eating, he sat down next to her and attacked the raw oysters that Diane was sprinkling with lemon juice.

"I thought you weren't hungry," she smirked.

Cal could only shrug as he forked a pinch of horseradish and stabbed another oyster. "These are really good."

"Mmmhmm. So, was that the boss?"

Cal nodded. He didn't like to admit it, but he was growing more comfortable with the notion that Diane knew what he did for a living. She still loved him despite the fact that he disappeared for weeks at a time and plunged headlong into gunfire whenever he could.

"I have to drive over to Eglin after lunch."

She didn't look surprised.

"Can I come?"

It had been Brandon who'd suggested that Cal bring Diane into the loop. She'd even been part of TJG's last two operations, serving in a supporting role where she utilized her impressive talents from her days as an enlisted Naval Intelligence analyst. They'd even talked about making the arrangement permanent, at least after Diane completed her last semester at the University of Virginia.

"Sure, why not? If he gets mad, you get to explain that you wouldn't stop crying until I let you come."

Diane huffed and rolled her eyes. "You are impossible, you know that?" She smiled when she said it, entirely used to the constant ribbing from Cal and his friends.

Cal shrugged. "I am who I am."

Two hours later, they drove through the main gate at Eglin AFB, the American flag waving at half mast as they pulled past security.

"Is that for the downed Blackhawk?" Diane asked, pointing at the flag.

"Yeah."

Cal had read the bios on all the fallen Marines. What a loss. They were good men, some of the finest warriors America had. One had even received the Silver Star a week earlier. Tragic that so much talent should go down in a training exercise. But that was life in the military. You never knew which day was going to be your last. So far, Cal and the majority of his companions had dodged fate's cruel aim, but it wasn't for lack of trying.

They pulled into the parking lot of a long nondescript building. Cal had never been there before, but the gate guard had given them perfect directions. He knew they were in the right place because of armored Humvees and military police cruisers surrounding the place. Luckily, a familiar face was waiting outside, and the man pointed to Cal and Diane, saying something to a burly black airman in full combat gear.

Travis Haden met the two visitors halfway, crushing Cal in a bearhug in the process.

"Good to see you," said the former Navy SEAL, who also happened to be Cal's cousin.

"Jeez, Trav. Save it for the ladies."

Travis placed a wet kiss on Cal's forehead and let him go.

"Diane, it's great to see you again."

His hug for her was much more chaste.

"What, no bearhug for me?" Diane asked, kissing Travis on the cheek.

"Are you kidding? Cal might not look like much, but he's a scrapper when it comes to defending your honor," Travis said, motioning for them to follow him into the building.

They walked past the amused looks of the security contingent, and Cal nodded to the Secret Service agents inside the door.

"We just met with the Blackhawk crew's families. He wants to swing by Lejeune on the way home, spend some time with the Raiders too."

"That's good," Cal replied. It was more evidence of how the Massachusetts Democrat had evolved from self-absorbed playboy to the Commander-in-Chief. While Cal would never admit it to Brandon, he was beginning to think that his friend just might go down in history as one of the best presidents who'd ever lived.

"He's in here," Travis said, although the comment was unnecessary. There were four gun-toting special operations troops with full beards standing watch outside the door. They nodded to Travis as he walked in the door, and gave Cal a once-over as he passed.

The door closed behind them and President Zimmer stood from where he'd been reading a thick file behind an old metal desk.

"Well hello, strangers," he said, coming around the desk to give Diane a hug, and Cal a handshake that turned into an embrace. "I'm sorry to take you away from the beach, guys."

"It's no problem, Mr. President," Diane said. "Cal promised me a hop in Air Force One."

Zimmer looked at Cal, who was shaking his head. The president chuckled.

"She's as bad as you are."

"Worse," Cal added, receiving a playful slap on the shoulder from his girlfriend. "Any word on what caused the crash?"

Zimmer shook his head, the smile fading from his lips. "They think it might've had something to do with the fog, but they're not sure yet."

Everyone was silent for a moment.

"So what did you want to talk about?" Cal asked.

"Did you know we went to Rome?"

"Yeah. We saw you on TV with the Pope. Good visit?"

Zimmer nodded. "The Pope is a good man. I'm glad I got to meet him." There was hesitation there, something in his eyes that made Cal wonder. He'd assumed the trip up to Eglin was about the crash, that maybe the investigators needed help.

"Is this about the Pope?"

"It is." Zimmer ran a hand through his perfectly sculpted hair. "Honestly, I'm not sure what to make of it. That's why I wanted to talk to you first."

"Okay. Give me the overview."

President Zimmer told Cal about the private conversation with the Pope, about the attack on the small Acapulco parish and possibly others. Finally, he detailed what he knew about the secret brotherhood of warrior monks that the Pope had tasked with finding his kidnapped flock of priests and children.

Cal looked over at Travis, then back to Brandon. "Is this for real? Are you seriously telling me that the Pope has monks that shoot guns and take down bad guys?" He said it in jest, but no one laughed. "Come on, guys, that was just a little funny."

Zimmer didn't even crack a smile. "And the part about jihadist soldiers running around in our backyard?"

"We've been talking about that for years. I'm sure you get reports on this stuff every week. I told you before, it's only a matter of time before they exploit our weaknesses along the border. And don't even get me started about our border with Canada."

"Trust me, I know all about it. My concern is that this is something new. Travis checked with the CIA, and there wasn't even a blip on their radar. If that's the case, we have an obligation to at least check it out."

"You want me to go down there?" Cal asked, not surprised by the president's coming request. He could see it on his face. Brandon's mind was made up.

"I do."

"When?"

"As soon as you can."

Cal shrugged and turned to Diane. "Well, babe, it looks like our time in paradise just got cut short."

CHAPTER 6

Cal didn't say much on the way back to the house. Diane knew better than to pry. Like a lot of men, Cal liked to digest information before coming to a conclusion.

She'd seen the reluctance on his face when the president leveled his request. It wasn't that he didn't trust the president, the opposite was the case, but the analyst in her understood that at times Cal thought he knew better than his good friend Brandon. Not to say that wasn't the case, but Diane might've been a little more subtle in her manners with the leader of the free world, even if he was a good friend.

But that wasn't Cal's style. While she'd instantly seen his drive when they started dating, it wasn't until they started working together that Diane saw the breadth of Cal's personality. His men trusted him because of his confidence. To say it was cockiness would be naïve. Cal Stokes lived and breathed the battles he fought. It was part of who he was. If others didn't like him, they could just pound sand.

It was why men like the president came to Cal for help and guidance. He admitted when he was wrong, asked questions when he didn't understand, and always passed the credit off to his men. She'd asked him once why he thought so many men trusted him, why they put their lives in his hands. He'd shrugged and said, "I guess it's because I'm a Marine, and I'm not afraid to figure it out as I go."

And that was what he was doing now, even as he guided their rental car back to the beach house. His eyes scanned, but his mind was calculating. Diane wondered what he would say when he gathered his men.

The house was empty when they arrived. After grabbing two Coronas from the fridge, Cal and Diane walked out onto the back porch. It led to steps that spilled out onto the white sands of their own private oasis. Cal heard the taunts before he saw them. They were playing eight on eight tag football, shirts versus skins.

Cal stopped and took a sip of his beer. He watched as the two sides collided at the line, and then, despite the deep sand, the mountain who was Master Sergeant Willy Trent broke from the line, heading for the end zone. Jonas Layton was playing quarterback and stepped back to pass.

Gaucho, a short latino with a deep tan and an eccentric dual braided beard, barreled toward him, somehow slipping through the offensive line. Jonas scrambled, heading toward the water, waiting for Trent to get open. And then he launched a perfect spiral that sailed downwind over the defenders' heads, and was snatched out of the air by the the massive Marine.

"Touchdown!" boomed Trent.

The skins team's arms shot up as they howled at their opponents.

"Twenty-one to fourteen," called Neil Patel from his beach chair on the sidelines. He had his prosthetic leg perched on a large blue cooler. The dark-skinned Indian had his ever-present laptop open, probably hacking into something he shouldn't or coming up with another multi million-dollar idea, even as he kept tabs on the game.

Cal hated to wreck the moment. He would have rather gone down and substituted for one of his men, but duty called. He whistled to get their attention. Heads turned his way.

"Bar's open in five minutes." He pointed back to the house. If any of the TJG warriors were disappointed, they didn't show it. He'd given them a heads-up about where he and Diane were going. They knew something was cooking and they were used to this life. One minute you were lounging by the pool with a cocktail in your hand, the next you were flying overseas.

Cal and Diane headed back into the house. The first to join them was Daniel "Snake Eyes" Briggs. The blonde haired Marine sniper was retying his ponytail when he stepped in.

"How did it go?" he asked, grabbing a bottle of water from the wine fridge.

Cal wished he'd had time to bring Daniel with him. Not only was the sniper his near-constant companion and pseudo-bodyguard, he was also the calming influence to Cal's fiery tendencies.

"He said to say hello," Cal replied, taking a seat at the end of the large sectional couch.

Daniel looked at Cal for a second like he was going to press, but he sipped his water instead and took a place next to the large kitchen island.

Soon, the rest of the twenty man team, including Diane, were present and waiting. These were professionals and Cal never had to preface any of his briefs with token jargon like, "What I'm about to say is Top Secret," or "This stays in this room." Those things were a given.

"I'll get right to it. The Pope, of all people, asked President Zimmer for assistance. It seems that a small Catholic parish in Mexico was attacked. Half of its members were killed and half were kidnapped. They suspect it's a group of unknown jihadists who did it." That got everyone's attention. They'd often sat around until the wee hours discussing the possibility of a terrorist incursion from the south. Cal knew what they were thinking: Could this be the one? "Apparently, the Pope has a group of warrior monks that he's dispatching to Mexico. The initial plan is to link up with them and see how we can help."

Cal had seen Daniel's normally cool eyes light up at the mention of the monks.

"Is this for real?" asked MSgt Trent, the sweat still running down his chiseled NFL physique.

"Which part?" Cal asked.

"The warrior monks."

Cal wanted to laugh, but he bit back the humor. "That's what the president said."

The room was silent for a moment.

Gaucho asked, "Where did it happen? In what city?"

"Acapulco."

Gaucho's eyebrows rose and Cal saw Trent glance at his best friend.

"What is it?" Cal asked.

"That's where my family's from," said Gaucho.

"Really? I thought they were farther north."

"Most of them are now, but we came from the coast."

That was something. The wheels cranked into a higher gear in Cal's mind.

"Is there anyone who could help us?"

Gaucho didn't immediately answer, and MSgt Trent frowned, staring at his friend.

"I don't think so," Gaucho finally answered. "No one that we could use."

Trent huffed. "That's for sure."

Cal looked back and forth between the former Delta soldier and the huge Marine.

"Do one of you want to tell me what's going on?" Cal asked.

Another looked passed between the two friends.

"Tell him, Gaucho," Trent prodded.

Gaucho nodded slowly.

"My uncle lives in Acapulco."

"Could he help us?" Cal asked, still not understanding Gaucho's hesitation. He'd just told them that terrorists were on their back doorstep. Any contacts would be more than welcome.

Gaucho shook his head.

"I don't think so."

Trent stepped in.

"I said, tell him, Gaucho." This time more forcefully.

Gaucho looked up at his friend. "I will, okay? Back off, Top."

Cal had never seen the two best friends at odds. Taking a page out of Daniel's playbook, Cal waited for Gaucho to explain. There was a trace of pain on his team leader's face, and Cal wanted to know why.

"My uncle was my hero when I was a kid. He's the reason I went into the Army, why I went Special Forces. He was a green beret back in the day. Did a lot of secret stuff that he'd sometimes tell me about. While the rest of my cousins were out playing soccer, I'd sit inside and listen to my uncle. It made us close. He was there when I graduated from boot camp, and even kept in touch after that."

Gaucho paused to take a deep pull from his beer.

"At some point he moved back to Acapulco. I'm not sure when. So naturally, when I was thinking about getting out of the Army, I flew down to talk to him. He'd changed. Instead of the loving guy I remembered, he was now surrounded by bodyguards and lived in some penthouse on the beach. I knew it was bad news: as soon as I pulled up, one of his guys frisked me up and down like I was walking into a Swiss bank. At first I thought that maybe he'd gone to work for the DEA or something; some undercover stuff could have explained it. But as soon as I saw his face, I knew the truth. There was a hardness there, like he'd done things that numbed his emotions. He hugged me like no time had passed, like I was still my younger self. He looked me up and down, appraising me with a smile. "You look good, Gauchito," he said.

"We sat down for a real first class lunch, prepared and served by some guy that kept looking at my uncle for approval. Once the small talk was out of the way, I asked him what was going on, what he was doing for work. He gave me this smile, like he had a secret he couldn't wait to tell me. He told me about moving back to Acapulco, and how hard it had been to find a job. He met a nice girl, and they were thinking about getting married. One night, when they were at some club, a group of thugs started making passes at my uncle's girl. He tried to ignore them, even asked her if she wanted to leave, but she didn't. Finally, one of the thugs was drunk enough to grab her and pull her towards the dance floor. My uncle said he tried to pull her back and head for the door. That was when the other guy pulled a gun and started shooting. My uncle's training kicked in, and pretty soon the guy was bleeding on the floor and his buddies were running for help. That might've been the end of it, but sometime during the fight, two of the guy's shots hit my uncle's girlfriend. She died on the way to the hospital.

"My uncle was pretty torn up after that. He told me he went to the police, but that they had interviewed the witnesses, and none of them could identify the attackers. He knew that was a lie because of the way the bartenders had given the thugs preferential treatment, like they came in all the time. Well, he decided to have a talk with a couple of the bartenders. They refused to talk. So what did he do? He found out where they lived and held them at gunpoint until they talked. After that, it wasn't hard for him to find the guys. The only problem was that they were tied to the reigning drug cartel. That didn't matter to my uncle. He started with the guy who'd taken the shots, and then he got the others. Their bodies ended up as shark food, thrown off a fishing boat my uncle rented."

Cal could see that nothing Gaucho had just told them necessarily disturbed the Mexican-American. Violence was part of their lives. It was what they trained for, and it was what they leveled against criminals.

Gaucho continued. "So he tells me all this, and I could understand, you know? But then his story took a weird turn. He said that the leaders of the cartel came after him, tried to kill him. Somehow he kept them at bay, dealing with two, then four, then ten man teams. I mean, that's what the Army had trained him to do. Finally, I guess after the death toll got too high, whoever was in charge of the cartel asked for a meeting. My uncle was allowed to choose the place. They met, and after an hour of friendly exchanges, they offered my uncle a job. They wanted him to train their men to do what he'd done, and they offered him money, lots and lots of money."

"And he took the job," Cal said.

"Yeah. But the story doesn't end there. After a year or two of training the cartel's troops, my uncle had it all figured out. So what does he do? He kills the leader and takes over. He's now one hundred percent on the dark side. I'm sitting there as he's telling me this, and it's like a stranger had taken over my uncle's body. Same face, same smile, but the heart and soul had changed. He must have seen the look on my face because he said, 'Don't be so surprised. This is the fucking real world, Gauchito.' And then he really shocked me, really made me realize he didn't know me at all. After all that, my uncle has the nerve to offer me a job, to do the same thing he did, training the troops."

No wonder this was a sore spot for Gaucho.

"What did you tell him?"

Gaucho snorted. "I told him he was going to hell, and that he could shove his job up his ass."

There were chuckles around the room, the mood lightening in the face of Gaucho's surprise revelation.

"And that's how you left it? He let you go?"

Gaucho shook his head.

"He let me go, sure. But not before he told me something that I'll never forget."

"What did he say?"

"He looked me straight in the eye and said that if he ever saw me again, he'd put a bullet in my head."

The room went quiet. Everyone waited on either Gaucho or Cal to break the silence. Finally, Cal laughed because it was the only thing he could think to do, and said, "Well, anyone else got any uncles in Mexico?"

CHAPTER 7

Metal grinding and the incessant hammering of factory workers below came in muffled clangs to the ears of the two men in the third story foreman's office. Everything was metal and dirty, except for the desk. Each sheet of paper was arranged neatly, and even the pencils and pens were standing at rigid attention in their lucite holder. Behind the desk, El Moreno listened as his client went on and on about their lack of progress.

"We should be at the border by now," said the jihadi. "If you cannot deliver, we will find help elsewhere."

Were there not so much at stake, El Moreno, the diminutive cartel jefe, would have put a bullet in the man's head. The leader, whose deep caramel skin was a result of African slave ancestors bred with Mexican Indians, smelled an opportunity. His fledgling cartel was muscling its way into coastal towns along the Pacific Ocean. Their progress in the last month alone eclipsed the moves he'd made in the previous year. The other cartels called them outcasts, peasants and even freaks, but El Moreno didn't care. He'd been called much worse, had been treated like a slave for much of his childhood. He could put up with the insults of his peers and even the complaints of this foreigner.

"We have paid you millions, and yet you continue to take tiny steps to our goal," the jihadi continued.

"Felix, I made you a promise and I do not go back on my word." He said it slowly, as if talking to a child. But the calm menace in his voice finally got through to the man standing across the small office.

"I do not doubt your word, but the men I answer to—"

"Are not here, Felix. Tell me, do they trust you?"

"Of course." The man huffed, puffing his chest like his honor was being questioned.

"And if you told them that you were merely being cautious, that the mission will be accomplished despite the needed delay, would they believe you?"

The hesitation on Felix's face was plain. Despite whatever boasts the man made, El Moreno knew that the terrorist held no real power. He was a pawn and nothing more. He'd just admitted it to a man who was accustomed to putting such knowledge to good use.

"What are you insinuating?" Felix asked, trying to regain a measure of his pride.

"Nothing, my friend. I am only reminding you that *you* are in charge, are you not?"

Felix nodded, reminding El Moreno of a circus monkey he'd once seen on a trip with his orphanage.

"Good." El Moreno pulled out a cigarette and tapped it on his desk. "Now, when are you going to tell me what you have in mind for the priests and children we've been keeping for you?"

"That is none of your concern. Your job is to ensure our safety, and get us to the border."

El Moreno nodded as he pulled out a cheap butane lighter and lit his cigarette. "That is true, but what happens under my roof is my concern."

El Moreno didn't really care what they were going to do with the priests this man had kidnapped. For all he cared they could kill them all. There was the issue of the children, however. Even he wasn't cruel enough to send lambs to slaughter.

But what he really wanted was a glimpse into the jihadi's plan. His men had overheard the terrorist talking about something the foreigners called the *three-headed dragon*. They made it sound like it was a kind of weapon to use against their enemies, the Americans.

Again, El Moreno didn't really care about what the Islamic fools did to Americans, although there was the underlying concern of what it might do to the demand for his goods, but he did want to know what their weapon would be. He'd supplied the foreigners with guns, vehicles and food after picking them up from a deserted bus station weeks before. There had been no shipments, minimal phone calls, nothing that could be considered a weapon.

He stared at Felix for a long moment, wondering what could motivate an intelligent man like this Spaniard to listen to the orders of some Islamic lunatic half a world away. El Moreno didn't care about the man's religion, it had no real bearing on their business relationship, but he did care about the actions that fanaticism could bring to bear. He often wondered what would possess a man to strap explosives to his chest and run into a crowded cafe. There was no payoff. Even when he'd been beaten, raped, and left for dead, never once had El Moreno thought of letting go. There was too much to live for.

His curiosity took over. "Why are you doing this, Felix? Why do you hate the Americans?"

Felix's faced colored. "Because they are infidels. I am bound by my faith to fight them to my last breath." He thumped his chest to accentuate the point.

Fool, thought the cartel chief. While his peers might send their troops to slaughter, El Moreno cherished his men, took care of them in ways he'd always wished to be taken care of. His actions trickled down and seeped into the streets. Now the downtrodden were starting to look to him as some kind of Robin Hood, a benevolent benefactor who wasn't afraid to walk the streets with them, take meals to their homes and eat with their families. El Moreno knew that if he had the resources of these single-minded terrorists, he might one day take over the drug trade for the entire country.

But now he was done with this conversation. Obviously the proud jihadi wasn't going to divulge his secrets. There was still time for him to pry them out.

El Moreno shrugged, trying to look contrite. "You are right, Felix. Now that I have had time to think about it, we are moving too slowly." He rose from his chair and walked around the desk. "Come, let us see how we can find this missing priest and get you through the American border by the time we promised."

CHAPTER 8

The TJG team came in on six different flights. Cal opted not to bring their own transportation, much to the chagrin of MSgt Trent. Top loved flying in TJG's swanky Gulfstream. It was one of the few aircraft that the huge Marine could fit in comfortably. Instead, he and Gaucho paired up and routed through Dallas, Los Angeles, and finally down to Acapulco International Airport.

After a twenty minute taxi ride out of the city, the mismatched duo stepped out into the blazing sun. A weathered iron gate awaited, and a nondescript two story house lay inside, weeds tumbling over long untended flower beds.

"Nice place," Trent said, grabbing his carryon bag from the back of the taxi.

"It may not look like much, but at least it's safe," Gaucho replied, handing the driver a fifty dollar bill.

Trent didn't know what Gaucho meant by safe. Hell, the rusted gate looked like he could kick it open without trying very hard. Trent was also surprised there wasn't anyone guarding the entrance. His questions were answered when he heard a tapping and looked up at the prominent second story window. Daniel Briggs waved to Trent, cradling his newly delivered M40A5 sniper rifle, a gift from a friend at Quantico. Trent relaxed and smiled up at his friend.

The gate squealed in protest as Trent swung it open. It really did feel like it would fall off its hinges at any moment. When they stepped inside, the pungent smell of incense greeted them.

"You think they've been holding mass?" Trent asked.

Gaucho shook his head and pushed past his friend.

"Hey, boss, we're finally here," Gaucho called down the narrow hallway.

Cal's form appeared at the end of the hall.

"Shhh," Cal said, holding a finger to his lips.

It was only then that Trent heard the chanting, low and even like worshippers praying in perfect sync. When they came into the far room, Trent's eyes took in the spectacle around the fireplace. There were four robed forms, all on their knees, facing a crude wooden cross that looked like something a child had pieced together from a fallen tree. Incense burned in a tiny bronze vessel that was shaped like a miniature teapot, a thin line of smoke reaching up to the stained ceiling. Cal was the only other person in the living room.

"What's going on?" Trent whispered to Cal.

"This is how we found them. They've been at it for almost an hour." Cal's lack of patience tinged his reply.

"Where are the rest of the guys?"

Cal pointed upstairs. "Getting comms up and unloading our gear."

"Briggs in charge of security?"

Cal nodded without taking his eyes from the four monks who had just completed a simultaneous bow.

Trent sensed that the prayer was coming to an end and a few seconds later, it did with a collective, "Amen."

The cloaked figures stood, threw back their hoods, and turned to face the newcomers.

"Mr. Stokes?" the largest of the four men asked, his accent slightly European, although Trent couldn't place where. His eyes were calm, but Trent could tell that under the bulky robes, this man was probably built like a body builder. He wasn't as tall as Trent, but the Marine estimated that the guy was probably at least six foot five.

"That's me," answered Cal.

The monk stepped forward, offering his hand. "I am Brother Hendrik. Thank you for coming."

Next, a smaller version of Brother Hendrik came across the room. This one's eyes were stone gray, piercing like a hawk's. "I am Brother Zigfried," he said in heavily accented English. This guy was either German or Austrian. Trent guessed the former.

The third man to come forward was Cal's size, and had the easy-going smile of an old friend. His hair was light brown and just beginning to bald. "I'm Brother Aaron," the monk said, nodding to Cal, Trent and Gaucho. He spoke in perfect American English. Trent didn't know what he'd expected, maybe a bunch of guys speaking Latin or Italian, not a mix of nationalities who looked more like an international SWAT team.

The last man to introduce himself was the shortest of the four and obviously Hispanic.

"I am Brother Fernando."

"It's a pleasure meeting you," Cal said, taking the time to look each man in the eye.

Trent wondered if Cal was thinking the same thing he was. The Jefferson Group had brought twelve men and had just as many in support back in Charlottesville. The Pope had sent four men. Only four men! Trent hoped that either the situation had improved or that there were more monks stashed somewhere nearby.

"As we discussed over the phone, Father Pietro should be arriving soon. He is understandably anxious to be under our protection," Brother Hendrik said.

MSgt Trent had discussed this Father Pietro with Gaucho. Both men wondered where the priest was hiding. If the poor guy had any sense, he'd probably been hiding in the darkest hole he could find. Gaucho said there were plenty of those in Acapulco, depending on how much money you had.

"My guys are getting things ready upstairs. Should we go up and talk?"

Brother Hendrik nodded and motioned for his fellow monks to lead the way. Once the four had left the room, Trent pulled Cal aside.

"I swear, Cal, when I heard that chanting, I thought you were having the rest of the boys sworn in as Catholics."

Cal chuckled. "You should've seen the look on Daniel's face when we came in. I don't know if I've ever seen him so surprised."

"Can you blame him?"

Cal shook his head and let out another quiet laugh. "I'm just worried that he'll decide to go back to Rome with them."

Trent and Gaucho looked at each other and then laughed with Cal. While Daniel was as spiritual a man as Trent had ever met, the massive Marine knew there was no way Snake Eyes could be torn from Cal's side.

"Come on," said Cal, clapping Trent on the back. "I can't wait to see what happens next."

———

Father Pietro shivered despite the oppressive heat inside the battered taxi cab. The steam and his passenger's unease didn't seem to faze the driver. He putted along like he didn't have a care in the world, as if this fare was supposed to last the rest of the day. The priest wished the man would press the gas pedal to the floor. The jarring ride into the hills already felt like it was taking hours. Father Pietro chided himself for not bringing a fresh supply of alcohol. At least that could have calmed his nerves.

But he wanted to make a good first impression in front of Luca's men. He had no idea what they would be like, and Luca had only told him when and where to be. It was just like his old friend to be cautious. That fact did not make his nerves rattle any gentler. The days of hiding had taken their toll. When he'd looked in the mirror after a much needed shower earlier that day, the priest wasn't surprised to see a haggard face that spoke of the fear that even now shook his body.

It wasn't like the old days when he'd laughed in the face of danger. This was different. There was something bigger happening. He could feel it, like an invading army marching over the horizon, stomping closer with each passing day. The days had given him time to think, but his thoughts always drifted to what he'd seen and what he'd done on that fateful night. Somehow, through the fear and drunken bouts, he'd found new clothing, and had even found shelter with a beggar who offered a place next to him under a crumbling bridge. It was the man's home, along with the ever-present ring of stray cats that shared his food and his bed.

He'd said a silent prayer for the man when waving goodbye. It spoke of the man's character that he had opened his arms and welcomed him without hesitation. This was a man who had nothing, who lived in the worst of conditions, who barely scraped by under the wary gaze of the rest of mankind. *What would mankind be like if they learned from the lessons of a humble beggar?* Father Pietro held onto that thought as the taxi struggled up the steep hill, finally coming to a stop in front of a dilapidated metal gate.

The driver didn't say a word, just turned in his seat and held out his hand.

Father Pietro glanced at the meter and thumbed out the appropriate number of bills, a parting gift from the beggar. "Thank you," he said, after getting a curt nod from the driver.

No sooner had the priest stepped from the vehicle than the taxi sputtered a choking cough of smoke and ambled on its way.

Father Pietro looked up at the high fencing, and into the crumbling courtyard. There wasn't a soul in sight. However, he could feel eyes watching him. Gulping down his fear, Father Pietro pulled open the creaking gate, and stepped inside.

———

"He's here," Daniel said, stepping into the room where Cal sat talking with Brother Hendrik.

Cal looked up. "You mind bringing him upstairs?"

"Brother Aaron, please go with Mr. Briggs," Brother Hendrik said.

Daniel was finding it hard to admit to himself that he was in awe of the monks. When he and Cal had first come into the house, finding the four men chanting in the living room, Daniel felt a familiar pull coming from the makeshift altar. Like so many other men and women, Daniel Briggs hadn't come home from war unscathed. He'd escaped bodily harm, but his mind and his conscience bore the pressing weight of his guilt.

It wasn't the killing that bothered him, or even the daily race against death. It was something deeper, like the devil was laughing at him, taunting him with his forked tongue. He'd felt cursed, like anyone who got within arm's reach would contract the worst malady possible: death.

And so he'd traveled the backroads of America, drowning his fears with a bottle of Jack here or a handle of Dewars there. As long as he moved and spurned all relationships, he thought he could outrun his demons.

In the end, he found the only ally who would always be there for him, who would keep the devil at bay. It was God who had finally come into Daniel's life and brought him the peace he never thought possible. That same peace was what he felt when he'd walked into that living room. It was like encountering your twin, someone who had experienced the same life, the same feelings, the same hopes and fears. He saw that plainly in the eyes of the four monks. They'd also battled their demons, and had come together as brothers under God. The only word that came to Daniel's mind was *miraculous*.

When he and Brother Aaron got downstairs, a man stood waiting. He had the look of a wounded animal, like a dog who cowered after being whipped one too many times by its master. He was covered in sweat and his ill-fitting shirt stuck to his chest.

"Father Pietro?" asked Brother Aaron.

The man nodded, taking a shaky step forward.

"I am Brother—" Brother Aaron began.

Daniel sensed it before it happened. Father Pietro's eyes rolled back and his legs crumpled. The Marine rushed forward and caught the fainting man just before he hit the tiled floor. Daniel could smell the lingering scent of alcohol seeping from the priest's pores.

He checked for a pulse and made sure the man was breathing. Both good.

"Get some water and a towel," Daniel said, lying the priest down on the floor.

Brother Aaron nodded and ran to the kitchen. He was back a moment later.

Daniel grabbed the moist towel and wiped Pietro's face. It was regaining some of its color. Daniel stopped. His eyes narrowed and he looked toward the front door. At the same moment, there was a commotion upstairs. Not yelling, just the hustled footsteps of men moving.

"What is it?" Brother Aaron asked.

Reaching for the pistol in his waistband, Daniel said, "We're about to have company."

Brother Aaron reached under his thick robe and produced a compact submachine gun. With one arm apiece, they dragged Father Pietro deeper into the house, gunshots already sounding from upstairs. Just as they pulled the unconscious man behind the kitchen counter, Daniel heard the sound of breaking glass, and a split second later, two olive drab grenades came skidding into the room.

CHAPTER 9

Following the priest's taxi was the easy part. The hard part had been finding him. They'd located him early that morning. Whoever the priest was, he at least had the sense to hide well.

There was little that money couldn't buy on the poor streets of Mexico. El Moreno had a certain affinity with the lower class, the pariahs. That was where he'd found the milky eyed captain who'd been entrusted with finding the rogue priest. After all, the religious man had apparently killed two of El Moreno's men.

Ricardo Lozano had always lived on the streets. He didn't know his parents, had rarely eaten something he hadn't stolen as a child. It was on one of his daily "shopping trips" three years prior that he'd first encountered El Moreno. Of course, he already knew about the brown-skinned man on the rise. The man would sometimes appear with a basket of pastries or a heaping sack of tortillas for the street urchins in the poorest areas of Acapulco. In exchange for this kindness, the men and women of the streets were El Moreno's eyes and ears. They were only too happy to provide information on so-and-so informant or this-and-that cartel. What wouldn't they give for a bit of food and friendship, two things that El Moreno gave in oversized helpings while rival cartels resorted to strong-arming and butchery.

Ricardo Lozano hadn't known much of El Moreno on that first day, but it was hard to miss the dark-skinned leader who dressed simply, a habit copied by his entourage. As Ricardo had watched the gang cross the street in front of Ricardo's favorite bakery, it was as if the world exploded. Machine gun fire erupted from rooftops and suddenly the area was filled with the sound of squealing tires.

El Moreno's men moved to protect their leader and paid the price. Ricardo had watched as one by one they fell, spilling blood as they ran, the unsettled dust in the road making the scene look like something out of a movie. Somehow, impossibly, El Moreno kept moving, firing as he went until his last man fell. For some reason (El Moreno would later call it fate), Ricardo ran to the man he'd never met, scooping up a submachine gun as he sprinted to the man's side.

Through fire and dust they retreated, Ricardo leading the way through the familiar streets. He'd saved El Moreno. He, the bastardo with one bad eye that the other boys always called Ojo del Diablo (eye of the devil), Ricardo Lozano stepped into the cartel world. For saving his life, El Moreno took the younger man under his wing. Despite his lack of experience, Ricardo listened and learned. Soon he was one of El Moreno's bodyguards, then in charge of protecting the cartel's inner circle. Now he was one of El Moreno's captains, like a field commander in the military.

He was proud of that fact. No one called him names anymore. He was a man of respect, a proven battlefield commander.

But as Ricardo ordered his men to unload from their vehicles, something itched at the back of his subconscious. He couldn't shake the feeling as they entered the front gate, wanting to take the priest by surprise. But then the windows on the second floor shattered and gunfire rained down on his men.

He had twenty men with him thanks to another kidnapping mission for the Spaniards. It was the only blessing Ricardo recognized as he took cover and ordered two of his men to rush the front door. They made it to the door, one soldier breaking the glass next to the door, the other man throwing two grenades into the house.

The explosions rocked the house, but the gunfire from above didn't relent.

"Knock it down," Ricardo screamed at his second in command. The man nodded and ran back to their SUV. It was a good thing they'd brought along a new toy El Moreno had given his captains. It was some type of cutting-edge explosive developed by the Russians. The first time he'd seen it, he thought it was a trick. How could one warhead, no bigger than an American football, level an entire building?

While he didn't understand why it worked, Ricardo knew it did. He would just have to tell El Moreno that there hadn't been a choice. Sometimes total destruction was inevitable in the face of troop loss.

He looked back and saw his man loading the thermobaric round in the RPG. Then he ducked down lower and plugged his ears. Ricardo counted down in his head. *Four, three, two, one...*

Nothing.

Despite the heavy gunfire, Ricardo picked his way back to where his man had been. When he got there, he found the RPG cast aside and a red hole in the man's forehead.

———

"Nice shot!" yelled Cal over the steady fire.

Daniel nodded, looking for more targets. After the initial barrage when The Jefferson Group and the monks leveled disciplined fire at the invading force, the enemy was getting smart. Daniel estimated that the attackers had lost half of their strength.

"We need to get outside," he said to no one in particular.

He was about to volunteer when Brother Hendrik tapped him on the shoulder. "We will go."

Daniel looked to Cal, who nodded.

Brother Hendrik ran for the door, his fellow monks on his heels.

This should be interesting, thought Daniel.

———

Down the stairs they went, hopping overturned chairs and debris. Brown robes flowing, the monks burst through the back door that spilled out into a small backyard. Brother Hendrik pointed to the six foot stone wall that wrapped around the house complex. His brothers nodded.

Brother Hendrik went first, secure in the fact that his fellow warriors and the Americans would cover his movements. He was over the wall with a jump and a pull, landing softly on the other side. There was a man with a machine gun at the far corner, obviously avoiding the onslaught from the second story. He was faced away from Brother Hendrik and went down with a quick burst from the monk's weapon.

Sensing his men behind him, Brother Hendrik strapped his submachine gun over his shoulder and grabbed the dead man's medium machine gun. After checking to make sure there was enough ammunition and that the weapon would function, he motioned to others, and they turned the corner in search of the enemy.

———— ◆ ————

Rounds were no longer flying past and over his head, but Cal could still hear the gunfire from the street. He got in a position where he could better observe what was going on. What he saw made him smile.

The four monks were leap-frogging from one enemy vehicle to the next, taking down bad guys like they'd been born for the task. When they couldn't get a good shot at one shooter, Brother Zigfried had the balls to jump on top of the hood of one of the vehicles while Brother Fernando produced a canister grenade from under his robes and threw it under-hand to where the bad guy was hiding. That made the dude run, and he was promptly cut down by a stream of bullets from Brother Zigfried.

On they went until no more enemies popped up to face the monks.

"Those are some badass padres," said MSgt Trent.

"Madre de Dios," said Gaucho, his eyes wide as he watched.

"Let's secure the street. I'll bet the cops will be here soon," Cal said, turning to head downstairs. For the first time since he'd talked to the president, Cal wondered what exactly they'd just stepped into.

Ricardo Lozano somehow resisted the urge to drop his weapon and give himself up. The sight of four robed figures systematically ripping through his ranks sent his mind reeling. He'd often wondered about the consequences of the life he'd decided to live under El Moreno. Was this his repayment? Had God sent his own messengers to pay Ricardo back for his sins?

He didn't know, but he wasn't going to stick around to find out. Without another thought, except to say a small prayer for forgiveness, Ricardo turned and ran as fast as he could.

Brother Zigfried took a knee, carefully following the retreating man in his sights. His finger touched the trigger.

"Let him go," came Brother Hendrik's voice.

Brother Zigfried hesitated. "But, brother, he was the last—"

"Yes," said Hendrik, watching the man disappear down the hill. "He was the last for today. Let him go back to his master and tell him of the Lord's messengers."

CHAPTER 10

His head throbbed as he came to. There were voices, muffled yet close by. They faded in and out for a time, like someone was turning the volume up and down on a television. He sensed them, but something in their tone made him think he was safe.

His first thought was that he'd been taken to a hospital. Then it hit him. The voices were speaking in Italian, not Spanish. Although he could've kept his eyes closed and enjoyed the overwhelming sense of safety, Father Pietro forced them open. Colors blended together in blurry blobs. He squinted despite the dim lighting.

Gradually his sight cleared. There were four men seated around a table, one speaking in Italian. They turned in unison as Father Pietro shifted his position, wincing at the searing headache.

"Welcome back, Father," one of the men said in fluent Italian.

The priest's breath caught when he realized the men were wearing the brown robes of monks.

"Where am I?"

"You are safe."

Father Pietro bit off a groan as he sat up in the bed.

"You're Luca's men?"

The largest of the four men nodded.

"We are the Brothers of Saint Longinus."

The priest searched his mind for any memory of the brotherhood. He couldn't recall ever having heard of it.

"Saint Longinus, you say?"

Another nod from the large one. Without thinking, Father Pietro examined the monks, assessing the outwardly formidable quartet. Strong, especially the apparent leader. The others might not seem as impressive as their peer, but Pietro knew better. They had the cool gaze of trained professionals. They were men who'd seen death, and likely dealt their fair share. He found himself wondering who these Brothers of Saint Longinus really were, and how his old friend Luca had captured their friendship.

"We are an ancient brotherhood. Brother Luca is the head of our order. He speaks highly of you."

Father Pietro thought that Luca might not think so highly of him if he could see what he had become. Sitting across from the four monks, Pietro felt like a lesser man, like a failure.

"How is my old friend?" the priest asked, wanting to change the subject. The last thing he wanted was to talk about himself. He'd avoided such conversations for as long as he'd served God, each day another ring of penance for his mountain of sins.

"He is dying." The big man said it matter-of-factly, like he'd already come to terms with the implications and sadness of Luca's death. But there was warmth there as well. This man respected Luca, cared for him like a comrade, like a brother.

Father Pietro said a silent prayer for his old friend.

"Then we should go. It has been too long since I've laid eyes on the old man."

A look passed between the four monks, like he'd somehow offended them. Pietro's stomach turned.

"I'm sorry. Have I said something wrong?" he asked.

"Our orders are clear, Father."

"And what are your orders? I assumed that you would be taking me back to Italy." That was all he'd thought about since that dreadful night. His plan was to give any information that might help in the investigation and then request a new assignment, perhaps one in Italy, without parishioners to tend to. Surely they would take his circumstances into account and let him live out his days in quiet solitude, atoning for his sins in relative peace.

"You are to remain here and assist us in finding our stolen flock. There have been more kidnappings."

Sweat sprang from Pietro's brow.

"I am happy to assist with information, but I am not qualified to help in any other way." He felt the panic clawing away at his insides. This couldn't be happening.

The muscular monk shook his head.

"That is not God's plan, Father."

The words shot from his mouth before he could stop them. "What do you know of God's plan?! What life have you lived that you should be the judge of what I must do?"

It was like the words shattered against an impenetrable wall of stone. The monk's face didn't change.

"It is not my choice, Father."

"Then whose is it? Who demands that I stay and help you?" His old anger simmered, long since tamped down into the farthest reaches of his soul, wrapped in iron bonds where it could no longer hurt others. But now it shook in its chains, demanding to be let out, howling for the light. Pietro let it come. "You know nothing," he hissed.

But still the monk looked unfazed.

"I know you are in pain, Father. Is that not why you changed your name, to distance yourself from your past? Is that not why Gabriel Fusconi became Pietro?"

Cold fury washed over the priest. His hands shook as he tried to form his retort.

"How dare you…"

"No, Father, how dare *you*." The monk rose from his chair, now even more imposing as he walked to the bed. His face wasn't the mask of fury Father Pietro expected, but still the calm facade of a determined warrior. Father Pietro glared at the man with every ounce of hatred he could muster, but if he felt a thing, the monk didn't let it show. He said, "You swore an oath to God. You promised to serve Him, to serve His people. Instead you've chosen to hide like a coward, to lose yourself in your weakness. That is not what God wants of you."

The words were like swift jabs to the priest's chest. He felt each one, saw the truth in the words, but didn't want to listen.

"So tell me, monk," Father Pietro stabbed back. "Whose orders do you follow now? Is it God who told you to keep me in Mexico?"

A smile made its way onto the burly monk's face. Pietro steeled himself for a glib reply.

"Normally we are bound by our vows not to divulge our master's identity, but Brother Luca has given me the assurance that you can be trusted."

Pietro was getting tired of the man's riddles.

"So, who is it? Who is this mysterious person that commands the warrior monks before me?"

The monk's smile stretched wider.

"His Holiness, our Holy Father, the Pope."

The villa they'd rented was swanky and built like a fortress. Commanding an impressive view of the Pacific Ocean, Villa Tesoro (Spanish for treasure) lived up to its name. With video surveillance inside and out, two sets of armored entry gates, and enough room to house a platoon, Villa Tesoro was exactly what Cal and his team needed: a safe place to plan their next move. Sometimes it was good to have a lot of money and friends who could find new accommodations on the fly.

The Pope's warriors had taken Father Pietro to a large guest room on the other side of the mansion. The Jefferson Group operators were congregated in a split level living area that overlooked an LED lit swimming pool that could've been an exact replica of the one at the Playboy Mansion.

Cal read the report Neil had sent moments earlier from TJG headquarters. With the help of the pictures they'd sent him of the dead men who'd attacked them hours before, Neil was able to discover their identities by accessing the Mexican police database.

"Neil says these guys are cartel gunmen. Some have records and others were rumored to have affiliations with a guy called El Moreno. Anybody ever heard of this guy?" Cal asked.

Gaucho raised his hand. "Yeah, I have. He runs the Guerrero Cartel."

"How much do you know about him?"

Gaucho winced. "More than I should. He's my uncle's number one enemy."

That got everyone's attention.

"Do you know this guy?" MSgt Trent asked.

"No. I just remember my uncle telling me about him."

"So what's his deal? Why do you think he was after the priest?" Cal asked.

"I don't know, but I can probably guess. From what I remember, El Moreno is new in the drug world. My uncle describes him like a lord describing a peasant, like the guy wasn't good enough to be in the drug business or something. Anyway, if I had to bet, I'm sure the Guerrero Cartel is leveraging whatever they're getting from the jihadis to step up in the world. It could be money, weapons, or both."

That seemed plausible to Cal. While the presence of Islamic extremists in a predominantly Catholic nation might've been a slim possibility in the past, who knew what upstarts like El Moreno were willing to do? More importantly, who they were willing to work with in order to get what they wanted?

"So how do we find this guy?" Trent asked to no one in particular.

"Neil said he's working on it, but El Moreno has been pretty good at staying off the authority's radar," Cal answered.

"What about the police? Could they help?"

Cal shook his head. "The boss wants us to keep the Mexicans out of it for now. I don't think they'd like to find out that we've been waging war in their playground. U.S.-Mexico relations are already bad as it is. Unless Hendrik and his brothers have some secret Catholic intelligence asset, I think there's only one option on the table." Cal looked to Gaucho, who returned the look with a frown. "You know who we need to contact, Gaucho."

The short Hispanic exhaled and tugged at his beard.

"Okay, but I'm not promising anything. My uncle did promise to kill me the last time I paid him a visit."

CHAPTER 11

Ricardo Lozano waited nervously for his boss. He'd had the unfortunate pleasure of having to call El Moreno while the leader was on a date. His master had been cordial over the phone, but Ricardo hated to disturb his boss when he was on one of his rare excursions into the upper crust of society.

It wasn't safe to speak over the phone, so El Moreno had instructed him to come to the hotel for a full debriefing. Ricardo knew he was stepping into dangerous territory, that the loss of so many men would surely ignite his boss's fire. He promised himself that he would take it like a man. He would not retreat from his responsibility. His faith was with his patrón.

As he waited in the penthouse vestibule, trying not to stare at the paintings displayed in gold gilded frames and the spotless sheen on the black marble floors, Ricardo replayed the disastrous raid in his head, no doubt that El Moreno would want to know every detail. He always did. The man had a mindset like what Ricardo assumed a college professor or a doctor might have. He missed nothing and remembered pieces of conversations that most other men would have missed.

El Moreno came into the room wearing a knee length black silk robe. His feet were bare and tapped lightly on the cold floor. Ricardo bowed his head.

"Jefe."

Without saying a word, El Moreno walked to his man and embraced him. Ricardo half expected a blade to plunge into his back, but none came. The short man placed a hand on Ricardo's shoulder and guided him into the living room.

"Tell me what happened." El Moreno's voice was calm, even soothing. It made Ricardo relax until a split second later when he remembered what he had to say.

"It did not go well, Jefe."

"Tell me everything."

Ricardo explained how one of the cartel's informants called with the information regarding the priest's whereabouts. A surveillance team was set up and for the better part of the morning nothing happened. Then, just after the lookout unit had switched over after lunch, a taxi arrived and the priest got into it.

"I called in the extra men who were still on the road from earlier."

"The ones running the errand for our guests?" El Moreno asked.

"Yes."

"So you had how many men?"

"Twenty, Jefe."

"Tell me what happened next."

Ricardo nodded, taking a hesitant breath before beginning again.

"If the driver or the priest knew that we were following the taxi, they did not show it. They made no stops until they arrived at their destination."

"Where was it?"

"In the foothills near Nueva Jerusalen."

El Moreno nodded. "Then?"

"The priest got out of the taxi and went inside the compound."

"What did you do?"

"I radioed the others and ordered them to go in like we always do."

"You expected trouble?"

Ricardo looked up, panic making his heart race. El Moreno's orders had been clear, "Bring the priest in alive."

His words came out in a tumble. "I cannot explain it, Jefe. I had a feeling, like someone was watching, waiting even."

El Moreno frowned.

"I understand. What happened next?"

"They started firing at us from the second story. I do not know how we lost so many so quickly, but two got to the front door with grenades. The explosion happened, but nothing slowed. We tried to use the RPG, but that man was killed as well. Everything was chaos. We took cover and tried to return fire. I couldn't see it, but I knew they were picking us off one by one."

El Moreno shifted in his chair, and then leaned closer. Ricardo avoided his gaze.

"I can see by the look on your face that this is not the end of your story." El Moreno still wasn't shouting. In fact, he seemed calmer than minutes before.

Ricardo shook his head, still trying to come to grips with what he'd seen.

"The firing changed. Whoever was in the house had sent men around the back to attack our flank. I had men posted there, but they must have been killed. I never saw the enemy until the monks appeared on my left, calmly shooting the rest of our men."

"Did you say monks?"

"I…yes, Jefe. I wouldn't have believed it if I hadn't seen it. There they were, four men in brown robes, firing machine guns moving closer to my position."

"So what did you do?"

Ricardo's head snapped up and he looked straight in his boss's eyes. If he was going to admit his failure, he was going to do it like a man.

"I ran, Jefe. I am ashamed to say it, but I ran."

"And they didn't shoot you."

It wasn't a question, just an honest observation, like El Moreno had already figured it all out.

"No, Jefe. They did not shoot me."

El Moreno nodded and was silent for a spell. Ricardo waited, ready to accept his fate. Finally, the cartel leader spoke.

"It seems there is more to this priest than we guessed. Come, Ricardo, I think it's time to have a word with our guests. There must be something they are not telling us."

El Moreno didn't bother calling before they arrived. He didn't want the Spaniards to concoct a story before he showed up. It would be better to see their candid reactions to his questions. He knew he'd been lied to by his foreign guests, but he didn't know how deep the deception went.

He wouldn't fault Ricardo. The man was a loyal soldier, a captain who would've taken a knife to his own throat if El Moreno had asked. That would be a waste. In the coming months, the Guerrero Cartel would need every good man it could find. Like any good general, the dark-skinned maestro knew that Ricardo wouldn't make the same mistake again. Word would trickle through the ranks describing El Moreno's benevolence. Others might see it as a weakness, but El Moreno had learned that men like Ricardo Lozano would rather brave a hail of bullets than to fail his master again. He would have paid anything to have twenty more of the same.

When they pulled through the warehouse gates and into the loading bay, Ricardo was the first out, still playing his role as protector. El Moreno smiled despite himself. Lesser men would have sulked and followed their master like a sick dog. Not Ricardo. Not the rest of the Guerrero men. It was a fact that made El Moreno proud and bolstered his step as he made his way to where the jihadis were lodged.

They walked up the old stairs to the second level. Ricardo banged on the metal door. It was locked from the inside.

"Who is it?" came the muffled voice from within.

"Open the door," El Moreno said.

A moment later, he heard the inner latch clank open, and the door swiveled inward.

The smell of rank body odor wafted out as the air shifted. It reminded El Moreno of his days on the street and the stinking beggars with whom he'd competed for food.

The leader, Felix, had opened the door.

"It is late," he said simply, shielding the rest of the former boardroom from view. His right hand was holding the door and his left was behind his back, no doubt holding a pistol.

"We have a situation," El Moreno said, watching to see if Felix's face registered true or feigned surprise. He got neither. Instead, the look of annoyance etched deeper into his ethnic Catalonian features. "We found the priest who killed your men."

That got the Spaniard's attention.

"Where is he?"

"*That* is the situation. You never mentioned that he had friends," El Moreno said.

"What do you mean friends? Do you mean to say that you lost him?" Felix's nostrils flared. El Moreno was beginning to tire of this one's bravado.

"I lost twenty men trying to get your priest."

Silence. Felix's eyes scrunched in confusion and then his face contorted again.

"Are you implying that I had something to do with their deaths?"

"I am saying that you will now pay us double for the men we lost, for their families, of course."

Felix brought the pistol from behind his back to the front of his body. Ricardo's weapon appeared in an instant, supplemented by the three guards who'd been in the SUV with them.

Felix spoke slowly, finally recognizing the threat.

"I am sorry for your loss, but I fail to see how this is my problem."

El Moreno smiled. "Let me explain how business works. If I incur certain, let's call them expenses, while engaged in activities that support our agreement, my organization is entitled to compensation for those expenses."

"That's not what we agreed. I never—"

"You haven't told me many things, I'm sure. For instance, what is so important about getting across the American border?"

"That is none of—"

"None of my concern? Oh no, Felix, it is. You see, if our relationship becomes known to the Mexican authorities, or worse, to the Americans, very bad things will happen to you and me. This is not your country and you are not sending mortars into the Gaza Strip. This is Mexico, and this is *my* land."

The jihadi took his time responding.

"Maybe it is time I found another partner. Perhaps your men are not up to the task."

El Moreno wanted to punch the man, but laughed instead.

"That would be wonderful. Please, try to find anyone else that could help you. But let me warn you, before you can adjust your plans, I will alert every federal authority I can think of and my fellow cartels to your presence. I assure you that while *I* am quite reasonable in my requests and welcoming to paying customers, *they* will not be so accommodating. So please, tell me what you've decided so that we can either conclude or continue our business."

There was another long pause as the extremist weighed his options, of which only one was viable. El Moreno was telling the truth. In fact, he knew that Felix's compatriots had attempted to contact two rival organizations, and had been told to stay out of Mexico. The other cartels believed that if terrorists were allowed free passage through their territory, that would in some way affect their business. They were probably right. The Americans could ignore the drug problem as long as the violence stayed south of the border. They wouldn't take as kindly to terrorists swimming across the Rio Grande.

El Moreno was willing to accept the risk because of the possible reward. Simply put, the Guerrero Cartel was the Spaniard's best shot.

"We will pay," Felix said.

El Moreno nodded, but couldn't let the man off so easy.

"And you're sure your masters will approve?"

Felix's chest heaved.

"I told you before, I am in charge,"

The Mexican put up his hands in apology.

"Very well. I'll take you at your word. We'll speak again in the morning?"

Felix grunted and shut the large door.

El Moreno turned for the stairs, his insides bubbling with excitement. What had started off as a potentially disastrous night had turned into something quite fruitful. Not only had he just negotiated a doubling of his fees, but he'd also pinned down two important points: 1) if Felix could approve such a large increase in payment, there must be many more funds available, and 2) he now had the jihadis right where he wanted them. It was only a matter of time before he had their money and their weapon.

CHAPTER 12

The phone call the night before had been short. MSgt Trent estimated it was probably under a minute. He couldn't read Gaucho's expression when he hung up the phone.

"What did he say?" Trent and Cal had asked simultaneously.

"He gave me directions to a helipad in the city. From there they'll fly me to wherever he is."

"I'm coming with you," Trent said. There wasn't any way, come heaven or hell, that he was going to let his best friend go it alone. *No way, man.* That wasn't the way it was done.

"Top, I told you, my uncle has always had a bug up his ass about security. What do you think he'll do when a seven-foot black guy shows up?"

"First of all, I'm six-foot-ten. And second, if you don't let me come with you, we're finding another way to do this."

Trent had looked at Cal, who could only nod in agreement.

Gaucho didn't fight it very hard. He knew what was right, and going into a cartel stronghold alone wasn't the best tactical decision. In the end he'd agreed, and Trent had slapped his friend on the back.

"Come on, man, don't look so glum. This'll be fun."

Gaucho's typical reply jab never came. All through the rest of the night and into the next morning, he pretty much kept his mouth shut.

So when they showed up at the helipad and faced the armed guard who was with the pilot, Gaucho had explained that he was bringing his friend. After a quick phone call, the two guests were ushered onto the aircraft.

There was more greenery on the ground than Trent had expected. Sure most of it was probably scrub and scraggly trees, since not much could survive in the heat, but at least it wasn't miles and miles of desert. Gaucho kept to himself as Trent took in the view. It wasn't long before they'd left the coast behind, and headed northeast away from the city.

There were little pockets of homes tucked into the ravines of the countless hills stretching toward the horizon, but not many. Once they'd left the hub of the city, the terrain below was mostly free of human life.

Sooner than expected, Trent could feel the helicopter banking left. In a move that surprised him and Gaucho, the pilot dove for the deck, the nose of the aircraft pointed into a deep draw. Trent held on as they made their steep descent. Just when he thought the pilot was taking them in for a free fall, he pulled the helo up and they cruised barely ten feet above the treetops, following the terrain higher up the draw.

When they popped up and over a hill, the pilot whipped the bird around 180 degrees and plunged to the deck. There was a sprawling ranch below, ringed with fence lines and dotted with horses and cattle.

It was obvious that the guy knew what he was doing and had probably made the same landing countless times before, because he touched down like a feather floating from the sky.

Trent took a steadying breath (he'd never completely enjoyed the flyboy tricks of helicopter pilots) and looked through the window. The house looked much smaller than it had from the sky, probably because it was only one story.

A man approached the aircraft at a fast walk and opened the hatch.

"Gentlemen, if you will follow me please."

The guy had a butler's outfit on, resplendent in his formal black-tailed tux. Trent would've laughed if they weren't walking into the lion's den.

Trent ducked his way past the still whirling helicopter blades and followed Gaucho and the butler up to the house. The place really did look like something you'd find in Wyoming or Texas. There was even one of those horizontal posts to tie up horses. Trent half expected to see cowboys riding up at any minute.

When they stepped into the house, Trent's eyes went wide at the decor. The vestibule was probably twenty by twenty, and all up and down the ten foot walls were the mounted heads of jackalopes.

"What the hell is this?" Trent couldn't help but ask.

"It's my uncle's idea of a joke."

"A joke about what?"

"He says that if man could invent the jackalope and make people believe that the mythical creature exists, then man can do whatever he likes."

Trent shook his head. He didn't really get the joke.

"Oh," Gaucho said, "it's also his nickname."

Trent snorted. "Do all these guys have nicknames?"

"Most of them do. It makes them into sort of celebrities down here. Did you know that rappers even write songs about cartel leaders?"

"Seriously?"

Gaucho shrugged as they followed the butler through the expansive kitchen. Trent's chef-trained eyes went to the enormous gas stovetop and the equally impressive hood. Everything was state of the art, from the chrome appliances to the ultra-thin television screens placed every few feet along the walls.

It was the same in the living room, where lush potted plants accented elegant leather chairs and modern art was mounted in tasteful gray frames. It looked more like something out of an expensive designer's magazine than a hideout plopped in the middle of Mexico.

The back patio was no less impressive. There was an enormous pool front and center. It looked like it had been carved from the hill itself. In the middle of the water was a large square fountain that held a statue of Jesus, and from his hands poured water like they'd been piped through the holes he'd received when nailed to the cross. Behind the water feature was an amazing view of the surrounding countryside. The only thing that disturbed the view were the armed guards patrolling the well-tended property, each offering a casual glance toward the strangers as they passed.

"Holy shit," whispered Trent.

Gaucho just stood there with his arms crossed.

"Your uncle will be here soon. May I get you anything?" asked the butler in lightly accented English.

"No, thank you," said Gaucho.

"I'd love some water, please," Trent said, getting a funny look from his friend in the process. "What? I'm thirsty, okay?"

Trent wished Gaucho would loosen up. He seemed more like Cal at the moment, intense and ready to pounce should someone say a word he didn't like. But that wasn't fair. Maybe that was the old Cal. His leadership role had matured and grown within The Jefferson Group; most likely, at least in Trent's opinion, this was due to the positive influence that Diane Mayer had on the stubborn Marine. If Gaucho wasn't in such a foul mood, Trent might have shared his thoughts with him.

Trent took a seat as Gaucho paced slowly back and forth across the porch. No sooner had Trent taken his first sip of cucumber flavored water than he heard a noise that made him turn. Hoofbeats coming closer. A minute later, a group of riders came into view, trotting onto the back lawn like they were just coming in from a cattle drive. The man in the lead motioned for the others to keep going, and he circled back toward the house.

The guy rode high in the saddle, like the way Trent assumed a nobleman might have. The horse clopped onto the stone patio and the rider tossed the reins to the butler. After dismounting, he scraped his cowboy boots on the edge of the pavement.

"Who's your friend?" the man asked. He looked like a ranch hand, strong in that wiry kind of way. He was clean shaven and stood at least half a head taller than Gaucho.

"This is Master Sergeant Willy Trent," Gaucho said, still standing with his arms crossed, his cool gaze not wavering from the man Trent assumed was his uncle.

"Not a Marine, I hope?"

Gaucho scowled.

"What did I tell you about befriending Marines, Gauchito? And you even picked a big black one!"

"You'll have to excuse my uncle, Top. He's always been a bit of a racist."

Gaucho's uncle shrugged as if being racist was just one of those things that men in his position were allowed to be. Even so, he walked over and offered Trent his hand.

"Since my nephew is too rude to introduce us, my name is Armando Ruiz."

"Willy Trent, Mr. Ruiz."

Ruiz let go of Trent's hand and motioned for his guests to follow him into the house.

"Were you offered something to drink?" he asked as he slid open the glass door.

"We're fine," Gaucho answered.

Trent coughed and gave his friend a "get it together" look.

"Mr. Ruiz, if you're offering something stronger than water, I'll have something," Trent said, trying his best to diffuse the simmering tension between uncle and nephew. In Trent's humble opinion, Uncle Armando just won Round One.

"Whiskey okay?"

"On the rocks, please."

While Armando Ruiz busied himself at the well-stocked bar, he pressed, "You said it was important."

"It is," Gaucho replied, one notch lower in his pissed off tone.

"So, what is it?" Ruiz asked, turning to deliver one of two lowball glasses to Trent.

"We met some of El Moreno's men."

"Oh? And how is El Negrito doing?"

"We left twenty of his men dead on the streets."

That got his uncle's attention. Ruiz chuckled and took a sip of his whiskey.

"Now *that* I wasn't expecting. I thought you were coming to tell me that you were still mad at me for saying I was going to kill you. I've gotten past that you know. You *are* family."

Trent hoped to see his friend relax, but he didn't.

Ruiz continued, "Are you going to tell me why you ran into these men, or should I ask Mr. Trent?"

Gaucho ignored the question and asked, "What have you heard about any recent church kidnappings?"

Ruiz's eyes lit up. "Ah! Is that why you're here? Has the American government finally taken an interest in the well-being of our country?"

"You can cut the *our country* crap. Your love for Mexico has to do with one thing: opportunity."

Ruiz grabbed his chest and took a step back. "You wound me, nephew. I am a proud Mexican. I serve Mexico just as I once served your United States."

"You can drop the act. You quit being that person a long time ago."

Ruiz looked at his nephew for a moment and shrugged. "Well, we all have to change some time. Like you, what is it that you're doing these days? Still eating snakes and swimming through rivers of Iraqi sewage?"

"I'm in the private world now. That's why we're here."

"And what is your mission? To save some poor souls that happened to walk in the line of fire?"

Gaucho smiled. "No. We're here hunting terrorists."

Ruiz lowered his drink from his lips. "Are you saying that El Negrito is working for those savages?"

Gaucho's smile widened. "That's exactly what I'm saying."

Ruiz turned and hurled his glass into the stone fireplace, crystal shattering into hundreds of little pieces. He whirled back on his nephew.

"Say what you want about me, that I'm a criminal or that I do things that make you sick, but I spent twenty years fighting those bastards. From the Philippines to every shithole we could find in the Middle East. That was before it was en vogue to fight terrorists. We saw the threat long before the American government would ever admit it. I did it then, and now I've done everything I could to keep them out of this country, too. Just last week I led my men into the desert where we heard a group of Saudis had taken up in an abandoned village, training for a trip across the border. We slaughtered them like lambs and then burned their castrated bodies in a blazing fire." Ruiz spat on the floor. "So you tell me, nephew, is this why you came? To tell me that this half-breed, this bastardo, has slipped into bed with these animals?"

Trent was completely taken aback by the outburst. The man who'd just moments earlier been as calm as Don Corleone was now seething with anger.

"Yes, Tío, that's why we came. But I'm also paying you a visit for one other reason." This was the Gaucho he knew. He'd somehow taken the reins from his uncle and turned the tables in their favor. The little shit hadn't even told him he was going to do that. Trent grinned in admiration.

Ruiz asked, "What's the second thing? What other news do you have to spoil my day?"

Gaucho walked over to his uncle and looked him right in the eyes. "I want you to help us track these jihadists and take them down before they can do any more harm."

His uncle relaxed and placed a hand on Gaucho's shoulder. "See, I knew we would one day be working together." He then turned to MSgt Trent. "My men and I are at your disposal, but on one condition."

"What's that?" Trent asked.

Ruiz grinned. "When we find these men and track them back to the Guerrero Cartel, I am the one who gets to kill El Moreno."

Trent downed the rest of his drink and then said, "You've got yourself a deal, Sir."

CHAPTER 13

The smell was starting to get to him. He should've listened to the Mexican who had recommended allowing the prisoners to get a bar of soap under a garden hose at least every other day.

"They will start to stink if you don't," El Moreno had said.

Felix shook his head and tried to concentrate through the stench of sweat and who knew what else. As if planning and executing a major attack against the Great Satan wasn't enough. Now he was playing innkeeper and babysitter to cattle who would most likely be dead in a matter of days.

He wondered if his masters had ever had to do the same, to go through the mundane in order to get to the glory. Felix never took the time to ponder the question before taking the circuitous route to Mexico, first on a plane from Madrid to Venezuela, then the mind-numbing hours of buses and trains through Panama, Central America, and then finally up the coast of Mexico until they'd arrived in Acapulco.

Felix knew they were lucky. He and his men were a new breed of holy warrior. His cousins in the Middle East had the Arabic features that set them apart throughout the world. As a native of Spain, Felix could blend in anywhere. He had grown up alongside the Catholic children who'd spat curses at him because of his religion. Going to university in Barcelona had been easier simply because of the more liberal leanings of much of the student body. There he'd almost been normal compared to the Moroccans and Asians who stood out regardless.

He'd learned to hide his religion, his passion. But that had changed during his final year in school, when his father paid for him and a close friend to visit Mecca and then America. Before leaving, Felix had been confused about America. Why would his father send him to a place called Detroit?

It all became clear in the end. The journey to Mecca had been less than luxurious. He was accustomed to living in the comfort of middle class society. On this trip, his father insisted that he travel with the masses to watch and learn. And learn he did.

His fellow travelers were mostly poor, some spending all the money they'd ever saved to make the sojourn, their Hajj or pilgrimage. They were humble and polite. They shared their meals with him and he came to understand the true gift of spiritual renewal. He cried at the end of his pilgrimage and prayed with his brothers as they circled the obsidian Kaaba in the center of Al-Masjid al-Haram mosque, the largest of its kind in the entire world.

Felix left Saudi Arabia with a full heart, his soul cleansed and yearning for something more than his business degree could give him.

His next stop was much different. Landing in the Detroit airport, he was at first overjoyed to see such wealth and prosperity. Everything looked clean and new. But then he remembered his lessons, and until he left aboard the hotel shuttle, he kept his eyes downcast so as not to allow himself to be corrupted.

After spending a sleepless night at a small hotel on the outskirts of Detroit, he was picked up the next morning by a small man who introduced himself as Walid and said he was a friend of Felix's father. Felix breathed a sigh of relief as he embraced the man, and then asked endless questions as his host drove to another city called Dearborn. According to Walid, Dearborn housed the largest Muslim community in America. Felix had never heard of such a place, but he took the man at his word.

Walid gave him a brief tour of the city. He pointed out the Arab American National Museum, various neighborhoods his brothers had invested in, and finally a modest mosque tucked into the corner of an aged shopping center. They parked behind the mosque and entered through the rear entrance. Felix still remembered the feel of the place, like a worn down tea shop that contained more nicotine stains than customers.

Soon they entered a small room, and at first all Felix could see was a haze of smoke. As his eyes adjusted, he saw three men sitting on wicker chairs. They turned to regard him. Like Walid, they were of Arabic descent, with dark skin and bushy hair.

"Is this the boy?" one of them asked Walid, pointing a fat finger at Felix.

"Yes."

"Come closer, boy. Let me take a look at you."

Felix stepped closer, trying to focus on taking short breaths so he wouldn't cough from the cigarette smoke.

"Walid said you've been to Mecca."

"Yes. I just returned," Felix said, trying to sound proud but feeling more like he was an insect being dissected under a microscope. Why had his father sent him to these men?

"And what did you think of your Hajj?"

"I found my purpose."

"And what purpose would that be?" the fat man asked.

Felix searched for the correct answer, and then said, "To serve Allah, and live by the example of the Prophet Mohammed."

The fat man and his two companions nodded in affirmation.

"We try to live humbly amidst the heathens in this country, but at every turn they swat us back like flies. Do you not see what we've been reduced to?" The fat man spread his arms and motioned to the dingy room.

A flame of anger ignited in Felix's belly.

The fat man continued. "We need your help, brother. We need warriors like you who can show the Americans that our people are the chosen ones, not them. They must learn to respect us, to fear us. Tell me, do you think you are up to the task?"

Felix nodded eagerly.

"Good. Now go back to your studies. Finish your Western education, and then we will find a place for you in our army."

He'd spent another three days in America with Walid as his guide. Walid had shown Felix how the Americans lived, how they assumed that their safety was guaranteed. They walked in groups and indulged in their vices as if Allah was not watching. It filled Felix with excitement, like a warrior looking down upon an undefended future conquest.

He was far from that moment now. Working out of the scrap metal factory owned by El Moreno, Felix longed to set his gaze on America again. But this time he would not be the observer; he would be the avenger, taking the fight to an unguarded enemy. It felt so close and yet so far away. If only he could get to the border. From there things would fall into place.

El Moreno nodded to the workers as he made his way through the factory. They subtly bowed, never stopping what they were doing. He paid them well and expected the best. They knew that and there'd rarely been the occasion to get rid of a willing worker.

He poured himself a cup of coffee from the communal pot that was always simmering, and grabbed a golden brown Pan Dulce, his favorite powdered Mexican pastry. His ever-present security team followed, weapons holstered in one of the few safe havens for their master.

As they ascended the stairs, Felix called from the second level.

"We must talk."

El Moreno calmly held up a finger and then pointed to his pastry. He was getting tired of the Spaniard's orders. Felix could wait.

He checked in with his secretary even though he didn't need to, and then sat down to finish his coffee and tasty snack. Really he just wanted his guest to sweat a little.

When he finally deemed that his stall time was sufficient, he emerged from his office to find Felix pacing. "I'm sorry. Were you waiting for me?"

Felix clenched his jaw but had the good sense not to say something stupid.

"Have you scheduled our departure?" Felix asked.

"Actually, I have."

For maybe the first time since the jihadi had met El Moreno, Felix relaxed like some burden had suddenly been lifted.

"When do we go?"

"Tonight, just after dark. Is that soon enough for you and your men?"

Felix nodded. "We will be ready."

<hr />

Gustavo Rosalez moved to the side as El Moreno passed him. He resumed his sweeping as soon as the security cordon went on their way, not once giving Gustavo a glance.

The slow broom strokes continued until he reached the restroom. Placing his dustpan on the floor, he swept up the debris, careful not to leave a speck on the concrete floor. He leaned his broom against the wall and entered the bathroom with the dustpan, depositing its contents into a metal trashcan.

There were two stalls and one urinal. Gustavo bent down to make sure neither stall was occupied and then entered the farthest one. After settling on the toilet to relieve himself, he pulled out his phone and composed a short text message. *They leave at dark.*

Once the message was sent, he deleted that conversation from his phone, and finished his business.

The coded message from the night before had been clear. The Jackalope wanted any information concerning El Moreno's guests. If the past was any indication, Gustavo knew Señor Ruiz would pay well for the information. This could be his second big payday in less than a month. Who knew that a humble factory janitor could make so much money by simply listening?

Gustavo smiled, flushed the toilet, and then went back to his work. He still had another six hours before he could make the long walk home. Maybe there would be more to hear before that happened.

CHAPTER 14

Daniel left the rest of his teammates to their lunch. Top was regaling the men with his story about Gaucho's confrontation with his uncle. Daniel had heard the story earlier, when Gaucho and Trent had arrived carrying white paper bags stuffed with Mexican street food. He'd eaten quickly, silently processing what the pair had told him and Cal. Things were about to get dicey, and Daniel wanted to be ready. But there was one part of the group that still didn't fit, a piece that still lay outside the proverbial puzzle. Father Pietro.

The priest had mostly kept to himself, sitting on the side of the pool and gazing out over the Pacific Ocean. When he wasn't there, he took to the room he shared with the monks. Daniel could see the battle going on inside the man's head, like he was trying to decide whether to keep living or just lie down and quit.

For some reason, and he knew better than to question it anymore, Daniel felt compelled to talk to the priest. While he didn't have any expectations that he could bring the man out of his funk after one conversation, Daniel knew from experience that sometimes all it took was a simple question, followed by a little patient listening, for a person to take that first step out of the fog.

Father Pietro looked up when he heard the knock on the door. Brother Hendrik rose from where he and his fellow monks were cleaning their weapons on towels on the floor. He unlocked the door and pulled it open.

"Brother Hendrik, I was wondering if I might have a word with Father Pietro." It was the quiet American, the one with the blond ponytail. The former warrior in Pietro recognized the calm calculation in the man's eyes. He also saw compassion there. Not that the rest of the Americans weren't kind. In fact, they'd gone out of their way to get him anything he might need despite his rookie mistake of leading the jihadis back to the safe house. The sophomoric act had put their lives at risk and had almost led to paying the ultimate price, but it seemed that they'd already forgiven him.

Brother Hendrik looked back at him, and he nodded.

The American stepped into the room, and the door was immediately locked behind him.

"My name is Daniel Briggs, Father," the young man said, offering his hand.

Father Pietro grasped it and looked into the man's eyes. This was a good man. He could sense it.

"It is good to meet you, Daniel. Please, shall we talk outside?" He motioned to the open sliding door that led to a comfortable patio.

Daniel nodded and preceded him out.

Father Pietro did not close the door behind him. There was nothing he wanted to hide from the brothers. They were good men as well, but their presence still unnerved him for some reason. He had yet to figure out why.

"What was it you wanted to talk to me about?" he asked, grabbing the railing next to where Daniel stood.

"I wanted to see if there was anything I could do to help," Daniel said. There wasn't an ounce of condescension in the man's tone. When Father Pietro looked into the American's eyes again, he realized what had first grabbed his attention. It was a look that he'd seen in very few people in his life. A rare quality that he'd at one time felt he could find: peace.

"You and your friends have already risked so much for me. I wish I could repay the favor."

"Brother Hendrik says that you want to go home, that you don't want to help us find the guys who did this."

Again, there was no accusation in Daniel's tone, just an honest statement needing confirmation.

"That is true," Father Pietro said, the words coming out slowly, like he'd practiced them.

"May I ask why?"

The night in the apartment flared in his mind. The machine gun fire. The smell of his own sweat and the sound of the last breaths of the men he'd killed. He closed his eyes and tried to force the images away.

"It is all too much. I don't have the strength." His soul ached. He'd tried for so long to be another person, to be a good priest, a devout follower of God.

Daniel didn't press, simply nodding his response.

And then for some reason, as if someone or something had taken over control of his body, the story came out.

"I was in my early thirties when they gave me my own team. I was a good soldier, a model within the elite ranks of the Ninth Parachute Assault Regiment. Have you heard of them?"

Daniel nodded.

"Those were the first days after your 9/11. The Italian government used us in many roles. We found and captured terrorists, Mafiosi, anyone who my government deemed a criminal. We were given the hardest takedowns, the most dangerous assignments. I did not mind. I was young and running into a house full of armed men gave me a thrill that I can even now feel."

Father Pietro took a deep breath and looked out to the waves rolling with the incoming tide.

"It was another classified operation. We didn't know where we were going until we crossed the border into Slovenia. The target was a bomb-making factory that was bringing its goods into Italy. The intelligence report said there would be minimal resistance, but that the ringleader would be at the location. My superiors wanted to bring him in for questioning, in order to see if the man would give up his customers.

"At first, everything went according to plan. There was minimal security outside the large barn, and we easily incapacitated those men. It wasn't until we stepped inside that a shot was fired. I had fourteen men, all handpicked by myself. We swept through the old place like we'd trained. Those enemies who raised weapons were put down. When we located the bomb maker, he retreated to an underground silo, where a farmer used to store grain. Well, he had a handful of men with him and, by the amount of firepower they were using, it was obvious they were not going to surrender."

Father Pietro watched the scene unfold as if he'd magically been transported back to that awful day. He continued, his voice almost mechanical, as if he were reciting an after-action report for a superior.

"I contacted my commanding officer who then gave me permission to terminate the target. My concern was that the bomb-maker had somehow rigged the entire building for detonation. It was one of the things he was known for. I ordered all but two of my men out, just in case. From the top of the stairs, each of the three of us pulled out two high explosive grenades and threw them down the steep stairwell. Even though the stairs went down almost two stories, the explosion still rattled the building and broke several windows. I took the lead, my men following behind. There was no sound as I descended the staircase. The explosives had apparently done their job. We didn't use that type of grenade unless the kill order had been confirmed. Typically we would have used what you call flash bangs.

"I had to turn on my flashlight as we neared the bottom. The explosions had taken out all the lights in the silo. The dust and leftover grain was still settling when we got to the bottom. It took a moment for me to get my bearings, to be able to see what our grenades had done. No one leapt up to greet us, and no bullets flew our way. What I found next was worse. Parts of the dead bodies of the bomb maker and his men lay nearby something that none of us had expected, a cruel surprise that our informant had neglected to tell us. We later found out that the bomb-maker was also getting into the slave trade. He had been harboring a shipment of young girls who would soon be making the trip to whomever had purchased them.

"There were thirty girls, all tied to rings mounted on the stone wall. One of the grenades must have landed right in the middle of them, because there were body parts everywhere. Thirty girls. Thirty girls, Daniel, all dead because of me, because of my actions, because of my decision to take another man's life. I swore right there as I fell to my knees, my weapons falling from my grasp, that I would never take another man's life. I would spend my life trying to atone for my sins. I see those bloody eyes every night. They come to me, pleading, begging for their lives. But I cannot help them. I cannot turn back time and bring them back. I must live with this pain. I must try to bury it and move on. I must..."

"Go on living," Daniel finished for him.

Father Pietro nodded.

"You've known this torment as well."

"I have."

"And does it still live inside you?"

"Always."

"How have you done it? How have you learned to hide from the pain, to forget your old life?"

Daniel smiled, the warmth in his voice like a welcome salve. "I embraced the agony. I realized it will always be a part of who I am, but that fact doesn't make me weak or damaged. It makes me stronger. I made the decision to get up off of the floor and take that first step. But I didn't do it alone."

Father Pietro would have cried if he'd had any tears left to shed. He looked at this young man, who seemed to glow in humble confidence, like he'd found the secret to eternal happiness and was now waiting for Father Pietro to ask the right question so that he could reveal it. He was desperate to know.

"Who helped you? Who showed you the way?"

With that curious smile again, Daniel pointed up at the sky, pulling Father Pietro's gaze heavenward. When he looked down, Daniel was still smiling, and hot tears started running down Father Pietro's face. How could one so young, in the line of work Daniel was in (he'd even heard the others calling him Snake Eyes), have the answer?

"Will you help me?" The question spilled from his mouth like he'd just exhaled after holding his breath for his entire adult life. Father Pietro reached out his hand and grabbed Daniel's arm, as if the act would transfer the young man's peace to him.

"Of course," Daniel answered, putting his hand on top of the priest's.

Father Pietro smiled and returned his gaze to the heavens.

CHAPTER 15

Hollow blips and the steady whir of a myriad of machinery greeted the Pope as he entered the converted apartment. He'd offered to lend one of his personal physicians, but Brother Luca had informed him that The Brotherhood had their own team of caregivers. They'd outfitted the master bedroom like a high-end hospital suite. Every device was digital and shiny. Apparently, The Brotherhood of St. Longinus was well-funded.

Luca's eyes snapped open and he struggled up in bed.

"Please, stay where you are," the Pope said, rolling over a chair so that he could sit next to his friend.

"I am sorry I could not come to you, Holy Father. These doctors have me hooked up to so many tubes." He adjusted the plastic oxygen cannula that ran into his nose.

The Pope waited for his friend to get comfortable, and then said, "How are things in Mexico?"

Brother Luca coughed into a handkerchief. "They tell me things are progressing. We should know more in the morning."

"Is there anything I can do?"

The monk shook his head. "My brothers can take care of it."

It wasn't that the Pope disagreed with him, but matters were getting worse. Too many parishioners had been killed or kidnapped. It seemed that the attacks had ceased, but that could only mean that the next phase of the enemy's plan would soon be implemented.

To complicate things further, the Mexican government was naturally alarmed. There'd been several inquiries to the Vatican regarding the attacks. So far, the Pope and Brother Luca had kept the secret of the terrorist actions to themselves. President Zimmer had also assured the Pope earlier in the day that the team he'd dispatched to assist the monks were the only ones that knew of the jihadi involvement.

It was only a matter of time before word got out. Some enterprising reporter would eventually pick up the story and start digging. Such was the new reality in a technological world.

The Pope exhaled. "Tell me, Luca, what do you think I should do about these fanatics?"

He saw a familiar twinkle in Brother Luca's eye, the same one he'd seen many times in their younger years.

"Prayers alone will not stop them, Your Holiness."

The Pope smiled. It was the same dilemma he faced from sunup to sundown. He was supposed to be the head of a rejuvenated Catholic Church. He tried hard to be a beacon of hope and an example of piety to the rest of the world. But

Luca was right. While it was easy to say that violence was never the answer, what should be told to those on whom violence rained down every day? Pray? Pray and you will be saved from the savages who took your mother and raped your sister? Pray and the army on your front doorstep will suddenly disappear?

No. He knew the truth, that most evil men could only be stopped by overwhelming force. On the face of it, it seemed like a contradiction. How could a good Christian wage war when much of God's message spoke of peace? Did that mean that every soldier who'd ever marched into battle was a sinner?

No. The answer was much more complicated. God had blessed warriors in the past, just as He would in the future. It was easy to condemn a man because of the gun in his hand. It was harder to look into the man's soul and find the good leading him forward on his mission.

And then there was the question of cause. Who was to say that one group's interpretation of heavenly blessing was superior over another? Were Islamic extremists correct when they declared that, in order to serve Allah, a holy war must be levied on their supposed enemies? Were clergy correct during the Inquisition when thousands of suspected heretics were rounded up and tortured, all in the name of God?

No. The Pope had studied religious persecution and violence since he'd first entered the priesthood. He'd come to the conclusion that should have been obvious. The crux of the matter was the simplest form of human emotion: Love. It all came down to love.

He secretly called it "the love test." He'd found that examining a person's motives became easier when you looked at them through the eyes of love. For example, was the decision to condemn all sinners an act of love, or merely a front to portray oneself as holier than others? The Pope knew from weathered experience that those who raised the anti-sinner banner were often the worst offenders, vying for power, celebrity, or just a cause they could put their name on.

So Brother Luca was correct. The jihadist threat could not be fixed with prayers alone. There would always be a need for warriors to protect the defenseless. While it might be a beautiful dream to imagine a world without violence, a utopia where harmony reigned, the opposite would always be true. If human history had taught the world anything, it was that evil men would always exist, fueled by power, greed, mental illness, or all three characteristics. As long as villains existed, the Pope knew there would be a need for men like the Brothers of St. Longinus.

The Pope sighed when he realized his mind had slipped onto his familiar rabbit trail, a quandary he could mull over for centuries if given the time.

"I was just thinking about what you told me when you first came to visit me in Rome," he said.

Brother Luca grinned, the gesture pulling the oxygen lines tight across his cheeks. "What was that?"

"You said that the greatest threat I would face during my time as Pope would be apathy."

"And have you found that to be the case?"

"Unfortunately, yes. It is easy for a person to say the words, to pray as if Jesus is standing before him, but the moment he leaves the church, he goes back to his old ways. The same can be said for governments, my own included. We talk about helping others, unconditionally opening our arms to the world, but do we really? No."

"I am surprised. I thought you were going to say that you were appalled by my recommendation to strike a blow against the jihadis."

The Pope chuckled. "I was more surprised to see you than to hear that you wanted to take the fight to those fanatics. You are, after all, the same Luca I met all those years ago on the streets of Argentina."

Luca nodded, the motion triggering another coughing fit. Once he'd regained his breath, Luca said, "What will you do? Will you tell the world what is happening?"

The Pope honestly didn't know. He didn't have the answer even though he desperately wanted one. With so much at stake, including ever-shrinking numbers of churchgoers, he was hesitant to do anything that might further discredit The Church.

And that's when it hit him.

Brother Luca watched as a subtle change came over the Pope. He first paled and, just as quickly, his color returned like a jolt of electricity had shocked his system.

"What is it?" he asked.

The Pope closed his eyes, ignoring the question. His lips moved and Brother Luca realized the pontiff was saying a prayer. He waited for his old friend to finish.

When he did, the Pope looked up, his eyes bright.

"I must go."

"I am sorry to have kept you." Brother Luca assumed that the Pope had just remembered an important meeting, or maybe he'd come to a revelation that didn't involve his dying friend.

The Pope brushed the apology away with a wave of his hand.

"I am sorry to leave you. I just had a…reminder."

Luca didn't understand. "What happened?"

The Pope smiled. "The Lord works in mysterious ways."

What did that mean? "So where are you going?"

"To Mexico."

If he'd been able and not tethered by tubes and wires, Brother Luca would have jumped out of bed.

"What?! I don't understand. We have things under control. My brothers—"

"I am a simple priest in the service of God, Luca. I go where He bids me to go."

"You are the Pope! Millions depend on you!" Luca searched his mind for any excuse that could stop the stubborn determination in the Pope's tone. "Easter is coming. What about Easter Mass? What about the thousands who have travelled to see you?"

The Pope shrugged like he was a twenty-three-year-old priest again, walking the dangerous byways of Argentina's worst slums. Not a care in the world, like the only sustenance he needed was God's love.

The pontiff rose from his chair and laid a hand on his friend's arm. "Right now, one man needs me. I must go to him. After all, is it not my duty to fight for every soul I can?"

And with that, the Pope left the room, leaving Luca to wonder how to explain this to the rest of the Brotherhood.

CHAPTER 16

They waited in an abandoned convenience store a block away from their target. The only thing that remained in the old store were the remnants of broken shelving and the droppings of animals and humans alike. Cal barely registered the smell of the place. There were too many other things to worry about.

Armando Ruiz had insisted on bringing his men and taking the lead in the operation. Cal hadn't liked the idea at first, but with Gaucho's blessing, The Jefferson Group contingent and the monks were playing a supporting role. Their combined firepower would only be brought to bear if everything went to shit.

Up until that point, it looked like Ruiz had things well in hand. Much to Cal's surprise, the cartel soldiers were polite and well-trained, a far cry from what he'd expected. He'd asked Gaucho about it and the short Hispanic had said, "My uncle always liked things tied tight. It's good to see he's still a pro."

Cal had to give it to the guy. He had the bearing of a crusty and gruff Marine colonel, but the unflinching acceptance from his troops spoke volumes of the reputation the criminal had within his organization. It was almost hard to hate the guy until Cal reminded himself that this was a drug lord he was thinking about.

He heard the clipped voices over the radio, barely making out two out of every ten words. They spoke in their native tongue and Cal was ready to turn his walkie off. Gaucho sat next to MSgt Trent, listening intently and giving the occasional translation like, "They've got eyes on the warehouse," or, "Every egress route is covered."

Cal felt useless. He was not accustomed to playing a supporting role. Even during his time in the Corps, he somehow always ended up at the front. He didn't volunteer for it. It just happened.

Daniel had set up on the roof. With nothing better to do, Cal left out of the back exit, and climbed the metal ladder. At least maybe up there he'd have a better view of what was about to happen.

"Vehicle noises inside the factory," came the voice over the radio.

Ruiz waited. It would only be a minute or two before he triggered the ambush. His instructions were simple: clear shots only and no mowing down vehicles. If they could take down the convoy without firing a shot, all the better. Not that the veteran soldier expected that, but his men knew his intent. There were civilians in the line of fire. No need to have their blood on his hands. He wanted one man: El Moreno.

"Factory doors opening," came another voice.

"Wait until they all clear the door," Ruiz ordered. The last thing he wanted was for the enemy to take cover back inside the factory. No, he wanted them in the open, where well-aimed shots could disable whomever they wanted. With shooters lining every possible way in and out, things could get out of hand quickly should his men get itchy.

"Vehicles moving." There was a short pause. Ruiz inhaled. "Six vehicles clear. Factory doors closing."

"Go, go, go," Ruiz said calmly. He flicked the safety off of his weapon and followed his bodyguards out the front door. He didn't hear any firing. That was good. Maybe El Moreno wouldn't put up a fight. Not that it would keep Ruiz from putting a bullet in the man's head, but it would keep things cleaner.

He could see his men up ahead. They'd pulled their own vehicles in front of the convoy so he could see past them.

"Update, please," he said over the radio, his pace quickening.

There was no answer. He broke into a jog.

"Update," he repeated, noticing that his bodyguards were now fully alert.

"Sir, they're just children."

"What?" he asked, skirting around the idling vehicles, his patience thin.

"The drivers, they're children."

Ruiz got to the first truck and stared up at the frightened eyes of a child. He must have been eleven or twelve.

His mouth was taped shut and his hands were secured to the steering wheel.

"It's the same with the others," one of his men said.

"All children?" Ruiz asked.

"Yes, sir."

"Get them out and back to the Americans. Quickly."

He marched off without waiting for a reply. When he got to the back of the convoy, he pointed to a soldier holding a large crowbar.

"What are you waiting for? Open the door."

It only took a couple of tugs for the man to get the side door open, Ruiz falling in with his troops as they streamed into the factory. Five minutes later, the "all clear" came over the radio. The place had been abandoned. They'd rigged the factory doors to open by remote. Ruiz shook his head. El Moreno had played them perfectly. He'd somehow slipped through the surveillance they'd put in place earlier.

"Sir, there's something you should see."

Armando Ruiz looked up at the man.

"What is it?" he snapped.

The man pointed toward the back of the expansive factory.

"It's back there."

"What is?"

"It's a note."

"What does it say?" Ruiz growled.

"It's for you, sir." To his credit, the man didn't cower. Ruiz's men didn't back down from anyone. He'd taught them that.

Ruiz nodded and said, "Show me."

They made their way deeper into El Moreno's complex. The place was tidy and in complete contrast to the crumbling exterior. He knew that his rival used the place as a metal works shop, producing counterfeit car parts that were shipped all over the world, mostly to America. Not for the first time, Ruiz wondered where the tiny man had found so many skilled laborers to fill the long assembly lines and cramped workshops.

"It's in there, sir," his soldier said, pointing to a room off to the right.

When he got inside, there were a handful of men standing around a large metal box. Ruiz realized it was a commercial grade walk-in freezer, the type used in food processing plants and shipping hubs. The men moved aside when he came into the room, and that's when he saw it.

A man was literally crucified to the huge steel door, using heavy metal cable as shackles around his wrists, ankles and waist. Adding to the macabre display, the dead man was hanging upside down. The man had been disemboweled, and his intestines, stomach and other internal organs hung down onto his bare chest and over his face. Surprisingly, someone had the foresight to place a metal bin under the dying man, and the receptacle now held the majority of the man's dark blood.

Ruiz stepped around the bucket of fluid and moved a strand of intestines aside. It was his informant, the janitor, Gustavo. Apparently the man hadn't been as careful as he'd been taught.

"Where is the note?" Ruiz asked, wiping his gloved hand on the hanging man's trousers.

One of his men produced a rolled up piece of paper and handed it to him. The message was typed, probably on one of those antique typewriters. The note was short and to the point.

Señor Jackalope,
I am sorry that we missed you. Unfortunately, I did
not wish to meet at a time of your choosing. But fear
not, I will see you soon. Please
enjoy the <u>treats</u> I left for you.

El Moreno

Ruiz looked up from the note.

"Was there anything else? He mentioned treats."

A burly soldier with a shaved head pointed to the dead janitor. "Did he mean that?"

"No. He specifically underlined *treats*."

"Sir, we haven't looked in the freezer," said another man.

The freezer. For a second Ruiz had thought El Moreno was referring to the children driving in the convoy. That wasn't his enemy's style. El Moreno liked to pretend he was one of the people, a poor man's Robin Hood, but Ruiz had seen the results of the man's barbarity. Those stories were well-concealed and rarely made it to the public.

Ruiz pulled the metal bucket aside, black blood sloshing and spilling over. The way now clear, he moved to the pull latch. With a quiet whoosh the door slid open, cold air hitting him in the face, sending white clouds into the warm room. It was dark inside the big cooler until he flicked on a switch just inside the door.

He resisted the urge to take a step back. Instead, he took a step forward and called back to his men, "Tell the monks to come. Now."

Brother Hendrik heard the order over the radio and left the storefront with his men. He whispered for his brothers to be ready, not that they needed the reminder.

Blank stares greeted them as they hurried through the factory and back to where they were being escorted. Brother Hendrik saw one man do the sign of the cross, mouthing the words to some unheard prayer.

The first thing he saw was the man hanging on the freezer door. Ruiz's men were trying to get the man down, but it looked like the steel cables were being difficult.

"Where is Mr. Ruiz?" Brother Hendrik asked.

The answer came from inside the freezer. "I'm in here."

Brother Hendrik motioned for his fellow monks to stay outside the container as he stepped toward the blast of cold air. He couldn't see past Ruiz due to the fog created by the mixture of frigid and warm climates.

"You wanted to see me?"

Ruiz nodded slowly, shifting to the side so the monk could pass. "I thought you should be the first to see."

Brother Hendrik stepped farther into the freezer, shapes taking form in the mist. He stopped as a burst of refrigerated air cleared his field of view.

In front of him lay a scene he'd only read about in history books. Standing neatly against the walls of the freezer, and lined down the middle of the remaining twenty feet of freezer space, were large metal crosses, no doubt made in this very factory. But what made Brother Hendrik say a silent prayer, what made him ask God for assistance, were the crucified bodies of black clothed figures, mocking representations of Jesus Christ himself.

He'd found the kidnapped Catholic priests.

CHAPTER 17

Treats. That's what he'd called them. From his first memory, that had been the only name he'd known. Sometimes there were variations like "My Treat," "Tasty Treat," or "Chocolate Treat." As a five-year-old, he hadn't known the sin in it. He'd felt that special relationship, something the lost memories of his past could never conjure about whomever had left him on the doorstep of the Catholic orphanage.

He couldn't remember when the touching had turned to hugging, or when the loving embraces had turned into the little games. Little games. It was those little games that first started the whispers, that got him noticed by the bigger kids who ran the orphanage. Most of them had known their parents, had experienced life outside the sheltered walls of the mission.

But not him. He didn't know there was anything wrong with the little games and the sweet candies pressed into his hands afterword. But he remembered the day the revelation hit, levied by the right hook of a fifteen-year-old orphan. The rest of his gang joined in, spitting on him, calling him names, cursing his birth.

It was the priest in question who'd broken up the beating, chasing off the attackers and holding the little boy to his chest. He sobbed as the priest carried him to the small clinic, and he wailed as the nuns mended his wounds.

It was his sixth birthday. There were no presents, no cakes, just the throbs of pain from the cuts and the deep bruises. The nuns said there was nothing broken, but he felt like he wanted to die.

More than the pain, the memories of what the others boys had said stabbed his heart, pierced his soul, and made him question everything about his young life. When he'd finally been well enough to leave the cot, he found the priest and asked him about what the children had said. The young man brushed off the boy's concerns and ushered him on to lunch.

He'd spent the rest of the day alone, shuffling around the walled perimeter of the playground, thinking. It was the first time he'd truly thought for himself, like the beating he'd taken had awoken something inside of him that he never knew he had. While his six-year-old mind pondered, the others jeered from the swings and occasionally tossed a handful of pebbles his way. He didn't hear them or see them. His brain processed all that he could remember, sifting the good and the bad into piles, like stones being sorted for play.

Gradually, the pile of bad outweighed the good. His chest felt heavy, like it was filled with the tangible filth of those dirty deeds. But then, in the most natural way, like someone had tapped him with a wand and proclaimed him changed, the disgust and guilt turned to anger. Seething, tearing, burning anger. It flooded his body and he let it happen. The warmth felt like home, like it was supposed to be there. He was whole.

The priest had been his first kill. He murdered the pedophile with a large rock from the garden. It only took six downward strikes. He remembered that fact vividly, just as he marveled at the way his tiny hands had the ability to take a grown man's life. Dripping with blood, he wiped them on the bedsheets and left for the last time.

El Moreno thought about everything that had happened since that day. Not once had he felt like a victim again. He'd literally taken justice into his own hands, and it wouldn't be the last time. He was soon one of the fastest pickpockets in town. When the small police force finally found out who he was, he moved on to Acapulco and staked his claim.

Even as a teenager, he'd taken children under his wings. He was never cruel to them. Soon he was running a profitable trade and raising a score of younger boys and girls. They never talked of God, only of the responsibility they had to themselves and each other. Not once did they look for a handout. El Moreno would take anything they needed. From food to clothes, he provided. Some of those same children were still with him today, forging a new path for the one-time outcasts.

So when the Spaniard had asked for El Moreno's permission to kill the priests, his request was denied. He alone wanted to be the one to send a message, that his organization was better than the others, that he didn't fear God or the repercussions. He'd already been to Hell and back and wasn't afraid to tempt the road again.

While Armando Ruiz wouldn't understand the connotation left in the note, El Moreno looked at it as yet another step forward, a dark blanket over old memories. He would never be anyone's treat again.

———————

Felix looked up from his phone and smiled. The next phase of their plan was a GO. His masters had been right, their faith unwavering. He thought about what it must be like to hold such power, to be so sure of your path that only death could take it from you. He marveled at the mystery of Allah, and how everything came to pass just as his masters predicted.

Even though he would never admit it to his men, Felix still harbored doubts. He found it hard to fully believe in something he could not see. While others walked through life with blinders, he kept looking all around, just as he had as a child when his father took him on business trips to Barcelona.

But Felix knew that curiosity and uncertainty were enemies to the true believer. He prayed every day that he could shake away his fears and embrace his masters' vision. All he needed was evidence. Maybe now he had it. After all, what otherworldly power did it take to precipitate the actions that were now coming to fruition?

Allah be praised.

Then there was the issue of the Mexican, El Moreno. They'd had their differences in the past, but now it seemed they were coming together, finally on the same page. Felix had at first been enraged when the cartel leader said he couldn't kill the priests. But when the slim smile spread across El Moreno's face and he said he alone would take care of that deed, Felix had felt real fear.

That worry had only increased as he watched El Moreno's workers craft the metal crosses and mount them inside the freezer. It was El Moreno himself who took the time to strangle each priest with a yellow extension cord, one by one as the others watched. Then, with the help of his men, he mounted the dead bodies on their displays, not an ounce of remorse on his face.

The act itself wasn't the problem. In fact, it showed Felix that the Mexican would have no qualms about the next phase of their operation. What worried Felix were the steps after that. He'd been told to keep things close, to only divulge information at the last practical moment. But El Moreno kept dropping hints. He wanted to know everything. And now, after watching what he'd done to the priests, Felix had no doubt what would happen to him and his men should they cross the line with the Mexican.

Felix looked out at the passing ocean and said a prayer that the pieces would fall into place quickly. The sooner he could finish his task and return home a hero, the sooner he could get away from the cherubic drug lord and his violent grasp. The steady stream of ocean air didn't cause the shiver that ran down his back as he stepped away from the railing. It was the thought of tiny hands wrapped around his straining neck that gave him chills.

CHAPTER 18

THE WHITE HOUSE
11:35PM, MARCH 14TH

President Zimmer toweled off after taking his second shower of the day. He'd found that taking one in the morning helped wake him up, and taking one before going to bed helped to wash away the smell of another day in Washington, D.C. He was finding it harder and harder not to be cynical. There were too many players who seemed hellbent on causing chaos.

From gun control to civil rights, the White House always had to have a comment. Some days he wondered how he'd ever get anything done. All Zimmer had to do then was remind himself that he had a good man at his side, a man who'd fought on the front lines and come to D.C. kicking and screaming. Travis Haden kept him grounded and looking forward. Not a week went by that the Chief of Staff didn't make some small comment that would nudge his boss back into the slipstream.

It didn't help that an endless influx of enemies cropped up daily. While Americans believed that their government could protect them, Zimmer knew that was impossible. There were just too many threats on the horizon and the United States was a big juicy target.

As he slipped into a freshly laundered robe, he looked in the mirror, noticing more gray hairs than before. Had there ever been a president who hadn't aged prematurely? They all looked fresh and clean when they took office, but the piling problems and constant strain stripped them of their innocence and their youth.

He finished his nightly routine and made his way to bed. A preview of the next day's schedule lay waiting. Zimmer exhaled as he grabbed the one-page report and pulled back the duvet. He'd just sat down on the bed when there was a knock on the door.

He took a deep breath.

"Come in," he said, trying not to sound annoyed.

A Secret Service agent entered the master bedroom.

"Mr. President, we have a secure call for you."

Zimmer wondered why they hadn't just patched it to the phone on his bedside.

"Who is it?" the President asked, grabbing his newly designed portable phone that the developer bragged was unbreakable. It reminded Zimmer of the old suitcase cellphones from the Eighties.

"It's the Pope, Sir."

He hadn't heard from the Holy See since their visit in Rome. Regular updates from Cal had kept Zimmer apprised of the mess in Mexico, so it wasn't like the two heads of state needed to talk regularly.

"Thanks. I'll let you know when I'm done," the president said, waiting until the agent left the room.

"President Zimmer," he answered, after waiting for the range of clicks and zips to die down.

"Mr. President, I am sorry for calling you at this hour."

"It's not a problem. I wasn't even in bed yet."

There was a pause as the connection settled again.

"I wanted to let you know that I am on my way to the United States, and then to Mexico."

That was news.

"Oh? I hadn't heard that you were coming."

"It was a last minute decision."

"Will you be coming through Washington? I'm sure we can shuffle my schedule around a bit."

"That won't be necessary, Mr. President, although I appreciate the thought. You and your men have done enough already. My representatives in Mexico tell me that your men are very good."

"I've heard the same of your men." That was true. In fact, Cal's exact words had been, "These monks are Class A pros." That was a huge compliment coming from the picky Marine.

That gave Zimmer an idea.

"Where will you be flying into? I assume you have your full compliment coming?"

The Pope didn't fly anywhere without his retinue. From the bubble car to the Swiss Guards, the Pope's crew rivaled even Zimmer's.

"No. We are coming in a private aircraft and I've brought a small contingent of security."

More news that Zimmer hadn't expected. What was the Pope up to?

"May I ask why you're coming?" Zimmer asked.

"The Lord has requested my presence." He said the words as if he'd just told the president that a neighbor asked him to coffee. Zimmer didn't know how to respond.

"And where exactly will you be going?"

"We land in Calexico, California, in the morning and then move across the border to Mexicali, Mexico, once the proper overtures have been made to a select handful of Mexican officials."

So this wasn't going to be an official visit. Even so, Zimmer wondered how incognito the Pope and his men could really be. It was one thing to walk unnoticed through the labyrinth of tunnels beneath Rome. It was something else completely to hop across a border with minimal interruption, especially for a man of the Pope's stature.

"What reason will you give the Mexicans for coming?"

The Pope chuckled. "Although I would like to say that men like us do not need a reason, I was thinking that a request to see the displaced orphans who are being shipped to your country might be sufficient."

Immigration. The word flared in Zimmer's brain. It was one of many thorns in the president's side. There didn't seem to be a good answer. And even while American politicians quibbled about the merits of amnesty versus tighter border security, more and more illegals were flowing across the border. That gave Zimmer an idea.

"How about this? The rest of my week is pretty light. Let me fly down and meet you. That way, if reporters start snooping around, we can say it was a mutual decision on our part."

"I would not want to inconvenience you."

"I've been meaning to get down to the border for some time. Maybe you can help me come up with a solution to our immigration problem." He said it as a joke, but cringed when he realized what he'd just said. The Pope was a man of open arms. If it were up to him, the border barriers would probably be torn down. That wouldn't go over well with even the most vocal amnesty proponents.

Luckily the Pope picked up on his joke and said, "In exchange, I would only ask that you give me a lesson in appeasing your constituents."

The two men laughed, Zimmer more from relief that his slip hadn't moved the needle of U.S. immigration policy.

"I'll get my people to work, and see what we can do to keep this under the radar," Zimmer said, already smiling at the thought of the look his Chief of Staff was about to give him.

"Very good. I look forward to seeing you."

The warmth in the Pope's tone came through the phone like a father's warm embrace. Zimmer found it hard not to get a little bit emotional. This was the Pope after all. With only a few words, the man had the ability to make him feel like a trusted friend.

"I'll see you tomorrow."

Zimmer ended the call and walked to the bedroom door. When he opened it, the Secret Service agent was waiting.

"I need you to get Mr. Haden up. I'm sure it won't make him happy, but tell him the boss said so."

The agent grinned and took the phone from the president.

"I'll use my kid gloves, Sir."

CHAPTER 19

They had disposed of the priests's bodies after a short prayer led by Brother Hendrik. That was hours ago. Now they were waiting for word from one of Ruiz's informants. Not only had El Moreno slipped through their trap, he'd also apparently slipped out of the city. Ruiz's network couldn't find him.

Gaucho's uncle didn't seem perturbed. Cal watched as the drug lord monitored his impressive collection of cell phones, laptops and police scanners. His Spartan hideout reminded Cal of a scene from *The Godfather*, when the Corleone family goes to war with other families of New York. They even had the mattresses to match the famous line "going to the mattresses." All they needed was fat Uncle Paulie cooking up a big pot of pasta sauce on the one burner.

Once again, The Jefferson Group operators were relegated to a supporting role. No, not supporting, waiting, something Cal did poorly. At least this time he had something to think about. The President had called earlier, informing Cal of the Pope's travel plans as well as his own. Cal could tell by his boss's voice that he would not be convinced to do otherwise. Brandon had explained it simply enough, saying, "It is technically my Spring Break after all." The only thing Cal had made him promise was that he'd stay on the U.S. side of the border. Encircled by his ever-present Secret Service cordon, the President would be one less thing for Cal to worry about.

The problem now was who to tell about the Pope. Daniel knew, of course, but Cal was having trouble deciding who else should know. Definitely not Ruiz. While Cal respected the man's leadership skills, the guy was still a crook. No, Ruiz would be the last to know, if at all.

But he had to tell the monks. They hadn't said a thing to Cal about the Pope's visit, so they must not already know. Cal had to tell them.

He made his way over to where they sat. Their conversation died when he approached.

"Brother Hendrik, I was wondering if I could speak with you for a minute," Cal said.

Brother Hendrik nodded and unfolded his large frame from the floor, his weapon coming up with him. He followed Cal to a quiet corner away from the chatter.

"I just got word that the Pope is flying into the U.S.," Cal whispered, always keeping an eye on Ruiz's men.

"I know."

Anger sparked in Cal's stomach. He searched Brother Hendrik's face for any shred of remorse. There was none.

"Why didn't you tell me?"

"Would you have told me if your president was doing the same, even if his closest advisors did not know?"

The monk was right. Technically the Pope's trip shouldn't interfere with their operation, just like President Zimmer.

"Well it just so happens that the Pope called my president, and he's on his way too."

Brother Hendrik's eyes widened for a split second.

"That I did not know."

So the Pope wasn't telling his men everything. He wondered what else the pontiff was keeping to himself.

"Look, I told my boss to stay out of the way. I sure hope you told yours to do the same thing," Cal said.

"I do not tell the Holy Father where he should and should not go. He is guided by a higher power."

That was all Cal needed, for the monks to bring religion into the picture and screw up every shred of operational security they had. Cal respected them and their church, but he wasn't about to let their spiritual leanings dictate how things were being run.

Just as he went to say something back, Gaucho interrupted, "Hey, I think they've got something."

Cal threw one last warning look at Brother Hendrik and the two men followed Gaucho over to his uncle's hasty command post. Ruiz was muttering something in Spanish into one of his many phones. He looked up when his guests approached.

"We found him," Ruiz mouthed, motioning that he'd only be another minute on the phone.

Cal waited impatiently, wishing that he spoke more Spanish than he did. He was pretty much limited to "Una cerveza, por favor" (One beer, please) and "Buenas noches" (Good night).

Ruiz set down the phone and pulled out a brand new map of Mexico. He'd used it earlier to show them the mostly likely routes he thought El Moreno would take to the border.

"Well, I was wrong. He boarded a large fishing vessel yesterday," Ruiz said, flattening the map with his hands. "The boat is most likely heading up through the Gulf of California."

"Most likely?" Gaucho asked.

"That's what they told the harbormaster, but they could have lied."

"So we really don't know where they're going. They could be halfway to San Diego by now."

"Not necessarily," Ruiz traced a finger up the Mexican coast and north through the Gulf of California that split the Baja Peninsula off from the rest of mainland Mexico. "This isn't news to your DEA, so I'll tell you. The best ports to bring anything in through the west side of Mexico are all along here, not on the Baja Peninsula."

"Why is that?" Cal asked, thinking that a more direct approach to the U.S. might make more sense.

"Various factors," Ruiz explained. "Two of the best reasons are the surf and weather conditions. The Gulf of California is naturally protected. That makes it much easier to travel and enter port."

"So where do you think he'll go? I see three or four places they could dock, and that's assuming they don't pick a random landing spot that doesn't even have a name on it," Cal said, trying to picture the terrain in his head.

Ruiz shook his head. "My gut tells me that he's short on time. If it were me, I'd either hit the port here in Guaymas, or make the run all the way up to Puerto Peñasco."

"And if you had to choose?"

"Puerto Peñasco," Ruiz answered without hesitation. "It's a newer version of Cancun and less than one hundred miles to the Arizona border."

Cal scanned the map and figured it was as good a choice as they were going to get. With no good ports north of Puerto Peñasco, at least they could use it as a chokepoint. There looked to be one major road going in and out. The other piece of good news was that Calexico (where the president told him the Pope was headed) and its sister city of Mexicali were well west of the Arizona border crossing. That would keep the Pope out of the picture.

"Okay," Cal said. "How do we get there?"

"We own a few planes. They'll be ready to go when we get to the airstrip."

At least they had Ruiz's assets at their disposal. Nodding his agreement to Gaucho's uncle, Cal wondered how long it would take before those assets might be turned on TJG and the monks. They needed to be prepared if that occasion arose. After all, if Ruiz found out who Cal and the robed warriors worked for, all hell would undoubtedly break loose.

Father Pietro had spent most of the preceding hours in prayer. He hadn't been there to see the scene at the factory, but he'd been with the Brothers of St. Longinus when they laid the murdered priests to rest. Their faces were covered, and he was glad of that. There were at least two brothers from his parish lying under the old paint-stained tarps. He did not know them well, and that fact shamed him.

If he had been a good priest, he would have taken the time to share a life with his fellow priests, to understand their joint mission to reach the people of Acapulco. But that hadn't happened. Since his talk with Daniel, Father Pietro had come to see what had become of his life. In no way did he believe he'd changed, but at least now he could see.

There was much that he was not proud of. More than the drink and his lackluster performance as a leader in the church, it was his cowardice that shamed him the most. He'd run to the church to hide, when, in fact, he should have dealt with his demons like a man. There'd been more than one occasion when he'd had the chance to confess, or just open up to someone, anyone, but he'd kept it covered instead.

Coward, he thought. He prayed that God give him the courage to take those first steps. Then he realized he already had, that God had placed men in his path that could help him see. The Brothers of St. Longinus and their storied pasts, who'd redeemed their old lives and forged ahead as anointed warriors for the Pope himself. Then there was Daniel and his quiet confidence. In a way it reminded Father Pietro of his old self, when he'd stood on a hill with his hands on his hips and dared the world to challenge his talents. It seemed that Daniel did the same in a humbler way, not with his talents, but with his faith.

Father Pietro did not know where his path would lead, but when the word came that they would be leaving in minutes, he rose without hesitation. For the first time in years, he looked forward to the adventure ahead, that there could be a new life for him yet. He grabbed his pack and followed the small army out the door.

CHAPTER 20

His security team wasn't happy, but they weren't about to fight him on this. With only eight men available for the last minute excursion, the Swiss Guards were tense. The Pope could see it in their eyes, the way they glanced at him half like he was crazy and half like there must be something else going on in order for him to break protocol.

The part of him that was still human, and not the leader of millions of Catholics around the world, almost lost his patience. He was not simply a figurehead to be toted around in a bulletproof box for all the world to see, like some strange circus exhibit. He was the Pope, appointed by the Cardinals of the church and God himself to tend to his flock.

As they'd flown over oceans and continents, he'd had to remind himself of that fact, a fact that many couldn't seem to grasp: He was a simple priest elevated to the highest holy position. There were days when he wished for nothing more than to wander the streets of Rome again, conversing with beggars, smiling at the vendors, and enjoying a shot of espresso in peace.

But that would never again happen. He was the Pope, and most Popes only left their lofty position by dying.

"Your Holiness, it is time," said the leader of their expedition, a clean cut Swiss Guard in his early fifties. The man was on a short list to take over the guard when the current chief retired. He was a good man, a soldier who had thwarted his fair share of attempts on the pontiff's life. In short, the Pope trusted him completely.

"Should I change?" the Pope asked. One of the concessions he'd had to make for the antsy team was that he would go incognito, leaving his normal attire in the aircraft.

"Yes, Holy Father," the Swiss Guard said respectfully. The Pope remembered that the man's name was Angelo. How fitting.

Five minutes later, the Pope emerged from the private restroom. He wore a dusty gray suit over an off-white button-down shirt, more casual than formal. Topping off the disguise were a pair of non-prescription gold wire rimmed glasses and a navy blue flat cap.

"How do I look?" he asked Angelo, who had looked up from another briefing with his men.

For the first time since they'd boarded, the Swiss Guard smiled. "You look like a businessman, Holy Father. A good disguise."

The Pope returned the smile and adjusted the blazer. It had been decades since he'd worn anything but what was prescribed for Catholic clergy. It felt foreign, but not in a bad way. A prickle of adventure ran down his arms as he went to find his seat. It had been too long since he'd felt so alive, so young.

He looked out the window as the pilot made his final approach. It was dark on the ground, so it was easy to see the well-lit line marking the U.S./Mexico border running east to west. There were the lights coming from Mexicali on the Mexican side of the fence, and far fewer lights coming from their destination, Calexico, California. He'd never been to the border town, and wondered again why he'd felt the compelling pull to make the impromptu visit.

The landing was perfect. Come to think of it, he couldn't remember ever feeling a bump in any of his flights as Pope. He wondered if that had more to do with the caliber of pilots or the importance of the cargo. Probably a little of both.

They taxied to the end of the small receiving area and the aircraft stopped. From what he could see from the window, there wasn't much of a terminal. Even though it was called the Calexico International Airport, it looked to be no more than a private landing strip for smaller planes.

Angelo was the first to the door. The Pope could feel the tension in the air, as if the moment the door opened the Swiss Guard expected a swarm of attackers to converge. They'd instructed the Pope to remain in his seat until the security team had a chance to check the area, and then they would all move to the registration building to procure the rental vehicles that were supposed to be waiting.

Seven men hurried out the door. One man stayed behind, a grizzled veteran who'd said little on the journey over. Angelo had instructed the man to stay no farther than an arm's length away from their charge. The Pope could see that the man was taking his task seriously. There was barely a hand's distance between them.

Angelo poked his head back in the cabin a couple minutes later and said, "It's clear."

The Pope wasn't an ancient man, but he still needed help getting down the ladder's steps. It was warm outside, a welcome change to the cold weather they had in Rome hours earlier. It reminded him of home, of days on the beach in Buenos Aires. He breathed in a flood of air as his guard guided him toward the short row of buildings up ahead. The airport itself was well lit, but the area beyond was an impenetrable dark.

The crack in the distance startled him even though he'd heard many gunshots in the past. It sounded like it had come from the border, too far off to be of concern. But when he turned to see Angelo's reaction, he saw the Swiss Guard on the ground, blood gushing from a hole in his neck.

The Swiss Guard assigned to watch the Pope dropped all sense of propriety, half dragging and half carrying the Pope to safety. They headed back toward the plane.

There were shouts and the sudden explosion of more gunfire and the Swiss Guard fired at targets the Pope could not see. When they were maybe one hundred feet from the plane that was revving its engines, something streaked overhead, causing both men to duck.

The Pope fell to his knees, scraping them through his new garments. But the pain was nothing compared to the blast that followed, as whatever had been fired slammed into their only way out, sending the aircraft up in flames. The force of the explosion rolled over them, and his protector did his best to shield him from debris.

"We must go," the guard said, hoisting the Pope to his feet even as the gunfire intensified all around them. He heard screams of pain and confusion, like the Swiss Guard was fighting an invisible foe.

He tried to put it out of his mind as they hurried away, the Swiss Guard grunting as he pulled the old man along. When they finally got to a small shed, the Pope was completely out of breath. His heart pounded and his lungs ached. His vision blurred in and out of focus.

"Stay here. I must check on the others," said the guard, who didn't stop to hear if the Pope might protest.

When the man left, the Pope strained to hear what was happening, but his inexperienced ears couldn't make out the balance of the ongoing gun battle. Another explosion rocked the once quiet airport, followed by screams and shouts, some in Italian, and others in Spanish.

The Pope felt weak and hopeless. At least if he had been younger he could have run. But now he was left to wait, an old man past his physical prime. What could he do? What *would* he do?

His hand slipped down to where he normally had his old rosary, a gift from a blind woman he'd once met in Buenos Aires. The beads were made of seashells and the crucifix was carved from a piece of driftwood. It was one of his most cherished possessions, a reminder that God could be found in the humblest of places.

But he'd left that gift in the airplane that was now burning at the end of the runway. Instead of finding the rosary, his hand tapped against something rectangular. At first he couldn't remember what it was, but then he realized it was the cellular phone Brother Luca had given him before leaving.

There were only two numbers programmed in the secure phone. Luca was too far away to be of any help, so the Pope opted for the second number. He pressed the call button, and waited for an answer.

There was a pause and then the sound of heavy breathing.

The President was finally dozing off when his personal cell phone rang. He was immediately awake. Maybe half a dozen people had that number, and none of them would be calling if it weren't a catastrophic emergency. But when he picked up the phone, he didn't recognize the number. He answered the call.

"Yes?"

There was a pause and then the sound of heavy breathing.

"Mr. President?"

President Zimmer couldn't make out the voice through the background noise.

"Who is this, please?"

"It is your friend from Rome."

"Your Holiness?"

"Yes. Mr. President, I do not have much time. To be brief, we are under attack. We landed in Calexico minutes ago, and almost immediately came under fire."

"Are you okay? Where's your security team?"

Zimmer heard the Pope cough. "They are engaging the enemy."

"Okay, listen. Let me get on the phone. I'll have my military there in no time. Yuma isn't far away, and the Marines—"

"Mr. President," the Pope interrupted, "there is not time for that. You must listen to me."

Zimmer gritted his teeth and cursed every extremist nut job the world had ever birthed. Trying to kill an American president was one thing. To kill a holy man like the Pope took a twisted soul and heaping helping of "I don't give a fuck."

"Tell me what I can do," Zimmer said, rising from bed and switching on the light.

"Trust in our men."

"What men?"

"The men we sent to Mexico. It is their mission that is most important."

"But you could be captured. They could—"

"I am well aware of what they could do to me. I put my faith in God, you, and our men. Will you do the same?"

What the Pope was asking him to do was ludicrous. In less than an hour, Zimmer could have the best special operations troops in the country swooping in for the rescue. Part of him wanted to ignore the pontiff's request, but for some reason he didn't. Maybe it was the certainty in the Pope's tone, or the fact that the possibility of otherworldly intervention had slowly crept into the president's mind.

So against his better judgment, he said, "I'll do it."

"Good. Now I must discard this phone before they realize what I have done. God bless you, Mr. President. I am sure we will see each other soon."

There wasn't time for Zimmer to respond before the line went dead. He stared at the phone in his hand for a second, praying that something miraculous would happen, or that the Swiss Guard would win the day. By the Pope's choice of words, the second option didn't seem likely.

After slipping on his robe and formulating his thoughts, he left his Air Force One bedroom suite to alert the team.

The Pope turned off the phone and dropped it into an old oil drum. He heard it plop into whatever liquid the vessel now contained.

The gunfire had faded, and now there was only the crackling of the burning plane. Somewhere in the distance he heard sirens. Maybe the American police would make it in time.

He did his best to find a hiding spot in the back of the shed, but there was little to shield him from view. Besides, as soon as he'd gotten comfortable, he heard the sound of footsteps running in his direction.

The first one around the corner was his protector, the gruff Swiss Guard who'd been tasked to stay with the Pope.

"There he is," the man said, pointing to where the pontiff's shoes were visible behind a stack of wood pallets.

Two other men, both masked and carrying assault rifles, came around the corner and eyed their prize before moving to pick him up off the ground.

"You are my Judas," the Pope said to the Swiss Guard, who no longer harbored any visible concern. He wondered if the traitor had killed his former comrades along with the masked attackers. "I will pray for you, my son."

The man's mouth stretched into a sneer. "I don't need your prayers."

Whatever fueled this man's hate ran deep.

"I will still pray for you," the Pope said as he was hoisted to his feet. And he did say a prayer for the man, that he might one day find peace. In his next prayer, as they stuffed him into the back of a van and placed a hood over his head, the Pope prayed that President Zimmer would keep his word, and that the warriors they'd sent to Mexico would fulfill their mission. He knew his time on Earth was not yet over. His only hope now was that God would give him the strength to do what he must. There was still a soul crying out for help, and he had to find it.

CHAPTER 21

Travis Haden peeled his eyes from the latest report on Iran. The Iranian government was talking a good game, but it didn't look like their puppeteering was letting up in other Middle Eastern countries. When would it end?

"Trav," the President said, one foot outside his stateroom door.

Travis nodded and took the folder with him, shaking the stiffness out of his legs as he walked.

"What's up?" Travis asked, tucking the red file under his arm.

The President didn't say anything, just motioned to his office. Travis nodded and followed his boss in. They had a minimal crew on the plane. Besides the Air Force personnel and the Secret Service, he and Zimmer were the only ones aboard. A rarity, but natural considering the last minute arrangements. The Chief of Staff hadn't been happy about getting the late night call, but he jumped at the chance to get out of D.C.

"The Pope called."

The President's eyes were doing that shifty thing. It was a small tell that he only showed among friends. Travis frowned.

"What happened?"

Travis was one of the few people who knew about the covert Mexican operation. Hell, his cousin was leading the U.S. delegation. For a second, Travis had the gut-gripping feeling that Cal was hurt.

"I think the Pope was just kidnapped."

Travis couldn't hide his surprise.

"You've gotta be kidding. What the hell happened?"

Zimmer told him what he knew, about the attack and that the Pope thought the fight was tilting the other way.

"And you're sure he wasn't killed?"

"I don't know."

"We need to call our people. They can get the SEALs in quick, maybe even some Delta. I've got a buddy that—"

The President held up his hand.

"We can't do that."

Travis thought that maybe he'd misunderstood.

"Don't worry, it'll all be hush-hush. These guys know—"

"No," Zimmer interrupted again, shaking his head, his eyes set. "We can't call anyone in."

"What? That's crazy. This is the Pope we're talking about!"

What could Brandon be thinking? If he was attacked, every American with a gun would probably be called in.

"I know." The words came out with reluctance, Travis could see that. "He said to let things play out, to let our guys in Mexico do their jobs."

Disbelief surged in Travis's chest.

"Look, I know Cal's boys are good, hell, I trained some of them myself, but this thing is bigger than any of us. If word leaks out that the Pope's been killed, can you imagine what would happen?"

He searched the president's face for comprehension. All he found was unease.

"I can't explain it, Trav. The way he said it...he knows what's going to happen. Even though there was gunfire on the call, he sounded levelheaded, like he understood where things were headed."

"I don't care how levelheaded he sounded, Brandon! That's the Pope! I'm going to make some calls, get the ball rolling. You stay here and I'll—"

"No."

The word felt like a slap in the face. Since going to D.C. at the President's behest, the two men had rarely disagreed. Despite the fact that the Commander in Chief was a Democrat from Massachusetts and Travis was a staunch conservative former Navy SEAL, they'd found common ground and forged an ironclad working relationship based on trust and mutual respect.

All Travis could do was stare at the man he now considered a friend.

"What if he's right, Trav? What if this is out of our hands? What if God wanted this to happen?"

That shook Travis more than he would ever admit. While he wasn't a practicing Christian, he did have a deep respect for God. Few who'd seen the scourge of war hadn't turned to God at some point, whether for comfort or that last ounce of bravery. But saying that circumstances should be allowed to roll despite the arsenal at their disposal was pure insanity.

"I'm telling you this as your friend and as your Chief of Staff. If the Pope dies, and the public finds out that you didn't lift a finger to help him, do you think they're going to listen about the last conversation the two of you had?"

The two men stared at each other.

"Faith," President Zimmer finally said, his voice even and calm. "Maybe we just need a little faith."

Travis would have laughed if Zimmer didn't look dead set on his decision. They'd rarely had "the religion talk." Sure, they crafted the President's "official" religious stance for the media, but both men held their spirituality in a private corner of their choosing. It was no longer en vogue to profess your religion on the national level. There were too many organizations ready to take pot shots if the opportunity presented itself.

"We can't do this, Brandon. It's not right."

"Take off your political hat for a minute. What if the Pope told you to trust his men, to trust our men, your cousin being among them. Do you trust them? Do you have faith that they can get to the bottom of whatever this conspiracy is?"

It was like getting called to the carpet by your commanding officer. Shit or get off the pot.

The words came from his subconscious.

"I should be with them."

It took the President a second to comprehend. He nodded.

"You mean with Cal."

"Yeah. With Cal, Trent, Gaucho and Daniel. Instead I'm up here, reading reports and serving as your glorified secretary."

He wished he hadn't said that last part, but the truth slipped through his normal restraint. To his credit, the President didn't look upset.

"I understand. Do you think I always want to be president? Sometimes I wish I'd met you and Cal earlier, like when I was in college. Maybe you could've knocked some sense into my Ivy League brain then and dragged me into the military."

"You don't mean that. You've had a good life."

Now Travis really felt bad. Brandon was a good boss, on his way to being a great president, maybe one of the best who ever served his country.

"I do mean it. I have a good life because of you guys. I'll never forget the sacrifice of so many of our brave troops. It's the reason I understand why the Pope asked me to wait. He has complete faith in his men. It doesn't hurt that he probably has an oversized helping of God on his side, too. I think we should wait, see what happens."

Now he sounds like a president, Travis thought, staring at the man who'd once been a spoiled politician full of his own inflated worth.

"Okay. So what do we do now?"

The President smiled, the warmth in his tone soothing some of Travis's misgivings.

"First, I suggest you let the agents on board know. I'm sure they can monitor the situation from here."

"Anything else?"

This time the President's eyes seemed a little sadder, but still resolute.

"Yeah. Call your cousin and tell him you're coming to help. You are one of them, after all."

CHAPTER 22

They arrived under the cover of darkness. Instead of flying into the small resort town's airport, Gaucho's uncle had them land at a hasty landing strip away from the coast, its runway lined with upturned LED flashlights set in little tin buckets. From what Cal could see, the place looked like a perfect smuggling hub: remote and perfectly hidden in a shallow valley. Improvements were minimal, but someone was definitely taking care of the dirt runway. He imagined some old guy out there every day, picking up pebbles and smoothing out rough edges. Not a bad gig for an old-timer, if you didn't mind living in the desert. From what he'd seen of Ruiz, the guy probably paid pretty well, too.

They were thirty men strong. While Ruiz said he would love to take an army north, even he had limitations. Even at thirty, keeping concealed would be close to impossible, but everyone agreed that the extra firepower was needed.

"Here come the vans," Daniel said, pointing into the darkness. Everyone turned that way.

It was a short hop into town, maybe twenty minutes. Ruiz had already gotten confirmation that a couple large fishing vessels had come in earlier. If they were lucky they could cut off El Moreno before he bolted north. Cal was concerned that they had no idea where the guy was going. The U.S. border ran hundreds of miles. If their thirty-man force couldn't snatch him, it might be like looking for a single grain of sand on a pristine beach.

The passenger vans rumbled closer, opting to turn onto the runway. Cal's phone buzzed in his pocket. It was Travis.

Cal answered. "Hey, Trav."

"Can you talk?"

"Hold on." Cal moved a few feet away from the others, Daniel following close by. "Okay. We just got to the port. We're about to hop in our transport and—"

"Cal, your plans just changed."

"What happened?" His mind immediately jumped to the worst case scenario. Had El Moreno somehow gotten past them and already bounded across the border?

"The Pope just got kidnapped."

"No way," Cal exhaled.

"Yeah. He got a call in to Brandon a few minutes ago. Said he and his security team were attacked. We thought he might've been killed, but the Secret Service guys with us are monitoring the police channels. The cops think it's a shipment exchange gone bad. No sign of the Pope, but a bunch of dead Swiss Guards who they still think are hired guns."

"Holy shit. Are the spooks coming in, spec-ops?" Cal assumed that the President had pressed every emergency button he had to get the Pope back. This could look bad for everyone involved.

"No."

"Wait, what?"

"We're not calling anyone in."

"Why the hell not?! Let me talk to Brandon. He's about to make the dumbest—"

"Cal," Travis interrupted. "The Pope asked Brandon not to call in the big guns."

Cal almost screamed at his cousin. He gritted his teeth instead and said, "So what the hell are you going to do?"

"The Pope asked for you and the monks to find him."

That almost surprised Cal more than Travis's admission that the President wasn't going to lift a finger to help the Pope.

"Look, Trav. What you need to do is shut down the border. Call the Mexican government, make them deploy their troops and we do the same on our side of the border. I'm sure they didn't go far."

"It's already done, Cal. It's you guys or nothing. Are you telling me you won't do it?"

"You know that's not what I'm saying. Of course we'll do it, but this has the potential to get really fucking ugly."

"I know that and so does Zimmer."

Cal knew it was no use to keep up the barrage. Like Travis said, the plan was set. The Marine's mind clicked over as he refocused on their new mission: save the Pope.

"There's one more thing," Travis said.

"Please don't tell me the Pope said we couldn't use guns."

"No. The last thing is that I'm coming to help. I got a hookup with the Marines at Yuma. They're going to insert me and four Secret Service agents wherever you think we should meet."

Most people would have scoffed at the idea of a paper pusher coming along on a rescue mission. But Travis was a

SEAL and barely forty years old. He'd somehow kept his elite level physical abilities despite his demanding job. He'd even heard from the President that Travis liked to sneak out on military installation visits to train with the troops. Cal bet his cousin hadn't lost a step. That didn't mean he wouldn't give him a hard time about it.

"You sure you can keep up, old man?" Cal asked, warming to the idea of his cousin joining their merry band.

"I'll smoke your ass, sonny."

Cal grinned. It was like old times. "Okay. Let me talk to Ruiz, and then I'll let you know where we want you."

"We'll be ready."

The Jefferson Group operators, the monks, and Armando Ruiz listened as Cal told them about the Pope. He left out any mention of the President. Shock and anger radiated from the Brothers of St. Longinus. Determined scowls were cast by the TJG boys. It was Ruiz that surprised Cal the most. The man looked like he was going to cry. Not like a couple of tears, but a full on blubbering meltdown.

The stoic leader somehow kept it together until Cal finished.

"So that's it. We need to get up to Mexicali as soon as we can. They're pretty sure the attackers slipped back through the border from Calexico. Now, the problem is transportation. Trav says they've shut down the airports in both cities, so flying straight in is a no-go. If we take the vans, I'm afraid to ask how long it would take."

Cal's eyes rested on Ruiz for the answer. The cartel leader had regained a measure of his composure and answered in a strained voice, "Four hours barring any traffic."

"That's too long. Any other ideas?" Cal asked the rest of the men. Maybe Brother Hendrik had a miracle up his robe sleeve.

No one answered. Instead, Daniel asked, "What about El Moreno?"

Cal had almost forgotten about the Guerrero Cartel and their terrorist companions.

"I think our priority is the Pope. Anyone disagree?" Cal asked.

Even the monks agreed.

"If we're lucky, they're part of the kidnapping," Cal continued. "I find it hard to believe this is a coincidence. Ruiz, do you think your competition could pull this off?"

Ruiz's eyes snapped up, like Cal was accusing him.

"Whatever my competition is, many of them are still men of faith. No, I don't think they would do this, but El Moreno would. Few people know this, but he hates the Catholic Church. I don't know why, but I'm sure it has something to do with him being an orphan."

Cal nodded. "That's good to know. At least now we have suspect number one identified. Any ideas on how we can get north?"

Ruiz spoke up again. "I have an idea, but you won't like it." He had a look on his face like he'd just remembered something he'd left hidden away.

"What is it?"

"The Mexicali Cartel owes me a couple of favors."

"But I thought they were the enemy," Gaucho said.

Ruiz shrugged. "Like any business, competition is fierce, but sometimes we work together on things. The Mexicali Cartel makes a lot of money ferrying other cartels' drugs across the border just like we help with import in Acapulco. Besides, Barachon won't like the fact that the Pope was kidnapped."

"Who's that?" Cal asked.

"The leader of the Mexicali Cartel. His brother is a priest, and Barachon has funded a handful of churches around his city. If there's anyone who would like revenge, it's him."

"Okay, but I'm not sure we should tell him about the Pope," Cal said, worried that the word could spread and make any rescue attempt impossible.

"The way I see it, our options are pretty limited, Cal," MSgt Trent interjected. "I say we listen to Ruiz and take our chances."

It was a crapshoot any way you looked at it. Cal gave the Pope a twenty-percent chance of survival. If the jihadis got their hands on him, no doubt an internet video was about to hit the waves. Had that been their play all along, to lure the well-meaning Pope to Mexico and snatch him to be the world's best piece of propaganda? It was bold as hell, but someone had already pulled off the hardest part. Time was ticking.

"Fine. Make the call," Cal said. "The faster we get there, the better our chances."

Ruiz nodded and moved off to call his fellow cartel jefe.

———

The conversation went smoother than Ruiz expected. Other than the shock on the other end, Barachon took it well. As Ruiz knew he would, the Mexicali *padron* wanted blood.

"You let me cut them into pieces, Armando. *Animales.* You let me do that, and I will give you anything you need," he'd said.

Barachon gave Ruiz the secret coordinates for one of his cartel's hidden landing strips. Each faction had them and this one happened to be very close to Mexicali. They'd said their goodbyes and Ruiz hung up the call.

He looked up at the sky, stars twinkling down in the predawn air. He said a prayer, then another. Maybe it was time. Could this be the sign he'd been waiting for? He'd first thought that divine intervention was in play when his nephew called. They'd been close, more like father and son than uncle and nephew. Ruiz was the strong male influence Gaucho needed as a child. In turn, his nephew had loved him unconditionally. On his long deployments with the Army, the fatherless soldier had always carried a photograph of a smiling Gaucho wearing a cowboy hat and the gunslinger's belt he'd given the boy.

Ruiz yearned for those days. He'd secretly watched his nephew and his American friends. They were good men. Ruiz said a final prayer and went in search of his nephew. They would have a few minutes before the airplanes were refueled.

"Gaucho, can I talk to you and Cal?" Ruiz asked. Gaucho looked up from where he was stowing his gear in the luggage compartment of the food transport plane. It bore the faded lettering Acapulco Produce, and was apparently one of his uncle's many business ventures.

"Sure."

They went to find Cal. He was talking with Brother Hendrik, who had just talked to his superiors in Rome. The monk was as heated as Gaucho had seen him. He looked like he would likely rip off the head of whoever had taken the Pope.

"We'll do everything we can, I promise," Cal was saying. Brother Hendrik nodded curtly and left.

"Cal, my uncle says he wants to talk to us," Gaucho said.

"Did he get in touch with Bajon?" Cal asked, skewering the proper pronunciation.

"It's Barachon," Ruiz corrected, "and yes. He has a secret strip outside of Mexicali. He'll be waiting with vehicles to get us inside the city."

"And the police? Do you think they'll be a problem?"

"He tells me they won't. The ones that are on his payroll will stay out of the way."

"Great. Anything else?"

Ruiz nodded slowly. "There's something I think you should know."

Oh shit, Gaucho thought.

Ruiz continued after making sure no one was within earshot. "I haven't been completely honest with you."

Cal's eyes narrowed. Gaucho had seen that look before. "Tell me."

Gaucho stared at his uncle.

"Did Gaucho tell you how I came to my current... position?"

Cal nodded.

"Did he tell you about my girlfriend and the men I killed?"

"He did."

"And he told you that I threatened him with his life."

"Yes."

Ruiz looked at his nephew, sadness etched into his weathered face. Gaucho had seen that look before. It was the Uncle

Armando that he remembered from his childhood, the man who helped raise the fatherless Gaucho.

"I had to do it," he said.

One plane engine sputtered to life and then another behind them.

"Look, Mr. Ruiz, we're a little short on time," Cal said, glancing at Gaucho with a "where the hell is he going with this?" look.

"Yes. I know. But I thought I should tell you in case something should happen."

Cal and Gaucho waited. What *was* the point of his uncle's rambling?

"I did come to Acapulco to start a new life. But when I got mixed up with the Guerrero Cartel, a DEA agent contacted me. He had informants within the organization and managed to save my life by warning me of an assassin who was coming to kill me. Well, once I took care of the assassin, the DEA agent offered me a job. He wanted me to play along with the cartel's overtures. Without any other prospects, I said yes. Pretty soon I was in so deep that there wasn't a chance I could leave. The DEA agent moved up the chain of command in his agency just as I did within the Guerrero Cartel. Sometimes we'd joke that one day I might take over everything. The first American to take over a drug cartel. Well, that joke became a reality. I had the shot, and I literally took it.

"The troops respected me, and my Green Beret background gave us more clout. Even the guys I'd passed over thought the fact that I'd been American was the perfect "fuck you" to the Mexican government and the United States. Well, I spent a long time reorganizing things. Murder is part of cartel life, but I forbade it when it came to civilians. I cleaned things up. It's not perfect, but it's a long way from where we were. Well, the whole time I was still sending reports to this DEA guy. In return, he'd provide us with intel on competitors and we'd seize the opportunity to raid or disrupt their operations. It was a win-win really. Things were going well. The Guerrero Cartel grew stronger with the help of more legitimate investments and new business. It doesn't hurt that there are more crooked politicians on the local and national level than we could ever have on payroll.

"So here I was, the lord of the land. Things were good. Violence was at an all-time low. I really thought that I was doing the right thing. It's crazy to say, but I felt like I was home. What is it they say? Just when you're comfortable everything goes to shit?" Ruiz chuckled. "Well it did. About a year and a half ago I found out the DEA agent I reported to had been killed in some raid in Ecuador. That would've been okay except that he was the only person who knew the truth. He was my handler, my benefactor and my only link to the United States. Without him I was stuck, stranded as the head of a drug organization in the middle of Mexico. I am a wanted man, a criminal."

As Gaucho listened, he saw the lies peel away. The masks his uncle had worn for so many years were slipping aside before his very eyes. If he hadn't known his uncle as well as he did, he might not have believed him. But he saw the truth in his eyes. There was the man he'd revered as a hero, something superhuman to a boy at play.

"Why didn't you tell me?" Gaucho asked, wanting to embrace his uncle, but afraid that in doing so his own emotions might come spilling out.

"How could I? Would you have believed me, especially after the last time we talked?"

Gaucho understood now. It had all been a show for the cartel. His heart ached for all the years they'd lost, all the hateful thoughts he'd projected.

"What will you do now?" Gaucho asked.

Armando Ruiz shrugged. "Stay, I guess. What else can I do?"

Gaucho didn't have the answer. He looked over at Cal, who looked like he wasn't convinced by Ruiz's story. "What do you think? Is there anything we can do?"

Cal didn't answer right away. Instead he kept his eyes locked on Gaucho's uncle. Finally he said, "Mr. Ruiz, if we get out of this alive *and* save the Pope, I'll do everything I can to help you."

Now Ruiz didn't look convinced. Gaucho had to remind himself that his uncle didn't know what The Jefferson Group was or who they worked for.

"Are you sure you could help? Do you know people in the American government?" Ruiz asked, a hint of hope in his voice.

Cal grinned and said, "Yeah. I think I have a string or two I could pull."

CHAPTER 23

El Moreno tried to watch Felix and his men with a dispassionate eye. He'd relayed the successful kidnapping with his typical downplay, but the Spaniards had worked themselves into a near frenzy. Even though they were crammed into the back of a repurposed delivery trailer, the extremists clapped their hands, raised them to the unseen sky along with their upturned faces, jabbering on in their adopted tongue. He couldn't help but think how easy it would be to kill them. If this was religion, it was a complete waste.

Not only were they rejoicing before their mission was complete, they looked like simple religious zealots. It was unprofessional and unsettling. El Moreno's mind once again worked through his options. There had to be a way to take advantage of the situation. Felix and his fellow Spaniards were not elite warriors of Allah. They were recent civilians who'd been given minimal training stamped by whoever was really pulling the strings.

He had to give it to them though. To concoct a scheme that could a) induce the Pope to fly to where they wanted, and b) bring only a scrap of his normal security, showed that someone in the jihadi chain of command knew what they were doing. Felix still hadn't told him how they'd known so much, and that could only mean that they had a man, or multiple men, on the inside. The intelligence had been precise and one hundred percent correct. Felix had confirmed the covert contact at the last possible moment, a crucial piece of information that had to be relayed to El Moreno's men in Calexico.

The tricky part now was getting to Mexicali in time. He'd instructed his hired guns to throw a hood on their prize, to bind him, but not too tightly. All they knew was that the man in casual business attire was worth a tidy payday. The last thing he needed was for the mercenaries to get curious. Hopefully whomever Felix had on the inside would keep them at a safe distance. Besides, the professional kidnappers knew what El Moreno would do should his package be damaged. It shouldn't matter what was under the hood. That was the cartel leader's business, not theirs.

Felix was hugging one of his compatriots, their eyes glistening with tears. El Moreno wanted to slap them and tell them to snap out of it. They had another two hours to go before reaching their destination and more to do once there. This mission was far from over.

"Felix," he said, trying to get the Spaniard's attention. "Felix," he repeated, a little louder this time, ignoring the annoyed looks from his own men.

Felix turned, his face glowing. El Moreno motioned for his guest to come across the storage compartment and sit next to him on the short metal bench that ran the length of the trailer. The Spaniard complied without his usual reluctance to follow even the simplest of suggestions from his host.

"Yes, my friend?" Felix said as he sat down.

El Moreno knew he had to be careful. The Spaniard's mood swings whipped in and out like an oversexed teenager. He was easily offended, a trait that had gotten countless up-and-comers killed for centuries untold.

"We should be in Mexicali just after sunrise."

"Good, good. Then everything went as planned with our guest's transfer across the border?" Felix couldn't keep himself from grinning like a sugar-filled child.

"Yes."

Felix nodded and even patted El Moreno on the shoulder, the first physical contact the two men had ever had. The Mexican resisted the urge to grab the man's hand and wrench it away.

"We will be heroes, you and I," Felix said. "They will write songs about us. You should come visit my country. Everything will change after this."

He really believes that, El Moreno thought.

"There is still much to do. Are you sure we can trust your man?"

The smile slipped from Felix's face for a second, but then he forced it back up.

"You worry too much, my friend. He is worthy of our trust. He is one of Allah's blessed."

The comment rolled right over El Moreno. He didn't have time for spiritual nonsense.

"Do you know him?"

"Why should that matter?"

"I only want us all to remember the potentially dangerous situation we may be stepping into. So far the American police still think it was a drug deal gone bad, but that could easily change, say, for example, should someone from Rome speak to the authorities."

Felix surprised El Moreno with his response.

"You are correct. I will defer to your judgment until we take possession of our prize."

That was too easy.

They still hadn't discussed what would happen after they had the Pope in hand. Felix had requested video equipment and Internet access, so El Moreno could only guess that they were about to make the religious figurehead into a propaganda piece. But what about the children? What was their role? Something in him squirmed.

"Tell me about the three-headed dragon," El Moreno said, trying to sound casual.

Felix's eyes hardened.

"Where did you hear that?"

El Moreno shrugged.

"I don't remember. I think maybe you told me?"

Felix searched the shorter man's face. He was too stupid to see through El Moreno's facade. His smile returned, but this time it was strained.

"Oh, that. Yes, it is just a nickname we have for the Americans, like how you call them gringos, no?"

El Moreno saw right through the lie. Felix did not have the gift of masking his emotions while the Mexican was convinced that he could even fool God, if there was such a thing. He decided to play along.

"I did not know that. I like it. I will have to use it."

Felix's face relaxed, like a boy who'd just gotten away with a misdeed. El Moreno smiled, further putting the Spaniard at ease, but inside all he could think about was how he was going to take advantage of the masterful strategy the jihadis had employed. After all, how many ways could you use the Pope as a puppet?

Felix returned to his seat, unease rattling in his head. The three-headed dragon. If his masters had been privy to the conversation, surely he would be dead. His father had pulled many strings to get Felix on this mission. He'd entrusted the family legacy to his son. His father, once a businessman nearing prominence, had slipped into hard times during the most recent worldwide economic collapse. Before that, religion had almost been an afterthought in their household.

But the Islamic community had embraced his father, welcoming him and his children with open arms. Soon he had more business than he could have ever dreamed, with much more on the horizon. He said he owed it all to Islam, to Allah, to the prominent masters who'd put their faith in him.

Before departing for South America and his journey to Mexico, Felix's father opened up to his oldest son with emotion that the two men had never before shared.

"This is a test, Felix. Allah is watching; he has chosen us to spread his message. With your bravery, and the courage of your brothers, the three-headed dragon will usher in a new era for our people."

Felix had never heard the term, and asked his father about the three-headed dragon. At first the older man pretended not to have said it, but Felix pressed. He was the favored son, the one who would carry on the family legacy. In the end, his father relented, but only after swearing his son to secrecy. Felix agreed.

"The three-headed dragon is our master plan, the way we will defeat the unbelievers and bring them to their knees. Just like it sounds, there are three parts. First, the physical. We must take the bloody battle to the enemy, make them cower and run. Second, the psychological. We must not only break their bodies, but their minds as well. When you have done these two things, you have come close to victory. This is what our brothers in Syria, Iraq and Yemen have accomplished to great effect. But even the condemned man still holds out hope. What do you think keeps a man from giving in even after his body is mangled and his mind is controlled?"

Felix hadn't known.

"It's his spirit. If you cut off the chance of eternal salvation, in essence, cutting off all spiritual hope, you have won. That is the third head of the dragon."

He'd asked his father how that could be accomplished if the only way to make such a thing happen was to kill a god.

"That is true," his father had said, nodding his head in agreement. "But what happens if the symbol of that god resides here on Earth? What if all hope of salvation lay within one man?"

Felix had seen the truth in his father's words, but it took him a moment to understand to whom he was alluding. Religions were so decentralized in the modern era that decapitating any single faith was...

No, it wasn't impossible.

"The Pope," Felix had whispered. His father nodded, his smile engulfing the room.

"Yes, my son. The Pope. A man who has long plagued our people. From the crusades to his support of the Zionists, the Pope is more than a man and more than a symbol. To the Catholics he is a physical representation of their God, much as their Jesus was. What would happen should something befall the Pope? Would it not serve to strengthen our cause?"

Of course it would, but Felix still couldn't grasp how such a thing was possible. Growing up in Spain, where most of the population kissed the very ground the Pope walked on, it was impossible for anyone not to recognize how protected that symbol had become.

It was only after he'd left his home and traveled through South America, receiving his final orders prior to taking his first step into Mexico, that Felix came to know the full plan. Three-headed dragon indeed. The world would tremble because of the bold actions of Felix and his fellow warriors. They would shatter faith across the globe and show the world which deity ruled them now. After that, recruitment would skyrocket. For those populations who did not capitulate, a swarm of holy warriors would invade their homes, trample their lives, and murder their loved ones. The three-headed dragon would portend their end of days.

For a moment, Felix wanted to tell El Moreno everything, to let him bask in the light of the truth. But that could not be. His masters had been very specific; the Mexican should only know enough to get the job done. Felix had already made one mistake in discussing their plan near the cartel. He knew that had been his pride, and that he would have to be more careful with his actions and with his tongue. If only he were able to speed up time. Now that would be a miracle. Then he could ride the wave of religious joy back to his home, the conquering hero embraced once more by his father and by his people.

CHAPTER 24

The sun was just tickling the horizon as Travis Haden waited for his friends. He rolled his shoulders back, still uncomfortable with the assault gear he'd borrowed from the Secret Service. The familiar itch of sweat breaking out under layers of kevlar and nylon swept his mind back through the years. His time with the SEALs were some of the most exhilarating of his life. Sometimes he wondered what would have happened if he had stayed in, but in the next moment he thanked God for his uncle's foresight in making him an integral part of Stokes Security International (SSI), the company still owned by Cal.

It was funny how things worked out. Never would he have thought that one day his service to his country would be as Chief of Staff to the President. The same thing could be said for what he was doing now. Never in a million years would Travis have imagined that President Zimmer would allow him to go on a real mission, to be part of a team outside the White House. But Travis needed this and, apparently,

Zimmer understood that. You could only cage a bull for so long before it bucked its way out. This was Travis's chance.

He inhaled the dusty Mexican air as one, then all four planes came into view. They flew in low, landed with practiced ease, and taxied to where Travis stood waiting. He was flanked by the four Secret Service agents in matching tactical gear, and Barachon, the cartel leader of Mexicali. The guy wasn't much to look at, with his sagging red face and overweight body, but when he shook Travis's hand, the American saw fire in the man's eyes. There was plenty of fight left in the aging gangster. The Colt .45 he carried in his waistband accentuated that point.

And yet, Barachon was gracious. He was a bit standoffish, but this was his turf after all. Travis knew they'd have to play by most of his rules.

A man Travis could only assume was Gaucho's uncle walked up first, embracing Barachon.

"Thank you for meeting us, my friend," said Ruiz.

"It is you who should have the thanks. To imagine such foolishness happening in my backyard." Barachon shook his head sadly. "Come, we have refreshments waiting."

While the two leaders moved off with their men to the desert camouflaged headquarters tent a few feet off the runway, the rest of Travis's friends made their way from the planes, followed by the robed monks.

Jeez, they look like they just walked out of a monastery, he thought.

"Well I'll be damned," said MSgt Trent. "Cal said you were coming, but I told him he was full of it."

"How are you, Top?" Travis asked, grinning up at the enormous black Marine.

"The sooner we get rolling the better, brother. My legs are still cramping from that ride."

Travis nodded, turning his gaze to Cal.

"Hey, cuz."

Cal smiled. "We couldn't keep you away?"

"Not a chance," Travis said, smiling now that his men were together.

"So what's the deal? Does this Barachon know anything?" Cal asked.

Travis nodded and pointed at the large tent.

"He said he wanted to wait until you guys got here to brief everyone. Let's see what he's got."

As was his way, Daniel Briggs went first, his finely tuned radar no doubt working overtime despite his mellow demeanor. Briggs was one of the reasons Travis rarely worried about his cousin. Like a well-trained Doberman, the Marine sniper sniffed out danger like he was born to do it.

The tent was large, but not big enough to hold everyone, so other than Cal, Daniel, Gaucho, Travis and the largest of the monks, the rest stayed outside.

Bottles of water and sugary pastries were offered to the guests. Travis took two bottles and one pastry, suddenly realizing how thirsty he was. He remembered his number one rule before combat: Drink 'em and smoke 'em if you've got 'em. You never know when you'd get the next chance.

"If you gentlemen would like to gather around this map, I will tell you what I know," Barachon said, taking the spot at the head of a rectangular plywood table. A large rendering of Mexicali was pinned to the wood. Travis took a spot next to Cal and looked down at the map.

He estimated the urban part of the city to be probably four miles east to west and about the same north to south. Based on the satellite imagery he'd seen on Air Force One, Travis knew there were plenty of places to hide.

"We may have gotten lucky," Barachon said. "This is my city. Other families know to get permission for kidnappings and they always come to me if they are moving across the border. Just after you called, I had my men check the security cameras at all our crossings. Nothing. But, we did find that one of our tunnels's security systems was not working. I had a team check it out, and someone had disabled the video cameras." He paused and shook his head as if this news was all he had. Then he clapped his hands together. "But God is good. Earlier this year we installed motion sensor cameras just as the American Border Patrol had done. We told no one of this, and I am glad of it." Barachon snapped his fingers and one of his men produced a manila envelope. He laid the contents on the map, clear photographs of men with guns in a tunnel, one at a time. "I know these men. They do work for me. They started out as coyotes, taking immigrants across the border, but they wanted more. It now looks like they no longer choose to obey my rules. I was good to them, even fair when they asked to expand their business." Again the sad shake of his balding head. He laid the very last photograph on the table, slowly, as if he feared it would explode. It was a clear shot of a person hunched over, a hood on his/her head, hands bound and closed in front, being led by two men. "Can any of you tell me that this is our Holy Father?" He made the sign of the cross as he asked the question, kissing the gold cross hanging down on his chest when he'd finished.

Everyone bent closer, but it was impossible to make out the hooded stranger's features.

"Brother Hendrik said he would be disguised, but who knows from this shot?" Cal said, turning the picture so the large monk could get a closer look. "Do you recognize anything? Could this be him?"

The monk picked the photograph up reverently, his eyes darting around the page. Travis could sense the near desperation in the way he held his breath, his arm shaking just perceptibly.

"I don't...I'm not sure." He turned to Barachon. "Does this match the timeline? Could there be another way across the border?"

Barachon shrugged.

"Anything is possible, but not likely. There are other ways across, but none as fast. And yes, the timing is the same. This must be him."

Brother Hendrik nodded, returning his gaze to the picture. "It has to be," he muttered. His eyes never left the photograph. "Mr. Stokes, could you ask my brothers and Father Pietro to join us? Maybe they will see something that I cannot."

Cal nodded and left the tent. A moment later the other four monks entered, along with a man in soiled workman's clothing. His face was drawn and haggard. Travis thought that the man might pass out, eyes twitching nervously, avoiding eye contact with those he walked by.

"Tell me if you see anything familiar, anything that will confirm that this is His Holiness," Brother Hendrik said, now joined by his fellow monks and the pale priest.

One minute passed, then two. One by one the monks shook their heads, stepping back from the table until only Father Pietro was staring at the high definition photograph. Then the priest's right arm rose shakily, one finger pointing at something on the printout. Travis leaned in closer to get a better look.

"What is it?" Brother Hendrik asked, straining to see what the priest was trying to show.

Father Pietro's voice shook as badly as his arm. "His fingers. Don't you see them?"

"Yes, there they are. I don't understand." Brother Hendrik's voice rose in frustration. "What do you see?"

It started out as a low chuckle and then Father Pietro coughed out a laugh, tears falling from his eyes like he'd just heard something so hilarious that even the dire circumstances could not hold back the mirth. Brother Hendrik's jaw clenched, his chin quivering.

"Tell me what—"

Daniel stepped forward, placing one comforting hand on the monk and another on the priest in near hysterics.

"Give him a minute," Daniel said to Brother Hendrik, his look fixed on Pietro. "Tell us what you see, Father. What are we missing?" His voice was soothing, like a doctor coaxing a patient into talking.

"Imagine, a fallen priest being the only one who can see that this is clearly who we seek." Father Pietro's finger stabbed at the picture. "There, his fingers. His smallest finger folded over his ring finger. Do none of you know?"

Complete confusion showed on Brother Hendrik's face.

"Tell us, Father. What does it mean?" Daniel asked.

Father Pietro steadied, a sudden resolve setting his jaw.

"In the days when Christians were persecuted, hunted down like animals, it was impossible for those early believers to wear anything that bore the likeness of Jesus of the blessed cross. Instead they found other ways to show their face to one another, like a secret handshake. This," he tapped the picture, "was one of those signs, the smallest finger folded over the next. It is not a natural gesture, uncomfortable even. A crude cross, but still a cross. I once heard the Holy Father tell the story of how those Christians first used simple signs to show their unity, their undying love for God. To him it was a constant reminder of where the Church came from, the lessons we should learn, and to always remain humble servants of God without the rich trappings of man. That sign, despite being surrounded by guns and men who could surely kill him, tells me that this is who we seek, the man who told me that in times of distress he would make this simple sign, a plea for guidance. Yes, this is His Holiness the Pope."

CHAPTER 25

MEXICALI, MEXICO
6:04AM, MARCH 15TH

El Moreno wiped the sweat from his brow as he walked into the cool underground compound. It was a storage space used to get crops out of the scorching sun. He could smell the remnants of years worth of asparagus even though the floors were swept clean.

"Where are they?" he asked the pair of guards who'd escorted them in from the farm above ground.

"In the back," one of the hired guns said, pointing toward the flickering light farther down the hall.

El Moreno nodded and motioned for his own men to lead the way. He'd told Felix to keep his mouth shut until they'd let the Mexicali mercenaries go. They would be used at a later time, but their constant presence was no longer needed.

Down the damp hallway they walked. Somewhere the sound of water dripping on metal could be heard, pulling them farther into the darkness. When they reached the room at the end of the hall, El Moreno's men went in first, always diligent about securing a space before their boss entered. When he was given the okay, he entered, followed by Felix.

El Moreno's eyes searched the dim space, his eyes coming to rest on a form sitting in a white plastic chair. His hands lay in his lap and the hood still covered his head. That was good.

One of the mercenaries came to greet him.

"Moreno, who is this man who guards your prize?" the mercenary said in a low voice.

El Moreno glanced over to where the man was pointing. He was talking about the Swiss Guard. Before he could answer, Felix decided to butt in. "That is my brother. Why do you need to know?"

The mercenary looked Felix up and down with amusement. El Moreno had no doubt that the shorter man could easily take the Spaniard.

"I was only wondering because he seems to have an attitude. The man refuses to talk to us."

El Moreno cut in before Felix could make matters worse.

"He is our informant, the reason you are getting paid."

The mercenary looked like he was going to push, but he thought better of it. "Do you have the rest of my payment?" he asked instead.

"Yes. I have it here." El Moreno patted the leather satchel on his shoulder, then he handed it to the man. "Thank you for your help. There will be more after we get across the border."

The man grabbed the bag eagerly, lifting the flap and leafing through the hundred dollar American bills inside.

"This man must be very important to pay such a sum. Tell me, who is he? A competitor? An American?"

El Moreno didn't like the man's line of questioning.

"Yes, a competitor who has crossed me for the last time. Now, if you don't mind, I would like to have a word with him."

The mercenary met El Moreno's gaze. The cartel leader didn't like the look he saw, like he was high on something. His options had been limited when it came to who he should hire. He couldn't go through the master of Mexicali, the aging Barachon. The old bastard hated him almost as much as that snob Armando Ruiz. He'd settled on this crew. Younger and more ambitious than their rivals, they were known to be reliable but a bit reckless. At the moment, El Moreno was getting a taste of the latter.

"Look, if you want us to take you and your cargo across the border, why don't you let me see who he is? Just by the look on your friend's face here," he poked his finger into Felix's chest, "I would say he is an interesting catch."

Yes, the man was either high or stupid. Not including Felix and the Swiss Guard, the mercenary was outnumbered two to one, and that was just underground.

El Moreno beckoned the man closer, so only he could hear. The man complied, more curious than scared.

"Take your men and leave. Now." El Moreno was used to having his orders followed. His demeanor left no space for interpretation. But the glazed eyes and the sagging grin of this mercenary wouldn't budge.

Loud enough for everyone to hear, the man said, "After you tell me who we kidnapped. You are in my town. I want to know."

One moment the man's head was there, and then El Moreno felt something splash his face, followed the sound of gunfire that made his ear ring. Quicker than he thought possible and before his own men lifted their weapons, the corrupt Swiss Guard not only dispatched the mercenary leader, but his four henchmen as well.

"What are you doing?" El Moreno hissed at the man, motioning for his soldiers to go take care of the rest of the mercenaries. All but three ran from the room, gunshots soon sounding from the storage space they'd first entered.

"He would not close his mouth, not from the first moment at the airport. The man was trouble." The stern faced former Swiss Guard didn't look worried. He took another magazine from his pocket and replaced the one in his pistol.

Felix walked forward like in a trance. In the most humble voice El Moreno had heard the man ever use, he said, "You truly are a Holy Warrior. What it must have been like to live with these unbelievers for so long."

Apparently the turncoat was a man of few words, because he only nodded.

One of El Moreno's men ran back into the room to report that the rest of the mercenaries had been dispatched.

"Good, now bring our cargo underground. We have some time before we leave. And remove these bodies before they start to stink," he said, pointing to the dead contractors on the ground, pools of blood already forming.

The man nodded and left the room again.

"Now, let's have a look at our prize," El Moreno said, stepping closer to the prisoner as he wiped the blood spatter from his own face.

Just as he reached for the hood, the Swiss Guard stepped in front of the seated man.

"It is for Allah's warriors alone to touch this demon."

El Moreno could feel his own soldiers at his back, no doubt waiting for his cue to cut the insolent fool to pieces.

"I believe I have earned the right to lay my eyes on him," he said.

The Swiss Guard didn't respond, but he did pull the hood from the prisoner's head, and stepped to the side.

And there he was, blinking like a babe just brought into the world, the light assaulting his eyes. The Pope stared up at him, and he stared back. Of course he recognized the pontiff. The man's likeness was posted in half the establishments in Mexico. You couldn't take a piss without seeing the Pope's face. He was usually smiling or waving, but not this time.

What surprised El Moreno most, other than the insane fear that maybe he would be burnt to a crisp by the holy man's gaze, was that the Pope showed no fear. He simply stared at El Moreno with a look that was somewhere between worry and pity, like a parent who was looking at a son who'd committed a heinous act that could not be undone.

"You are far from Rome, Holy Father," El Moreno said, curious to see what the head of the Catholic Church would say.

"I am, my son." He said it matter-of-factly, like the trip had been inevitable, his choice even.

He is not afraid, El Moreno thought, unable to think of another thing to ask, the probing flown from his head.

"What is it that you want of me? Do you mean to murder me?" The Pope asked, his eyes moving from man to man, as if calmly daring them to fire the killing round at that very moment.

Felix was the one to answer.

"We have better plans for you, old man. Yes, you will die, but not before you see your beloved people crumble to their knees, not for your God, but before the might of Allah's warriors."

"And this is how you see Allah's will?" the Pope asked. "By the sword you must win instead of by the heart?" He shook his head sadly. "I pity you, my son. Let me help you."

Felix's face colored, his hands trembling. El Moreno thought the Spaniard was going to hit the man, but the Swiss Guard stepped between them.

"Now is not the time. We have preparations to make."

Felix shook his head, but he calmed.

"You are right. Now is not the time."

How interesting, El Moreno thought. The fox in the henhouse probably had more clout with Felix's masters than the Spaniard did. No wonder, the man had probably been under deep cover for most of his adult life. The Mexican drug lord had to respect that. And yet, he recognized the threat. Felix was manageable. This elite warrior standing guard over the Pope was an immovable object, a stone sentinel who was undoubtedly more dedicated to his cause than Felix.

That made up El Moreno's mind. Turning away from the two jihadis like he was going to address his men, he slipped the pistol from his waistband, hours of practice with his custom made H&K, the grips made especially for his tiny hands. The weapon felt natural in his grasp, an extension of his will. As he swiveled, his will moved down his arms, through his fingers and depressed the trigger, the pull lessened by the expert gunsmith who ran the Guerrero Cartel's armory. The Swiss Guard didn't even have time to turn as the rounds blasted through his neck, and then ran up the back of his head, brain matter exploding out the other side with the help of the 9mm rounds, knock-offs of the infamous Patriot Popper ammunition purchased by the American government. Overkill really, but El Moreno wasn't complaining.

He marveled at the way his shots turned the man's body into human Swiss cheese.

When his handgun clicked open, the magazine spent, El Moreno looked up at Felix's shocked face.

"Like he said, he was going to be trouble."

El Moreno left the Spaniard to his gawking and ordered his men to get to the rest of their preparations. He had Felix right where he wanted him, against the ropes, reeling, unarmed, and unsure of what the crazy Mexican might do next. According to the Spaniard, there was one more delivery coming, the final piece of the puzzle. El Moreno hoped it would give him the answers he wanted, as well as access to whatever weapon Felix planned on using. He was still up in the air about whether he would let the jihadi keep it.

We'll just have to wait and see, he thought to himself.

CHAPTER 26

It was decided that their makeshift task force should be split into three. According to the cartel master Barachon, there were only three farms in the vicinity of the border crossing used by the kidnappers that could hide the number of people with whom El Moreno was thought to be travelling north. No one had any better ideas, so they split into three groups: the monks and some of Ruiz's men in the first; Gaucho, Trent, Ruiz and his men in the second; and Cal, Daniel, Travis and The Jefferson Group operators in the third.

The plan was to go in at the same moment, just in case all three locations were being used, and one decided to alert the others. While Cal would've liked to send out scouts either from within his own ranks, or loaned from Barachon, he knew they didn't have time. He and his men could feel time slipping by, each second moving them closer to disaster.

Brother Hendrik and his men were ready. Even Father Pietro looked determined, although he'd still opted not to carry a weapon. Instead he carried a backpack full of extra ammunition, just in case they got into an extended gun battle, a scene not uncommon south of the border.

They drove through town in their dented pickup trucks, passing rickety abodes and dirt soccer fields, but no one gave them a second glance. As they approached the dirt road entrance to the farm, Brother Hendrik radioed the other two teams to let them know he was in position. They confirmed his call, and each said they were near their own targets. Less than a minute later, the signal came over the radio to enter the suspect property.

Brother Hendrik eased the pickup back onto the road and gunned the engine. The tires bit into the dry earth and the small convoy sped down the lane. He scanned the way as he drove, always ready to veer off the path should the need arise. It didn't.

He skidded to a stop one hundred yards from the metal farmhouse, weapons already trained on the lone building. The warrior monks led the way, now stripped of their robes and wearing the desert tactical gear they'd brought for the operation. As the others fanned out around the one-story shack, Brother Hendrik went for the screen door. It was hanging open, creaking back and forth in the slight breeze.

He waited for the rest of the team to signal that they were in place, and then slid inside the door with Brother Zigfried, the dour German, following right behind. There were two rooms in the simple building: a bedroom and a living room with a kitchen tucked in the far corner. Other than a family of stray cats that went skittering at their approach, the place was empty.

"We uncovered a cellar door behind the property," came Brother Aaron's voice.

"Wait until I get there," Brother Hendrik said, making his way back out the front of the structure and around to the rear of where he'd just been.

The rest of the team was waiting, weapons trained on the wooden doors with a heavy metal Master lock in the middle. Someone had moved a pile of hay bales to the side, stray stalks of which were scattered over the doors.

"Open it, quietly," Brother Hendrik ordered.

Brother Fernando, the Mexican monk, moved forward, pulling a bolt cutter from his back. With more than a bit of effort, he snapped the lock in two places and kicked it away, careful to keep as much of his silhouette away from the doors as possible.

Brother Hendrik clicked on the light from his mounted flashlight, and grasped the top door. He counted down from three in his head, and then swung the heavy door up and over, his weapon instantly trained into the darkness. There were stairs leading down, and he took them without hesitation. Down a full floor they went until they hit concrete, lights shining into the space, illuminating empty milk crates and broken farm equipment. The space was smaller than the farmhouse above it, and was empty except for the used items that were piled along the far wall.

Brother Hendrik exhaled. He was not one to lose hope, but he felt their chances of saving His Holiness slipping through his powerful grasp. As he moved to join the others, who were already making their way topside, his boot slid over something slick on the ground. He shined his light down on the ground and saw scraps of cardboard that he hadn't noticed before. There was no writing of identifying markings on the scraps, so he left them.

He scanned the area again, but didn't see any boxes. With a shrug, he left the trash where it lay and headed back up the stairs. He had to tell the other teams that Objective One was all clear.

7:53AM

Master Sergeant Trent gripped the wheel as the pickup bounded over the rough dirt road, dodging potholes and trying to keep a constant speed. Gaucho sat in the passenger's seat, holding on for dear life, his steely eyes focused ahead.

Somehow none of the six vehicles lost a tire or an axle before getting to the Quonset hut situated just off the road. Trent and Gaucho made it there first, followed closely by Ruiz and his men. Just as the monks had done, they surrounded the two story building, and then Gaucho led the assault force inside. He and Trent ran up the wooden stairs as Ruiz cleared the first level. It was a simple storage silo, and bare except for frayed string on the floor and a faded picture of the Virgin Mary taped to the wall just inside the front door.

It took them less than five minutes to do a thorough sweep of the surrounding area, and they did not find an underground storage facility like they'd heard Brother Hendrik announce over the radio.

"Let me guess, Cal and Daniel get all the fun," Trent grumbled, kicking a rock across the road.

"You know how it is, Top. He and Snake Eyes are like magnets for that stuff."

Just as he said the words, Gaucho pointed back down the road. There were vehicles coming their way.

"Looks like Humvees," Trent said.

"What the hell?" Gaucho added, looking at his uncle.

"They look like Mexican military," Ruiz said. "Barachon should have taken care of that. Let me call him."

The Humvees were doing the same dance they had done, dodging the large holes on the lane. But what worried Trent the most was the .50 cal machine guns pointed their way. There were four vehicles in all and enough firepower to take his team out in short order.

Without any other option, Trent did what he always did, he met the problem head on. He stepped out onto the road, waving both hands over his head to make sure the speeding newcomers would see him. They did, and so did their gunners.

Gaucho joined Trent on the road, and they both watched as the Humvees spread out, now driving toward them on line. Trent half expected to be cut down at any moment. These dudes meant business, and proved it by firing a volley over his head. The Marine winced, but kept his hands where they were.

Now a few of the soldiers were shouting and every man except the gunners and drivers was coming out to face them.

"They want us to get down on the ground," Gaucho said.

"Do you think we should?" Trent asked, not taking his eye off the soldiers.

"Hell if I know."

The soldiers were still shouting, but the two friends didn't move. A moment later, Trent heard Ruiz's voice and then saw him walk forward, his hands also raised.

"Gentlemen, I think there has been some mistake," he said, addressing the soldiers.

One of the soldiers came closer, his muzzle pointing right at Ruiz's chest.

"We have orders to take you in. Now tell your men to get on the ground or we will shoot."

"I have Colonel Molina on the phone," Ruiz said, holding up his cellular. "He would like to have a word with whoever is in charge."

The soldier hesitated, but then took the phone from Ruiz. The conversation was brief, and soon the phone was back in Ruiz's hand.

"I am sorry for the inconvenience, Señor," the soldier said, backing away and finally lowering his weapon. "We have been recalled to headquarters."

Ruiz nodded and watched them load back into their vehicles and leave.

"What the hell was that about?" Trent asked when Ruiz rejoined them.

Ruiz frowned.

"It looks like our little friend was expecting us, and somehow paid off someone in the Mexicali chain of command. Barachon is looking into it."

"And who is Colonel Molina?" Gaucho asked.

"He's the garrison commander and that young man's boss," Ruiz said, pointed to the Humvees that were now filing back toward town.

Trent shook his head.

"Is it always like this?"

Ruiz shrugged as if it didn't matter. Trent gave him one thing, he was as calm as they came. The Marine in him hoped Cal could pull some strings for Gaucho's uncle before this thing was over. It would be a shame to leave him hanging.

———◆———

7:55AM

The rest of the TJG contingent moved in just like the other two teams. There were no sentries to meet them and the sprawling ranch-style home was completely bare. Once the house was cleared, they took a cue from Brother Hendrik and searched the surrounding farmland. It didn't take them long to find the metal hatch hidden behind a random pile of rocks, no doubt dug up years ago from the long lines of plowed fields.

The hatch was something you might find on a ship, with the wheel in the middle that unlocked the inner latch. One of the men whirled the wheel while Cal, Daniel and the others waited. The latch clunked, and the man holding the door waited for Cal's signal.

"Open it," Cal said.

The operator heaved, pulling the circular hatch back, exposing the round hole. Cal expected to see a ladder, but instead found a thin line of steps, along with a waft of air smelling like rotten vegetables. It assaulted his senses. Daniel moved first, rushing down the stairs into the blackness, Cal three steps behind.

They found the bodies immediately, nine of them thrown in an unceremonious pile. There was little blood on the ground, but it wasn't hard to find the penetration wounds that had killed them, some in the chest and others in the head.

While two men kept an eye on the bodies, Daniel and Cal moved deeper into the space. It ended fifty feet from where they'd entered, and there was nothing else there, no secret doors, no more bodies, nothing.

"Dammit," Cal said, making his way back to the bodies. He'd already heard the results of the other two raids. El Moreno, one. The Good Guys, zero.

The Mexicali chief had seemed so sure. What had they missed? Was there another farm that El Moreno was hiding out in?

The answer came a couple minutes later, after Daniel made the educated guess that the dead men in the storage space were most likely the mercenaries who'd kidnapped the Pope. He said he recognized two of the faces from Barachon's still photographs from earlier. Cal didn't see it, but he trusted the sniper's assessment.

Cal's phone rang. It was Ruiz. Strange. Why hadn't he called over the radio?

"Yeah?" Cal answered.

"You heard about the Humvee thing?"

"I did."

"Well, there's more. Barachon just called. He said he's got some bad news."

Cal closed his eyes. "Tell me."

"Someone in his organization was working for El Moreno. The guy confessed to taking a bunch of people through a new tunnel early this morning. He let them out on the American side. The thing is still under construction, and Barachon thought it was unusable. That's why he didn't mention it."

"You think he's telling the truth?"

"He kept apologizing and we saw how he felt about you-know-who, so yes, I do think it was an honest mistake. He didn't say so, but whoever took El Moreno's money is probably begging for their life right about now."

Cal didn't doubt it. He exhaled, willing his limited patience to take over. His supply was dwindling.

"Okay. It looks like our plans just changed, again. You keep your guys in Mexicali, just in case. I'll tell my guys to saddle up. We've gotta get back across the border."

CHAPTER 27

A little over twenty miles north of Calexico, things were settling down. After the journey from Acapulco and the run-
in with the mercenaries, everyone was spent. They'd made
it into the U.S. easily enough, despite their cargo. The children were behaving themselves, for the time being, thanks to
the women he'd brought along for the sole purpose of caring
for the many boys and girls. They were quiet when ordered
and only the occasional whimper left their lips. El Moreno
watched them as they slept. Some were pretending to be
asleep if only to avoid his gaze. No one complained about
sleeping on thin mats on the concrete floor. At least now they
could stretch out instead of being crammed into a cargo hold.

But despite his success so far, El Moreno had a dilemma.
The Spaniard had yet to tell him what the plan was. That didn't
sit well with El Moreno. He and his men had done everything
they'd promised, and in return Felix kept the details of the
coming climax to himself. The Mexican drug lord thought
that the loss of his Swiss Guard spy would wake the Spaniard

up, loosen his tongue a bit, but it hadn't. If anything, it had done the opposite.

So while the soldiers of the Guerrero Cartel got some rest, the jihadis sat huddled in a corner, conspiring and planning. El Moreno looked around the room again, trying to put the pieces together. He'd always assumed that the children were bargaining pieces, or possibly some sort of diversion for the Spaniards, but that didn't feel likely. Something else was going on that made his insides squirm. It was the way the other jihadis looked at each other, like men going off to war knowing that they would never return home.

The buses would arrive that afternoon. Felix said he wanted to leave at sunset. He hadn't said it would be their final farewell, but El Moreno sensed it. The jihadis had a room prepped with video equipment. Not a fancy setup, just a tripod, a small video camera, and a simple set. A white sheet would be used as a backdrop behind an old metal chair.

That room was where they kept the Pope, tied to a chair, now guarded by one of Felix's men and one of El Moreno's. After the incident with the Swiss Guard, the Spaniards were leery about leaving their prize with the unpredictable Mexican or his men. Not that El Moreno would have done anything to His Holiness, but uncertainty had always been his ally. He wielded it like a fog machine, his enemies and friends never really knowing where he might strike next. In and out he moved, darting like a skilled swordsman through the haze.

But now, all his tricks were played. Unless the jihadis pulled another surprise entrance, introducing a verifiable weapon or bringing in new players, El Moreno's time was running out. He couldn't figure it out. The Pope, the children, and a few crates filled with blankets, clothing and hand soap. What the hell were they doing?

———————

Felix watched El Moreno out of the corner of his eye. He'd hoped to have been rid of the man by then, but the little Mexican insisted on escorting them to the mission's successful completion. It was what he said, but Felix knew that the only thing El Moreno wanted was more money and whatever weapons the jihadis intended to use. Little did he know that the three-headed dragon was not something you could easily bottle and sell. In fact, the taste of success was so near that Felix had to bite his tongue in order to keep from throwing the truth in the cartel leader's face.

He knew better, and kept reminding himself that a noble holy warrior does not brag, but instead carries his duties out with solemn reverence. Felix wondered if that was how the heroes of 9/11 had felt as they crashed their planes into their targets. Luckily he wouldn't have to share their fate. His masters said there was more to be done, other missions that required his specific talents. That thought kept him moving, kept his mind from being distracted by the dangers and the toil. Hard work was not something that came easily for Felix. It had taken every ounce of desire to retool his urges and reshape his priorities.

During his teenage years, and even at university, he lived a comfortable life. When the call came to serve his people, Felix jumped at the chance, envisioning mowing down hordes of unbelievers and lopping off heads with maniacal fervor.

What he found was the exact opposite. Yes, there had been the excitement of the attacks in Acapulco, but then there were the hours and days spent planning and waiting. The waiting was the worst! Like much of his generation, Felix wanted everything done at the speed of the Internet. Push a button and the task is complete. Make a call and your chores were done. But not in the real world. As the leader of his small band, everyone looked to him for the answers. If they were hungry, they looked to him. If they were tired, they complained to him. If they wanted to talk, they talked to him.

It was exhausting work and the Spaniard couldn't wait to have some well-deserved time off when he returned home. Surely his masters would put him up somewhere nice. He had always wanted to visit Monaco. Maybe he could convince them that the wealthy kingdom on the sea was the perfect next target. Yes. The idea calmed him, imagining the lapping waves and the luxurious accommodations provided by a thankful people.

Felix's mind snapped back to the present, realizing that one of his men was asking him a question. The idiot still didn't understand the breadth of the plan, something he had digested easily. Maybe next time they could give him more than these simpletons. After all, didn't the hero who brought the world's Christians and the United States to its knees deserve the best?

———

The Pope moved his hands to increase the circulation to his fingertips. That was the problem with getting older. He assumed that a young man tied loosely to a chair would not feel the aches and pains that racked his body at regular intervals. It was a small discomfort, and he once again reminded himself that too many throughout the world dealt with far worse on a daily basis.

As he often did, he let his mind slip into prayer. These were not recited words repeated verbatim, but an opening of his mind, a search for peace and guidance. He was in desperate need of both in ample quantities. He also prayed for the same to be granted to the Brothers of St. Longinus, and the brave men sent by President Zimmer.

Through the darkness, and in and out of various modes of transportation, the Pope had listened. If he had learned anything in his life it was that the simple act of opening one's ears often paid higher dividends than the converse act of opening one's mouth. He'd accomplished much over the years by nodding his head and letting others do the talking.

But listening wasn't helping him now. The guards were tight-lipped and after the confrontation with his nefarious Swiss Guard, the rival leaders of the kidnapping party had been careful to say nothing in front of him. But they had left his hood off after arriving at their current location, and the Pope took to watching as well as listening. He noticed small things like the looks passed between the jihadis and the Mexicans. He saw the cool demeanor of the shorter Hispanic leader, and the darting eyes of the jihadi.

Finally, he caught a glimpse of the children. They were scared, and more than one of them stared at him in recognition as they passed by his open doorway. He did not know if leaving the door cracked was a careless mistake made by one of the guards, or a subtle reminder by their leaders. Either way, he would have given his life had he known that the lives of the children could be saved.

And so with nothing more to do, the Pope watched, listened and prayed. God would make His will known soon, of that the pontiff was certain.

CHAPTER 28

To say that the mood in the room was deflated would've been a major understatement. Every piece of the puzzle came together, and then *POOF!* it was gone. Hours of scouring every net they could think of had turned up nothing. Whoever this El Moreno was, the guy wasn't stupid. Cal tried to put himself in the thug's shoes, imagining where they could go next.

The good thing was that the enemy's options were limited as long as they stayed as a group. But as the minutes flew by, that seemed a fading reality.

"If I were him, I'd split up as soon as I could," Cal said, receiving nods from everyone from President Zimmer on down. The team leaders and the President were crowded into a makeshift command post they'd set up in a displaced Marine major's office. The career logistician had been none too pleased until the Marine colonel tasked with escorting the President's men told the bony major to move out.

"But where does that leave us?" Zimmer asked. "They could be hundreds of miles away by now."

Cal saw the strain on the President's face. He'd made the call not to raise alarms and now he would pay the price. Whatever had come through the border had the potential to destroy many lives. The good news was that it probably wasn't a nuclear threat. Zimmer had told them that the active sensors the Border Patrol and Department of Homeland Security had installed over the last decade were now fully in place. If anything higher than a trace amount of radiation came across any border or through any port, they'd know about it. That didn't make anyone feel better, but the risk of a dirty bomb made even the toughest warriors squirm.

"I don't get the play," Master Sergeant Trent said. "Why risk coming across the border when you already have the Pope? Wouldn't one of those death videos work just fine?"

And there it was, the thing that no one wanted to think about. If they were taking the risk, that meant there was more, possibly much more. That gave Cal an idea.

"Mr. President, what if we sent out sort of a toned down alert? You know, kind of like we did after nine-eleven with the truck drivers. One of those "Be on the lookout for" kind of things. Maybe an Amber Alert?" Cal said.

Zimmer nodded his head slowly. "What would we tell them to look for?"

"Tour buses, RVs, convoys, that sort of thing."

"It's worth a shot. When do we sound the real alarm?"

Cal looked down at his watch. "Let's say midnight. If we don't have them by then, let's pull out all the stops." He looked around the room at his friends. Everyone seemed to agree with him except for Brother Hendrik. He seemed more nervous than before, his hands clenching as he sat thinking. "Brother Hendrik, do you have anything to add?" Cal asked, hopeful that he might.

The monk looked up in surprise, as if Cal woke him from a daydream. Without answering, he shook his head and went back to clenching his fists, lost again in his thoughts.

"Cal," Travis said, "I think we should ask the Marines if we can have a few helos on standby. That way, if we do get word, we're ready to bolt as soon as we hear."

Cal nodded his agreement. "Top, can you talk to the colonel and see what he can get?"

"No problem," Trent said.

"And, Trav, can you handle the alert?"

"Got it," Travis replied.

"Okay. Let's see what we can find. Either way, in less than ten hours, all hell's gonna break loose."

As the meeting broke up, Daniel excused himself to take a short walk. The fresh air would be a welcome change from the cramped quarters of the last two days, and the sniper needed time to think. He felt his normal peace slipping and he knew it had everything to do with the fact that the Pope himself was in peril. Normally, it was easy for Daniel to push his personal feelings aside. He'd done it for years in an unhealthy way, but he now knew how to harness the light and the dark in his soul. Like his own personal Yin and Yang, harmony allowed him to do many things that his peers could not.

This time things were different. The certainty he usually felt about the outcome of an operation now felt like a shifting target. You take a shot and the silhouette magically disappears before the round hits downrange. It bothered Daniel more than anything had bothered him for years.

He walked past the MPs standing guard and stepped out into the Yuma afternoon. A few laps around the building might loosen things up, get his mind realigned. He started praying as he took the first step down the sidewalk.

As he rounded the first corner, Daniel heard footsteps behind him. He looked back and saw Father Pietro trying to catch up with him. Daniel stopped and waited for the priest, smiling when he reached him.

"Hello, Father. Can I help you with something?" In the last day, Daniel had seen a change in the priest. Ever since he'd recognized the Pope in Barachon's picture, there'd been more confidence in his step, more steel in his gaze.

"Yes. I was wondering if I could ask you a question." There were still dark bags under the man's eyes, but he now stood upright, his lips no longer quivering when he spoke.

"Sure," Daniel answered, glad that the priest had found him.

"Brother Hendrik told me about your plan, and I was wondering if I might be allowed to come with you."

Daniel looked at the priest for a few seconds, and then answered, "We'll probably only have room for operators, Father." He hated to tell him no, but there was no way Cal would let the priest come along, despite any progress he'd made. The best place for Father Pietro was right there in Yuma until the whole thing was over.

"Yes, I thought you might say that and I understand. But I have been thinking and praying, of course. I believe God wants me to be a part of this. I won't carry a weapon, and I promise to stay out of the way and help in any way I can."

His eyes pleaded with Daniel, not in a pathetic, "I need this or I'll die" kind of way, but with a fervent tone that told the world that he was going, and would do anything in order to board with the rest of the warriors.

"Let me talk to Cal."

Father Pietro smiled, and nodded his thanks. Daniel watched him walk away, his sure step punctuating the man's newfound determination. For some reason that made the way clearer for Daniel. The unease he'd felt minutes before now seemed to fade away, like Father Pietro was indeed part of the solution. He made up his mind. One way or another, he was going to convince Cal that the priest should go. Daniel knew his friend wouldn't like it, but the sniper had plenty of chips stocked up to ask for this one favor. After all, when was the last time Daniel's call hadn't resulted in a win?

CHAPTER 29

The buses were running behind, almost an hour late. The drivers had called, of course, but that still didn't make El Moreno feel any better. After the snafu with the idiots at the border, his trust of independent contractors was at an all-time low. Part of the problem was that he was so far from his home turf. He'd already filed that issue away for later endeavors, planning to stay close to the Guerrero stronghold or using more force in the future.

He checked his phone again, frowning at the time. But then he heard a rumble. Less than a minute later, four buses pulled in front of the low brick building. They were of varying makes and sizes, and each one bore a different identifying logo or name. One was painted white and sported *St. Augustine High School* in navy blue writing. Another had a bleeding heart logo with *Marymount Catholic Church* painted in blood red over it. The other two buses were comparable, and all Catholic. Another similarity was that the windows were tinted almost black, so that nothing and no one could be seen from the outside. That had been a careful consideration for El Moreno, and initially he wanted to use tour buses. Felix had insisted on the painted Catholic modes of transportation instead. "More of a statement," he'd said. It was a little more hassle, but El Moreno's contacts said they could make it happen, for an increase in fee, of course.

El Moreno waved to the first driver and motioned to the back of the building. It would be easier to have the men load the cargo and the children there. While the vacant former shipping terminal was mostly shielded from prying eyes, it was better to be cautious, especially during this last leg of their journey.

As the buses drove to the back, El Moreno entered through the front door, his thoughts slipping back to his options. He hadn't found anything that could be used as a weapon, and he now realized that Felix had skillfully kept whatever he would soon implement to himself, at least until he was free of El Moreno. That would happen the moment they pulled away in those buses, any chance of gaining the upper hand on his rivals a fading dream.

He had part of his millions from the jihadis, but money had quickly become a smaller and smaller part of his expansion plans. Ah well, maybe they would do business again. And while he'd at first worried about the welfare of the children, seeing himself in their eyes at times, the pathetic weakness he'd once endured, his professional mind now saw it as a business transaction. Without the children, the remaining sum would not be paid. Despite whatever reservations he held about giving the children over to the jihadis, the thought of losing millions was worse. Once the final deposit was confirmed, he would take the money and walk away.

They'd been ready for the buses, so by the time he made his way through the building, everyone was gone or streaming out the rear exit. When he passed the room where the Pope was, he saw the old man still sitting there, watched by eager guards who were ready to be done with their boring duty. El Moreno nodded to them as he passed and picked up his pace. Getting the fifty-seven kids loaded into the correct buses would take no more than a couple minutes, but he wanted to watch the process. Maybe there was still time to extend their business relationship, one more chance to find out what Felix's plan was.

When he got to the parking lot, the children were mostly loaded. He noticed that the drivers were still in their seats. El Moreno waved for one of them to come out, but the man gave him a strange look and avoided his gaze. A cloud passed overhead, blocking the sun and shading the area in an unnatural dullness.

Something in El Moreno froze. His eyes swept the line of drivers. They either had their eyes focused dead ahead or were looking at their laps. He couldn't see into any of the buses, and therefore couldn't see his men who had escorted the prisoners on. Cursing under his breath, he just made it to the first bus, his foot moving up to climb the first step, his right hand on his gun at the small of his back, when he heard a voice behind him.

"Put your hands up, slowly." It was Felix. He could feel the Spaniard's glee even before he turned and saw the damn smile on the jihadi's face. There was an AR-15 in his hands, its muzzle extended by a suppressor, and it was pointed right at El Moreno.

"What are you...?"

The words disappeared as a quick burst from the automatic weapon hit him in the stomach. He fell backwards, hitting his head against the bus, and dropped to the ground, his vision beginning to blur.

Shaking his head before the real pain began, he felt rather than saw Felix grab the pistol from his back. He tried to push the Spaniard away, but his arms were like floppy tentacles, his fingers going numb as he attempted to save the weapon.

His stomach started to burn, and then his back went into tiny spasms, like someone had punched him in the kidney. El Moreno clenched his teeth and attempted to rise, his legs moving but refusing to support any weight. There was a tapping sound, and then muted gunfire that sounded like it was coming from the inside of a barrel. Then there were screams, children's screams, lots of them. They filled his ears and made him nauseous.

He was able to prop himself on one elbow, his vision going in and out like he was looking through some weird kaleidoscope. Men were being thrown from the buses, his men, he realized. Again he tried to stand, getting a kick in the back from someone he hadn't noticed beside him.

His head was bobbing now, his body telling him to close his eyes, to sleep away the pain that now ran up his back and down his legs, like someone had taken razor blades and drawn lines down the length of his body. He focused on the pain, like a screeching beacon he wasn't supposed to touch.

The last thing he saw before the light faded was Felix pointing down at him, his companions at his side, laughing at the fool they'd caught by surprise.

It had been too easy. His masters told him about the vast network in Los Angeles. There were apparently many followers who lived among the nonbelievers in one of America's darkest dens of sin. He'd only made one phone call, alerting his brothers of the men El Moreno had hired to drive the buses, and the Los Angeles-based jihadis had taken care of the rest.

They'd stowed away in the buses, weapons hidden but still trained on the hijacked drivers, waiting until the children were loaded. Then, once Felix had taken care of the Mexican, he gave the signal for the drivers and the rest of El Moreno's men were killed.

The screams from the children were only natural, but their extended internment, along with the sight of more weapons, silenced them soon enough. In one bold move, Felix had taken care of the head of The Guerrero Cartel, saved his masters millions, and secured their final passage.

After he was sure El Moreno was well on his way to hell, he ordered his men and the ten newcomers from Los Angeles to clean up any mess they'd made in the buses and to load the rest of the shipment. Each bus had to have the same amount of children and supplies. It was all part of the plan.

Once everything was loaded, all the bodies of the dead except El Moreno, who Felix wanted to leave where he lay, were placed inside the building.

Felix went back into the hideout, kicking open doors as he went. When he got to the Pope's small prison, El Moreno's last man was lying in a pool of blood, a single bullet in his head, legs still twitching. Without a word, Felix's man untied the Pope and led him out behind his leader.

"Put him in the white bus," Felix said.

His man nodded and escorted his charge to the appropriate vehicle.

Felix took a deep breath and entered each bus, bidding his brothers farewell. They knew the plan and would execute it as they'd discussed. There would be no further communications. The enemy could track cell phones and probably even radios. After they left, they would be on their own. If they were able to get away after their tasks were complete, their new friends from Los Angeles would take them to freedom. Should they somehow get caught, they were ready to die and the children would die, too. He hugged each man and told them he would see them soon.

Once his ritual was done, he boarded the fourth bus that would take him and the Pope to the most important destination. Felix tapped the new driver on the shoulder. It was time for the final show.

CHAPTER 30

Brother Luca scanned the precise report he'd just received from his men. Using the pictures provided by Brother Hendrik, they'd actually identified most of the bodies that'd been found in Mexicali. Just as their American counterparts had found out, the dead men were mostly Mexican criminals, thieves and murderers with long rap sheets. It was the lone white male who'd confused them all. The man had no identification and he couldn't be found in any of the international crime databases.

Then it had clicked. Someone remembered the missing man from the Pope's security team, the one who'd disappeared along with His Holiness when they'd landed in Calexico. Everyone, including Brother Luca, had assumed that the man had either been kidnapped or killed, his body disposed of separately. Again, the second option seemed true, but without any other leads, Brother Luca instructed the Brothers of St. Longinus to see what they could find out about the dead white man.

When the photograph was shown to the Swiss Guard, they recognized him immediately. They even supplied the monks with a name: Yan Mettler. The commander of the Pontifical Swiss Guard confirmed that Mettler was one of the men assigned to the small detail. It took a personal call from Brother Luca to pry the rest of the information from the protective commander. Due to the Pope's abrupt departure, and the pontiff's demand for complete secrecy, the Swiss Guard did not know the full story. They did not know, for example, that the Pope was missing. That detail flustered the career soldier and almost sent him running for the phone. Brother Luca calmed him down and explained that the Americans were helping in the search, and that it was imperative he be given any information the commander had on Yan Mettler.

Finally, the commander relented and read it over the phone. "Born in Zurich, Mettler was the only son of a single mother. She died when he was twelve and he was sent to live with his aunt and uncle in Berne. He enlisted in the army at age eighteen, and when he'd fulfilled the requirements for his current post, he applied. I knew the man. He kept to himself, but was a hard worker. No blemishes in his record. A shame to lose him, really."

He didn't know why, but something had bothered Brother Luca. You never knew the real desires behind a man with no attachments.

"Would it be possible to search wherever he lives, just in case it gives us any clues?"

That question got the commander riled up again.

"Is there something you are not telling me, something that should concern me even more than the loss of our Holy Father?"

Brother Luca didn't want to fluster the man further, so he just said, "Surely you wouldn't want any stones to go unturned, commander."

The Swiss Guard leader had grumbled, but promised to conduct the search personally. A return phone call came less than an hour later, the commander's voice speaking as if he'd just found a ghost.

"It was under the bed, no effort to be hidden."

"What was it?" Brother Luca had asked, his ears straining to hear the man's voice.

"There were old pictures of his parents, messages to friends, and a letter to us."

"What was it? What did it say?" He wanted to jump through the phone and shake the man.

"He lied. Somehow he hid it from us, from everyone."

"What did the letter say, commander?"

"He was a traitor, a wolf in our home."

"Get it together, commander! What did he say?"

Another pause, as if the commander was rereading the note.

"He said he had always been a believer, hiding under the robes of the Catholic Church, that he was a holy warrior, destined for greatness, and that the filth and corruption of the Catholic Church would lead him there."

For some reason that hadn't shocked Brother Luca. In fact, it emboldened him.

"I'm sending three of my brothers to help you. Would that be acceptable?"

The commander had agreed, and Brother Luca dispatched his men. Meanwhile, he had his investigative division dive into Yan Mettler's life. What had he done for the last three months, six months? They searched public video feeds and hacked into private telephone records. It didn't take long for a pattern to appear.

Mettler had mentioned the corruption of the Catholic Church, but Brother Luca assumed he had meant it as a whole, one of those sweeping statements that extremists make. But that wasn't the case. The trail led to one place.

"Get me out of this bed," Brother Luca barked at the nurse.

"But, Brother Luca, you should be resting."

"I'll rest when I'm dead, girl. Now get these tubes out of me and get me a wheelchair."

Fifteen minutes later, Brother Luca and four of his men, all heavily armed under their robes, stood outside the modest residence. One of the monks knocked on the door and a sleepy-eyed servant answered a few moments later.

"May I help you, gentlemen?" the young man asked.

"We would like to see your master," Brother Luca said from his wheelchair, where he was wrapped in blue hospital blanket.

"May I ask who you are?"

"We have a message from His Holiness."

The young man nodded, still looking at them warily. They were in the heart of the Vatican, one of the few apartments kept for high ranking officials, so obviously the visitors had already been screened by no fewer than three guard forces. The servant opened the door and escorted them to a sitting area.

"I can start a fire," said the servant, pointing to the fireplace.

"That won't be necessary," Brother Luca said. "Now, if you'll please wake your master. We have important news to relay."

The obedient nod came from habit and the servant rushed off to do as Brother Luca commanded. The monk wondered how he must seem to the young man, a shriveled troll surrounded by muscle-bound bodyguards, no doubt.

Five minutes later, the Cardinal Secretary of State of the Holy See, Cardinal Nofri Deliso, entered the room. He was a nondescript man, a bit mousy in the face, but with an average build. He had a scrap of hair above each ear and wore those thick black glasses that had gone out of style years ago. Despite his outdated appearance, the Cardinal had been one of the preferiti, one of the Cardinals known to the public to be a popular vote in the last papal election. He now held the post that oversaw the foreign policy for the papal kingdom. In short, he was a very powerful man.

"Cardinal Deliso, could you please ask your attendant to give us some privacy?" Brother Luca asked respectfully.

One of the Cardinal's eyebrows rose, but he nodded and told his manservant to leave the apartment. Brother Luca waited until he heard the front door close.

"I'm sorry to disturb you at this hour, but we have come on behalf of His Holiness."

The Cardinal's expression did not change.

"You did not mention who you were," the Cardinal said.

"We are loyal servants of the Church, Your Eminence."

"And you say you come with word from His Holiness, the Pope?"

Brother Luca couldn't suppress the gurgling cough that came up his throat. While he tried to calm the fit, Cardinal Deliso murmured, "You do not look well."

He said it with the air of someone who knew of such things, who had looked death in the face many times and now gazed upon it like a detached physician.

"I am dying," Brother Luca said, finally getting his breathing under control.

"What a shame. Now, what is it that you needed to tell me?"

The Cardinal's tone had a slight edge to it now, like his time had been wasted enough and he wanted the monks to leave.

"When was the last time you talked to Yan Mettler?" Brother Luca asked, sucking from the oxygen mask in his hand.

"I do not believe I know a Yan Mettler."

There wasn't even the briefest sign of recognition in the Cardinal's eyes. Brother Luca liked that. It made the joust more interesting.

"And what do you know about the Pope's trip to Mexico?"

"I believe he mentioned something about it, but I do not recall what it was in reference to."

Brother Luca nodded, and then looked to his companions. "Sit him down."

One of the burly monks pulled up a chair, while two more grabbed the Cardinal by his arms and shoved him into the seat. It was obvious that the man had rarely, if ever, encountered physical coercion because his face paled. But just as quickly, the fear was replaced by bluster.

"I will call the guard on—"

"Hit him. Once."

The larger of the two monks standing next to the chair connected his fist with the Cardinal's stomach. Brother Luca could see that the man hadn't put much force behind it, but the Cardinal still doubled over. It took him a minute to regain his breath and look back at Brother Luca.

"I wish I could have done that myself. Now, you were about to tell me how you convinced the Pope to fly to Mexicali."

The Cardinal's eyes flashed with terror.

"You can't do this to me. Do you know who I am?" He was trying to sound brave, but his voice shook like a child who was about to fall into tears.

"I know who you are, Cardinal Deliso, but you don't know who we are. Let me tell you. We are the Brothers of Saint Longinus, a very old and very secret order devoted to the protection of the Pope and the Catholic Church. I personally am a very old and dear friend of His Holiness. He saved my life a long time ago, and I will do anything to save his. Do you understand?"

Whether it was the men standing around who looked like they could beat him into a bloody pulp or the weapons they were now showing openly, the Cardinal nodded.

"Once I tell you, will you let me go?"

Brother Luca shook his head. Cardinal Deliso waved his hands as if the monk didn't understand.

"I do not mean to let me go, but to live out my life in exile. That I am willing to do as my penance."

Brother Luca nodded and motioned for the Cardinal to proceed.

Deliso ran a hand over his stubbly chin and started talking, "I do not have to tell you how contentious things can be in the Church. Sometimes I wonder how we have survived all these centuries, when man is pitted against man, priest against priest. We argue like old maids about scripture and policy. There are days when I would not be surprised if the Earth ripped open and the Church was simply devoured by the will of God."

He paused, and then chuckled.

"The Pope and I have known each other for many years. I would not say that we are friends, but we have learned to work well together. Much changed during the last papal election. Sides were taken and lines were drawn. I was the front-runner, the conservative who would bring back the traditions of the Church. It would be good to have an Italian Pope again, another sign that the Church was going back to its roots. But then a dark horse appeared and momentum grew. He was not a newcomer, but an unexpected addition to the preferiti. He lived simply, and professed to enjoy his life as a priest more than as a bishop or Cardinal. In my sin, I grew to hate him. He was elected in an overwhelming fashion. I was caught by surprise and the bitterness enveloped me."

When he didn't look like he'd continue, Brother Luca said, "What did you do about it?"

Cardinal Deliso looked up and shrugged, like it had happened so long ago that he might not remember the details. He said, "I travel all over the world as Cardinal Secretary of State. I meet with many governments. I forge new friendships and mend old wounds. That is what I do."

"*What* did you do?"

"The Islamic extremists will always hate us. I wanted a way to use that to strengthen the Church, to embolden God's followers to grow their faith. I was provided a contact here in Rome."

"Yan Mettler?"

"No, it was a code name, Gilgamesh."

"And what did you discuss?"

"Very little. He told me about the attacks in Mexico and that they were part of the plan. He said they needed the Pope in a certain location and said I could get what I wanted if I helped."

"And what location did they give?"

Cardinal Deliso put a hand over his eyes.

"Calexico. It is in America, just across the border from Mexico."

"And did they tell you what they were planning?"

"I did not ask."

"How did you convince His Holiness to go?" Brother Luca asked, barely restraining himself from launching across the short space.

"I did not have to do much. He came to me for guidance. He said The Lord had spoken to him and that he felt compelled to fly to Mexico. He asked me what I thought and I said that he should follow God's will. Because I know that area better than him, he asked where he should go. I told him Calexico."

Brother Luca's next question came out in a ragged rasp, "Have you had any more contact with this Gilgamesh?"

Cardinal Deliso shook his head.

After taking a few breaths from the oxygen mask, Brother Luca said, "Then that is all I need."

The Cardinal's eyes sparkled with hope. "Then you'll let me resign, spend the rest of my days in exile?"

"Yes." He looked up at the large monks. "Brothers, please escort the Cardinal to his bedchamber and help him pack his things."

"God bless you, Brother. God bless your forgiving heart," the Cardinal gushed, helped to his feet by the sentinels at his side.

Brother Luca gave his brothers a look and before the Cardinal could react, they whipped him around so his back faced the wheelchair bound monk, slammed him to his knees, and held him there.

Brother Luca bent over, placed his mouth right next to the Cardinal's ear and whispered, "Enjoy exile, Your Eminence."

Without warning, Brother Luca looped the thin garrote over the Cardinal's head, his aim perfect. It bit into the man's neck as the monk pulled on the wooden handles, even pushing with one of his feet in the middle of the struggling man's back.

He counted to one hundred, well past the possibility of there still being life in the corrupt Catholic leader. His grip loosened and his brothers caught the body, lowering it to the floor.

Brother Luca's breath came in gasps, the exertion too much for his failing heart and lungs. He managed to look to his men and say, "You know…what to do."

His chest felt like someone had lowered a thousand pound weight onto it. He clutched at his shirt, and then the pain left him, dispersed by his last dying thought. As he slumped to the side, he knew he'd done his duty, that his last act had been in the service of the Church and his good friend. For the first time in his life, Brother Luca did not fight and he let the light take him.

CHAPTER 31

Armando Ruiz took a tentative sip of the glass of tequila. Barachon said it came from an agave farm he'd acquired the year before, the former owners opting to stay on in exchange for a cut of the profits and their lives. His host laughed at that fact. Ruiz joined him.

Killing was easy. Anyone could be killed. What he learned from his years within the Mexican drug world was that killing had to have a purpose. While regular citizens might stare in horror at the television screen as the well-coiffed news anchor relayed the sad tale of twelve more senseless murders, Ruiz looked past the obvious. The deaths weren't senseless. They served a purpose. Whether a cartel wanted more turf or some upstart was carving his own claim, there was almost always a purpose.

Many pointed the finger at the Cali Cartel in Colombia and their infamous leader, Pablo Escobar. Yes, the man was a murderer, and yes, toward the end of his life he had become paranoid and killed needlessly. But that wasn't the whole picture. Ruiz had studied Escobar's rise, marveling at how the kingpin wiped out his enemies while winning the hearts of many Colombians. There were still towns that celebrated his memory, erecting wreaths and crying as if Escobar had only died the day before. The man was a legend, a model, both good and bad, of what a cartel leader should and should not be. So just like billion dollar corporations around the world, rival cartels studied their counterparts.

Ruiz watched as Barachon poured another round. It was the first time he'd spent time with the man and he could see how the man had gained his nickname. The former Green Beret was sure that his host could outdrink a man twice his size. He had the liquor collection to prove it.

"Do you think they will find him?" Barachon asked, making the sign of the cross, as he did every time he made mention of the Pope.

"I pray that they do," Ruiz answered solemnly.

The two men clinked their glasses together once more, each downing the contents without a wince. Barachon was pouring more as Ruiz set his glass back on the table.

"We should do this again, Armando. I like you. We should be friends."

Ruiz smiled, and nodded his thanks.

"Nothing would please me more."

Even though the casual onlooker might think the two men were good friends, what people might not see was the underlying tension. While Ruiz and Barachon might appear courteous and even brotherly, that was only a show. Ruiz had no doubt that the smiling man sitting across from him would not hesitate to put a bullet in his head if he knew it would benefit his business. The man that forgot that fact deserved to die. And as he often reminded himself, dying was part of the drug trade, a necessary evil to support the business.

So as he waited for word from his nephew, Ruiz played guest to his rival, his senses always alert, his weapon and his men always ready. Barachon was trying to get him drunk, but too many had tried that ploy before. Ruiz would not be manipulated.

As Barachon downed a solo drink, Ruiz's phone buzzed on the table. He looked at it, but didn't recognize the number. Curious and wanting an excuse to break from the drinking, he pointed to the phone and then to the next room. Barachon nodded, and shooed him out.

"Hello?" Ruiz answered, making his way out the door and into the sunroom.

"Ruiz?" The voice came in a rasp.

"Who is this?"

"Your friend…from…Acapulco." The voice was gasping now.

"Moreno?"

Ruiz heard coughing, and then the voice returned.

"Yes. I…lost him."

Ruiz froze.

"What happened?"

El Moreno tried to laugh, but it came out as more of a gurgle followed by a weak cough.

"They took him."

"Why tell me now?" Ruiz asked, still leery about his rival's motives.

There was another pause, and then El Moreno said in a whisper, "For the children."

Ruiz nodded his understanding.

"Tell me everything."

Less than five minutes later, Ruiz had five sheets of notes filled out in a small pad of paper. Even through his spasms and gasps, El Moreno's mind was focused. He'd told Ruiz about the buses, along with the names that he remembered. He told him about Felix, the Spaniard, and the video equipment that went unused. He even mentioned something called the three-headed-dragon, although he didn't know what it was other than some type of weapon.

"I am dying, Armando." The words were slurred, as if El Moreno had been drinking the same tequila as Barachon.

"Tell me where you are. I'll have them send help."

Another gurgled chuckle.

"No. They will find me when I am dead."

"But—"

"No." The retort was clipped but firm. "Leave me. It is time to see if this hell is real. Maybe I will see you there?"

"You may have to wait," Ruiz replied, not necessarily upset that man was dying, but still respectful.

"Yes. Goodbye, Armando."

The call disconnected and Ruiz exhaled. Now to see if the man was lying or not.

———

El Moreno looked up at the sky as he dropped his phone to the pavement. He was lying on his back and the position offered a perfect view of the clouds rolling by. The blue looked so blue, like someone had taken one of those fancy camera editing tricks and made it so only he could see through the lens. It reminded him of his first memory of the ocean, dark in some places, but azure in most. A tiny cloud floated by, for some reason its outline colored indigo.

He tried to move his legs again, but there was nothing. The pain was a dull throbbing, like his body was giving him a last ounce of peace, hiding the burn in his useless legs and toes. A breath in and a breath out. He noticed that he couldn't taste the blood in his mouth anymore, and wondered if that was because there was none left, or because he could no longer taste.

The thought flew from his mind as another puff of cloud meandered lazily by, this one looking darker than the others. For a moment he thought it would stop and hover down around him. Is that what death felt like, a dense darkness claiming you for heaven or hell? But the cloud passed on, once again revealing the startling blue. El Moreno looked at it one last time, closed his eyes, and then let himself go.

———

MCAS YUMA
5:20PM

Once he realized what his uncle was telling him, Gaucho asked if he could hold on a second so that he could put him on speaker phone. It only took a minute to round everyone up, including the whole TJG team, the monks and Father Pietro. President Zimmer stood with the rest of them, eager for news. Their low-level alert hadn't turned up a thing, and the deadline was drawing near.

"Okay, we're all here," Gaucho said, turning up the volume on his phone.

Ruiz rattled off everything he knew, including the two names on the buses that El Moreno had remembered.

"He wouldn't tell me where he was, but I'm sure your people can use this number and trace it back to him," Ruiz said.

"That should be easy," Gaucho answered, along with nods from Travis and the President. "Did he tell you what he thought they were going to do?"

"He didn't know."

"And you believe him?" Gaucho asked.

"I know it's hard to trust, but I do. Unless he's one of the best actors I've ever heard, that man is either dead or dying."

Gaucho looked up at Cal.

"Kids and supplies loaded on Catholic school buses. What the hell is that about?"

Cal shook his head, then pointed at the phone and made a cutting sign.

Gaucho nodded and said, "We need to get our assets in place. I'll call you when we have more."

"Okay," Ruiz replied. "Be careful. I didn't like that little bastard, but if these guys took him by surprise…"

"I know. Thanks again for the help," Gaucho said, ending the call.

There was silence for a moment and then Cal spoke.

"What did the Marines say they could give us?"

MSgt Trent was playing liaison with the Marine staff and said, "They've got four Ospreys and a few Predators on standby."

They already decided that traditional fixed-wing aircraft wouldn't do them much good. It wasn't like they could take out a target in the middle of California using smart-bombs. The long-range capabilities of the Ospreys and the intel gathering skills of the Predators would work for what they'd need.

"I figured we could go in one of the Ospreys, and they already have enough grunts to fill two more Ospreys. The colonel says they might be able to get their hands on some Marine Raiders."

That was good. Cal didn't have anything against the common Marine grunt, hell he had been one himself, but he'd rather have special operations trained troops for what they were about to do.

"Have them scramble all the Predators and give the pilots descriptions of the four buses," Cal ordered. "Daniel, call Neil and have him track down El Moreno's phone and then he can fan out from there with traffic cameras and his usual tricks."

Trent and Daniel left to complete their tasks, and the rest of the audience left the cramped room to head to the aircraft.

Cal nodded at President Zimmer and then met Travis's gaze.

"You staying or going?"

Travis grinned. "Race you to the Pope."

CHAPTER 32

Three Ospreys lifted into the sky, the one with the TJG men, the monks, Father Pietro and Travis leading the way. The Predators were launched minutes after they left the command post, and data was already being relayed on the screen in front of Cal. Just as everything came online, a new message came across his screen. It was from Neil Patel back in Charlottesville. Just as they'd known he would, the tech genius had found the location of El Moreno's phone. Cal clicked on the message and then forwarded the map coordinates to the command and control people handling the Predators.

The plan was to build a web with El Moreno's last known stop being the center. The Predator crews were pros, and the intelligence team supplying them with routes had years of experience conducting a search. If there was one thing that over a decade of war did, it was hone military output to a gleaming edge.

Two minutes out of Yuma, the call came over his headset that a Blackhawk helicopter full of eager Delta troops, fresh from weapons training on Santa Catalina Island, was heading their way from the coast. Cal told them to divert towards Los Angeles and loiter until they knew more. He received the affirmative and they kept flying north.

Neil's hacking found the first bus, the blue one. It had just gotten off of Interstate 8 in San Diego, and was now headed onto I-15 North. It was stuck in traffic.

Cal called the Marine first lieutenant on the second Osprey and told him where to go. Every team commander had the same ability to talk to Neil, so Cal was confident that the pared down platoon of Marines would have the intel they needed. With a pair of Predators hot on the new trail, there should be plenty of real-time data to go around soon.

—————

5:57PM

1st Lt. Greg Heron took the news stoically. He'd been surprised when his company commander had ordered him to choose twenty Marines and report to where they'd been training with the Ospreys the day before. Lt. Heron was even more surprised to see the President and his Secret Service detail upon arriving. Heron's Marines didn't have to be told to be on their best behavior. The grim faces of the assorted operators on the tarmac silenced them just as well as a screaming gunnery sergeant.

The details of the operation came from a guy in what Heron called "contractor gear." Basically a mix of kit, web gear and weapons that didn't match anyone else in the crowd. A lot like the handful of civilian contractors he'd met in

Afghanistan. He said his call sign was *Alpha*. The guy didn't mince words and basically told the Marines that the only people they could kill were the bad guys.

"There are kids on those buses and we are more than likely going into an urban area. I know a lot of you have done this kind of thing before, but this time it's not Iraqi or Afghani civilians that could get caught in the crossfire, it's Americans."

The plan was simple: locate the vehicles, and one Osprey would be tasked to take down each bus. They had no idea how many tangos would be in them, but what mattered was rescuing the children and securing the cargo. There should be enough firepower to do the job.

One of Heron's Marines raised his hand. The guy in contractor gear pointed at the corporal with an impatient glare.

"Is there anything we should know about the cargo, Sir?"

The guy actually smiled and said, "Didn't your drill instructor ever tell you that when the Marine Corps has information available, then, and only then, will it give it to you?"

The corporal smiled back. "So you're saying you don't know, Sir?"

A grin and shake of the contractor guy's head. "Now why on God's green Earth would a Marine staff sergeant ever admit to a Marine corporal that he didn't know something?"

This had finally broken the tension, and there were chuckles from the team of contractors, the Marines, and even President Zimmer.

The guy continued. "Tell you what, Marine. I'll give a thousand bucks to the guy who figures out what is in the cargo."

"And a weekend in Vegas?!" came a call from the other platoon of Marines.

The guy chuckled.

"If the President will sign off on it, I'll even pay for your date."

They boarded the Ospreys and took off into the dimming light. Lt. Heron didn't know why, but for some reason he felt better that there was a Marine somewhere in this hodge-podge command structure. As they turned West and headed for San Diego, he looked down the aircraft at his Marines and thought that they probably felt the same way.

———————

6:32PM

The Predators caught up with the blue bus as it exited the I-15 North onto El Cajon Blvd. From there it took a left on Park Blvd and left onto Polk Avenue. It pulled into a parking lot behind a stucco building. The operator of the first Predator switched to thermal video and zoomed in on the bus. Half of the seats looked full of white dots. Zooming in more, the video captured four more figures, two in the front and two in the rear, standing up and stepping into the aisle. As they moved, other items became visible as they swept over the white dots. Weapons.

"We have four confirmed tangos with weapons, five if you include the driver," said the intelligence officer looking over the pilot's shoulder.

The information was instantly patched to the Ospreys. The Predators took up a high altitude pattern. Luckily, the sky was clear of cloud cover and the drones could stay over the objective for quite some time.

6:40PM

Lt. Heron consulted with his platoon sergeant and told the guy in the lead Osprey, Alpha, that he was going to have his Osprey touch down a couple blocks from the objective. While fast roping onto a ship or tall building looked cool and they had the equipment to do it, there was no way the enemy could miss the Marine aircraft coming in. The Osprey and the Marines would be easy targets if they hovered in for insertion.

No. The better way was to touch down farther away and hoof it on foot.

He explained to the pilots what he wanted to do and got a "Two minutes," in return. Lt. Heron relayed the time to his Marines, who were already ready, but went to the task of checking the man next to them. More than one idiot had fouled up an insertion because a loose harness had snagged onto the edge of a bench or he'd forgotten to properly mount his night vision goggles.

There were no issues this time as they streamed out of the back of the bird. Weeks of practice had made it second nature, even to the least seasoned Marine. They double-timed down a block, the Predator guide giving Lt. Heron clipped updates the whole way. People stared as the Marines ran by, and some pulled out phones thinking it was another exercise. None of the Marines stopped to smile, following their point man as he weaved his way across traffic.

They got to the building behind their objective and that was when Lt. Heron realized what it was.

"Alpha, the objective is a church. I repeat, a Catholic Church."

He didn't wait for a response, his troops already taking up supporting fire positions. Once they were set, Lt. Heron bolted from cover with six of his Marines, the report from his headphones competing with the thumping of his heartbeat in his ears.

"Tangos are escorting prisoners out of the bus. Last tango is out of the bus."

Even as the words hit his ears, the infantry officer was seeing it.

"Get down on the ground!" he yelled, still running, toward the bus and the line of children being escorted toward the back of the church.

Everyone, the group of children and the armed men, turned and then time slowed. He didn't hear the screams of the children as they fell to the ground. He felt the recoil of his weapon as he hit the first man with two rounds in the chest and then aimed a little to the right and took his buddy down too. One of his Marines, probably Lance Corporal Brizinski, the rabbit of the platoon, sprinted by him, firing as he ran. Heron's eyes shifted right and saw two more men go down, but not before they got a few rounds off themselves, their fingers glued to their triggers as they fell back, bullets flying high in the air.

Sucking in air like it was an ice cold beer on a warm summer's day, Lt. Heron supervised the ensuing inspection. Three of the five tangos were dead. The two others were shot but would live, according to his corpsman.

The scene secure, Lt. Heron climbed onto the bus to see about the mysterious cargo. He found boxes of blankets, some hand-me-down clothes, and some containers filled with that commercial hand soap you see in restaurants. He relayed the information to Alpha.

"Are you sure there's nothing else?" Alpha replied.

"We can tear the bus apart, but there's nothing that looks obvious," Heron replied.

"Okay. Now listen. The cops are gonna be there soon, but our people will be on top of that. I need you to do me a favor. You think you can take the two tangos back to the Osprey?"

Heron looked down at the bad guys who were cuffed by the hands and feet but were receiving excellent medical attention.

"I don't know. They should probably get to a hospital," Heron said.

"If you tell me they're stable, we'll have time for that later. Are they stable?"

Heron asked the corpsman who gave him a thumbs-up.

"They're stable."

"Good. Now for the favor. How much interrogation experience do you have?"

"Not much," Heron answered truthfully.

"But you learned some either in your workups or at TBS, right?"

"Sure."

"So like every Marine lieutenant I've ever met, you've been trained to figure it out on the fly?"

"Yes, Sir."

"Great. What I want you to do is get them back on that Osprey with only the Marines you need and you know will keep their mouths shut, and find out what those tangos know. You think you can do that?"

It wasn't something he'd really thought about before. They'd taught him at Officer Candidate School (OCS), then The Basic School (TBS), and finally at the Infantry Officer's Course (IOC) that enemy combatant prisoners are to be treated by the rules governing the Geneva Convention. But somehow at that moment, he guessed that his instructors might be okay with letting him get a little creative.

"I'll do it," Heron replied.

"Thank you. Now get a notepad. Here's what I need you to find out."

CHAPTER 33

The Marine platoon commander was good. It took him less than five minutes to get the information Cal needed. He switched his headset so he was only speaking to the men on his aircraft.

"They just confirmed that bad guy number one did board the white bus. Bad news is that the joker who talked didn't know where they were going. In fact, none of the others knew more than where their respective vehicles were going. Another piece of good news is that the Pope is alive and he's riding with bad guy number one. Last piece of info: other than the blue and the white bus, there's also a purple and a yellow bus. They really went all colors of the rainbow on this one."

Cal looked down the line, expecting questions or comments, but none came. At least Brother Hendrik looked like his nerves had settled. Word of the Pope's current status must have been a relief to the monk. He hadn't said much since leaving Mexico.

"We'll loiter and wait for word. If anyone has a..."

His headset dinged, indicating an incoming message. The computer screen said there was another positive identification from the Predators. A purple bus was spotted on Interstate 10, heading northwest towards Palm Springs. Cal watched as the camera zoomed in. It was still too far to get a clear picture, so he waited until the infrared turned to thermal and the video cleared.

Almost identical to the first bus, there were white dots lining the seats on both sides of the aisle, the back clear except maybe for the suspect cargo. Lt. Heron's men had yet to detect anything wrong with the first batch of random goods. Maybe it was all a diversion. Go for the kids and sneak away with the Pope. Everyone on the mission knew it wouldn't look good if the Pope was killed on American soil. Cal had mentioned that to the President, suggesting that this could all be a ploy to align much of the Catholic world against the U.S., but Brandon shook it off, saying that his priority was getting the pontiff back.

Cal switched over to the frequency that allowed him to talk to the second Osprey with half a platoon of infantry Marines. "Longhorn, this is your baby. Use kid gloves," Cal said. He wondered what the hulking platoon commander would do. He'd proudly proclaimed his undying allegiance to his alma mater, the University of Texas when he'd tried to crush Cal's hand on the tarmac.

"Roger that, Alpha. Longhorn, out," came the thick Texas reply.

Cal didn't roll his eyes, but he wanted to. He had some good friends who were Texas Longhorns, but something about the big Marine reminded Cal of brand-spanking new butter bars he'd experienced in the Fleet. There'd been more than a little bravado in the Marine's tone before takeoff, like he was itching for a fight. He wondered if Second Lieutenant Meadows would act as cool as his fellow platoon commander. Hopefully he had a good platoon sergeant who would keep the reins on tight.

———————

7:22PM

Marine Second Lieutenant Matthew Meadows, "Hoss" or "Hoss the Boss" to his friends, punched his fist into his opposing palm. He could feel the battle coming. While he didn't have the luxury of a video feed like Cal, he'd still listened to the radio chatter. Sure Lt. Heron had done a tour in Afghanistan and the Marines seemed to love him, but Meadows knew in his soul that he'd been bred to be a warrior. He'd done his best to whittle down his platoon to those whom he knew he could trust, most combat veterans with at least one tour overseas. He felt the tide swelling behind him.

Twenty minutes later, the pilot gave the two minute warning to landing. Meadows stood up, his helmet almost thumping the top of the hold. The former offensive lineman for the Texas Longhorns bellowed, "Saddle up, Marines. It's time for battle."

The Marines didn't look as enthused as he felt, but he took it for nerves, something he rarely felt. He prided himself in his courage, his ability to jump into the fray no matter the danger. Somehow he suppressed a savage growl as the Osprey dropped from the sky, his insides burning with bloodlust.

Soon he would be tested, and deep down he knew he would never be caught wanting.

Two minutes later, the bird touched down, the ramp already lowered, and the Marines flooded out. 2nd Lt. Meadows led the charge, breathing through his mouth as he ran, his nostrils flared like a bull's. Just like with Heron, this bus had pulled into a church parking lot. The Predator jockies had already relayed the information that the cargo had been offloaded, and that the tangos were tucking tail and leaving.

That was all the better for Meadows and his Marines. The last thing any of them wanted to do was shoot a kid. Meadows tasted blood and realized as he ran that at some point he'd bit his own tongue. Maybe next time he'd wear a mouth guard, like when he'd played ball. He grunted to himself and kept chugging.

And then he saw them, a ragged group of four men carrying weapons headed back to the purple bus. They were probably a hundred yards away, the length of a football field, but Meadows didn't care.

"Get down on the ground, assholes!" he yelled.

They hadn't noticed the Marine until that point. The bad guys turned, leveling their weapons. Meadows fired first, almost laughing as he depressed the trigger on full auto. Against what his instructors had always said, but who the fuck cared when the shit hit the fan? He felt like Rambo, charging the Vietcong on another rescue mission behind enemy lines.

For some reason none of his rounds seemed to be hitting the targets, but he didn't mind. That happened in the heat of battle. Something in the back of his brain told him to lower the barrel, because most shots flew high. He was so intent on keeping his finger pressed on the trigger that he didn't even feel the three rounds crash through his skull, ending his charge prematurely.

——•——

Staff Sergeant Evans cursed for the second time. The first had been when his platoon commander opened his big mouth. Now the lieutenant was dead. Evans knew it wasn't his fault, that sometimes it was just your turn, but it didn't make him feel any better dodging the body of his former platoon commander as he rushed by.

"Corpsman up!" he shouted over his shoulder, letting off a controlled double tap from his rifle. One man went down. Three left. He heard someone scream behind him and knew that another Marine was down. Evans cursed a third time. He'd seen too many Marines die during his eight years in the Corps. "SAWs up!" he yelled, calling for the squad automatic weapons that were manned by some of the strongest men in the platoon. They weren't as big as their platoon commander, but they never complained about the extra load and they were always there when you needed them. "Don't shoot the church!" he reminded everyone. The last thing they needed was civilian casualties.

Evans heard the long rattle from one SAW, probably Corporal Drake firing from the hip. That devil dog could fire from the hip better than most Marines fired the SAW in the prone position. It was a beauty to behold. Sure enough, another tango went down. Two left.

By now he and his Marines had taken cover, leveling fire and maneuvering with their platoon mates as they closed in on the church parking lot. They'd done it countless times since joining the Corps, and now it was paying off. Evans saw another tango drop, the side of his face exploding in a burst of blood and bone before he fell. One left.

The last guy had found the best hiding spot, behind a heavy metal dumpster. Instead of poking his head out, he waited, and so did Evans. As his Marines kept the man pinned down, Evans focused on the edge of the dumpster. *Just give me one look*, he thought.

Tango Number Four must have been getting restless, because he shifted so that Evans could just see the outline of his shoulder. He didn't hesitate, taking the shot and knowing it would find its mark. At less than fifty yards, the Marine veteran felt it before he saw it. The man staggered out of cover just long enough for Evans to shoot another two rounds into the man's torso. Game over.

The four bad guys were dead. SSgt Evans was surprised to see two black guys in the bunch. As an African-American himself, he often cringed at the sight of so many of his race flock to the extremes of Islam. These guys looked American, while the others looked European or something. He ordered one of his Marines to take pictures of the dead guys and email them to Alpha while he and the rest of the boys headed to the church.

Getting into the church was easy. Rather than kick in the door or use explosives, Evans pulled out a set of locksmith tools. His father was a locksmith and at a young age Scotty Evans was picking locks all over the neighborhood. It was a good trick when you were messing with people in the barracks as a PFC, but it came in damn handy when you were looking for high value targets in Fallujah.

It took him twenty-two seconds to do both locks. He always counted, a habit he'd picked up from his father. His point man went in first, Evans right behind. It was pitch black inside, so they switched on their rail mounted lights. They'd come in the back way, so there were offices that were all empty as they cleared them one by one. Next came the modest chapel, a simple affair with that late 1970s style of wood and hard angles.

Evans stopped, putting his fist in the air. The rest of the Marines froze. He tried to focus through the heavy breathing and then he heard the whimpering. It took him a couple seconds to figure out where it was coming from, but then he looked down underneath the pews to his left. His flashlight illuminated a pair of eyes, wide with terror.

SSgt Evans lowered his weapon, so only the edges of his light touched the child. Then he saw there was another. When he knelt down, he saw more. Relief flooded through him. He had two kids, about the same age as the ones he was looking at now. He felt his throat tighten.

"It's okay," he said. "You're going to be okay."

CHAPTER 34

Cal nodded. He'd watched the entire exchange via the Predator feed. He'd seen the first Marine go down and now knew that it was the big Texan, who they'd already pronounced dead. There were three more wounded, nothing fatal.

Now that they had taken two of the convoys down and half of all the children were safe, things seemed to be falling into place. After days of failure, this felt like how things should be. Find the target and destroy it. Kill the bad guys and save the innocent hostages.

Two down, two to go.

He wasn't worried about the Delta guys. They did this kind of thing in their sleep. As long as Neil or the Predator sweeps could find it, he was pretty sure the soldiers would take care of business.

And as far as the complement of his Osprey went, there was no issue there either. He knew The Jefferson Group men personally, had taken down too many objects to count with most of them. He knew what they were thinking, and vice versa, without even trying.

The monks worked the same way and had quickly figured out their role within the team. Cal's boys would do the heavy lifting and the monks were called in to pinch hit. They were cool with that, and so was Cal.

The only wild card, if you could even call him that, was Travis. His cousin was obviously getting his kicks out of being part of the crew again. Hell, he hadn't lost that battle-hardened look since they'd met up in Mexico the day before. Travis was ready, and he knew most of Cal's men. The only thing that worried Cal was that Travis used to be the head man, the alpha dog, before Cal took over and Travis moved to Washington to serve the president. It wasn't that he didn't trust Travis, it was just that Cal wondered what Travis was thinking. It wasn't that Cal couldn't play second fiddle at times, but these were his men. Travis would never try to take over Cal's role, but Cal didn't want the former SEAL to feel like this might be his last chance at action and possibly do something a little too risky.

But as soon as the thought came, he brushed it away. Travis was a professional, a lethal operator who'd not only proved himself with the SEALs, but who'd also taken the warriors of Stokes Security International to a whole other level of readiness.

Cal caught Travis's eyes and gave him a nod. For some reason in that moment, his mind fluttered back to when they were kids. Especially the time when they'd gone camping with their dads, and Travis convinced him to sneak off for the day. They'd found a cliff to jump off of into some freezing spring water and Cal had twisted his ankle in the process. Travis half carried him back to camp and got a royal ass-chewing from his dad. That's how it had always been. Travis, the older cousin, coaxing little Cal to follow along.

Now the roles were reversed. Cal was in the lead and Travis didn't want to be left behind. He nodded at Travis again and looked back at his computer screen as another alert flashed in bold.

8:12PM

The Delta team ambushed the yellow bus just before it passed into Diamond Bar along the Pamona Freeway. Three members of the entourage ran ahead and stopped traffic using road flares they'd taken from the Blackhawk crew chief. That stopped traffic pretty quickly and not many drivers honked after seeing the three guys with guns, waving burning sticks.

Three hundred yards to the east, traffic ground to a halt. The yellow school bus was stuck.

Captain Bob Anderson watched from behind a tree as the driver of the bus conversed with his friends. The trick was to get in without hurting the kids. That meant speed above all else. Luckily, with more and more cars surrounding the bus, there was plenty of cover to get them in. He let time tick by. As a native of Long Beach, Anderson knew what happened when traffic just stopped: drivers got pissed and some of them would get out of their cars to see what was going on.

Sure enough, another six minutes later he saw the first passenger open her car door. Then the driver behind her opened his and stepped out, obviously asking the lady in front if she could see what the hell was going on.

Anderson waited until more impatient motorists changed tactics and then he signaled for his men to hit the pavement. Luckily, they were dressed in their most civilian attire. Even at close range, it would be hard to tell that they weren't anything but curious travelers.

Sure enough, his entire team made it to various points near the bus. Anderson took the lead, his weapons hidden behind his back. He rapped on the bus door. The driver ignored him. He knocked again, this time yelling, "Hey, can you see what's going on up there?" The driver shook his head and kept his gaze forward.

Anderson knocked again, this time harder. "Hey, I'm trying to get my wife to the hospital. You sure you can't see what's going on?"

This time the driver reached for the door handle, and a WOOSH sounded as the bus door opened.

"I can't see anything, man," the driver said, already starting to close the door. Anderson stepped in, one of his guys grabbed the door to hold it open and let in the others. The driver went down with Anderson's first shot. The next two took two apiece. Numbers three and four at least got their weapons up, but Anderson took down the one on the left and the operator behind him took out the guy on the right with their silenced rounds.

Another day, another dollar, Anderson thought, scanning the bus for more targets. All he found were the frightened faces of children.

8:44PM

"That's three of four," Cal announced. Somehow they'd done it without civilian casualties. With as many targets as they had and the landscape they were operating in, that was a frickin' miracle.

But, of course, they had the hardest one left. He'd purposely left that one for him and his men. The obvious reason was that the other three teams didn't know about the Pope. They knew about the kids and about the terrorists, but only the guys on Cal's Osprey knew about the highest profile hostage.

Again, everything was going according to their hasty plan. They'd gotten the intel from Ruiz via the dead El Moreno (the detail they'd dispatched to Brawley had confirmed the man's death, along with eighteen of his people), and now they were taking the rogue buses out one by one. It was methodical, like knocking down dominoes one at a time.

That didn't mean they'd come out smelling like roses. They already lost one Marine and there were more wounded, not to mention the trauma those poor kids were going through. Add to that they still didn't know the jihadis' true motives. It could all be for show, just to prove that they could get their hands on someone like the Pope and take him through a porous border into the U.S., but why? There had to be a reason. These clowns never did anything without a reason, whether it was to induce fear, subjugate a population, or just wreak havoc. All you had to do was look in the dictionary. The definition of terrorism was *the use of violence and intimidation in the pursuit of political aims.*

That's what people didn't get. There was always a motive, and Cal never forgot that.

As he watched the computer screen and listened to the ongoing chatter over the waves, he wondered what those motives might be, and if they were in time to hold off the potential killing blow.

CHAPTER 35

Kathy Anday-Fallenius was just wrapping up her work when she heard the rectory's doorbell ring. She was the last one there, thanks to the upcoming community bridge tournament. It was an annual affair and, as the resident bridge expert, Kathy always had a hand in it.

Her church was in a safe part of town, nothing like some of the neighborhoods she'd visited doing mission work in nearby Phoenix. Even so, she was always careful. Her husband had taught her that, God rest his soul.

The bell rang again as she hurried to see who was at the door. Probably some poor congregant looking for a late night visit with the priest. But Father Gerald had gone home, so that meant she'd have to either call him or somehow figure out a way to help. She hated turning away those in need.

She could see whoever was at the door go to press the doorbell again, but he checked his hand when he saw her. He waved and she waved back. She saw a white school bus in the parking lot behind him, but she couldn't make out the name on the side.

Kathy unbolted the door and cracked it open.

"May I help you?" she asked.

"I am sorry to disturb you at this hour, Ma'am, but we have half a bus full of kids the diocese got from the border." The man spoke reverently and he had a slight accent. But accents were common in Arizona, where much of the population was Hispanic. He stood a respectable distance from her, his hands clasped in front of his body.

"And the diocese told you to bring the children here?" Kathy asked. She hadn't heard anything about it. It wasn't like Father Gerald to drop the ball on something so important.

"Yes. Here is a letter with instructions." The man handed her a rolled parchment. "We also have supplies and money to get the children settled, at least until we can find them permanent homes."

"Are they all orphans?"

The man nodded gravely. "Many parents will do anything to see that their children have a chance to live better lives than what the south can provide."

Kathy understood. The church often played host to displaced families and even had a program dedicated to helping illegals get their citizenship. There were many in need, and Kathy knew you only had to look in order to find them.

"Let me call Father Gerald and make sure we can—"

"Please," the man said. "The children are tired and hungry. Many need to use the bathroom. Can we bring them in now and you can call your priest as we unload everything?"

Kathy wanted to do the right thing. What could it hurt? Maybe the diocese hadn't called Father Gerald. Maybe it was all one big mistake. Or maybe this was the miracle she'd been praying for. She was only in her early fifties and she'd never had children. Maybe God could bless her and one of those orphans on the bus.

"You're right," she said. "Bring them in. We can set them up in the choir room for now."

The man smiled and ran back to the bus.

Kathy couldn't help staring. She somehow kept the tears from falling as she watched the nineteen children file in. Their eyes were wide, like they'd been through the most horrific journey imaginable. She estimated that the youngest was probably three and the oldest was twelve or thirteen. No one made direct eye contact with her. Kathy could understand that too. She was a stranger and they were far from home.

They took turns using the various bathrooms in the church. While she supervised the children, the five men from the bus unloaded the supplies. There were boxes of used clothing (a blessing because Kathy knew the church didn't have enough for nineteen children), blankets and sleeping mats. There were even a couple cases of bathroom soap. She was familiar with them because they were the same brand she sometimes replaced in the bathrooms. Kathy asked the man in charge about the soap and he only shrugged and said, "I think it was some kind of surplus. I'll make sure my volunteers install them before we leave."

She almost stopped them, but what could it hurt? Although the church did well financially, they were always looking for better ways to cut costs and keep down spending. Because she wrote most of the checks for the monthly bills, Kathy knew they were buying that same soap for anywhere between ten and twenty five dollars apiece. Having a couple extra cases would save them a few hundred dollars, and that was a good thing.

Once the children were settled, the supplies were stacked neatly in the hall, and the soap dispensers replenished (luckily she'd remembered to have them save the old ones and put them in the supply closet), the man with the accent said farewell.

"God bless you for what you're doing," Kathy said to him as he turned to go.

He looked back and gave her a funny little smile, then nodded and got back on the bus.

Kathy waved her goodbye and then realized that she hadn't called Father Gerald. The delivery would be all anyone would talk about for the next five years. What a wonderful opportunity to help those poor children.

———◆———

Felix smiled as the bus pulled out of the church parking lot. He could only assume that the rest of the deliveries had gone according to plan. Even if one hadn't, the others would easily make up for it. From what his masters had told him, it would only take one to be a success. If more than one succeeded, so much better.

The dominoes were about to fall. All he needed to do was tip that first one over.

CHAPTER 36

Cal read the note on the screen. It sent cold tendrils snaking up his back. The jihadis had planned well. The Delta team was the first to discover the letter. An almost identical one had now been found at the two other scenes. They each had the proper seal from the corresponding archdiocese of the given church This had the markings of the Archdiocese of Los Angeles. Cal read it again.

Due to the increasing pressures placed on parishes along the Mexican border, the Church has tasked us with placing these children within our own archdiocese. As we are sure your parishioners will understand, this is a noble cause as these children deserve nothing less than our enthusiastic assistance.

As the volunteer team will tell you, the archdiocese had also included a shipment of supplies to get things started. You should also be given a thousand dollars for discretionary spending for the initial care of these young orphans. Please ensure that you use these supplies, as they were donated by loving supporters who would like nothing more than for them to be utilized.

Follow-up instructions will be provided within the coming days. Should you need immediate assistance, please call...

They'd checked and the phone numbers matched except for the very last number. A convenient oversight, and one that would be ignored by whoever they might find on their late night delivery.

The bastards had even done that part right. By taking the children in at night, they were almost assured an easy drop-off. The guy Lt. Heron had interrogated even told them that should they find no one at their designated church, they were to break into the building, stash the kids in a secure room, and lock them in. A call would be placed, and someone would show up to find them.

Simple.

So what was their goal? No one had found anything. The kids were getting a thorough check, and so far, other than the obvious exhaustion and fear, they were good. Travis had suggested that they get the rest of the supplies to a HAZMAT facility for inspection, and the first shipment had just arrived. Travis told the commander of the team of experts to comb every thread of those blankets and to put any other work aside until it was done.

Things were rolling, blocks were being checked, but they still didn't have the last bus or the Pope.

Cal tapped his cousin on the arm to get his attention. "Trav, can you figure out a way to alert the Catholic churches in California, Arizona and Nevada?"

"Sure. What do you want me to tell them?"

"Just tell them to contact us once they get the children. Don't freak them out, but give 'em a story about how we're the follow-up crew or something. You've been in Washington long enough to come up with a bullshit cover."

Travis rolled his eyes, but nodded.

As his cousin got working, Cal's eyes went back to the computer. He reread the letter again. There had to be something he was missing, a coded message, anything that could help him figure out what this was all about. Until that happened, the Pope was still down there somewhere, carted along by the twisted machinations of the Spanish jihadis.

OUR LADY OF JOY CATHOLIC CHURCH
CAREFREE, ARIZONA
9:25PM

The bus pulled into the empty parking lot and Felix got his first view of the Church complex. There were seven buildings that made up the church and corresponding preschool. While there were similarities to the Catholic places of worship he'd seen in Spain, this one and the others he'd chosen in America just seemed different. Whether it was the affluent culture or the fact that his skin crawled at being so close to the belly of the beast, Felix didn't like it. The fact that it made him uncomfortable pushed him farther. If he'd learned anything from this journey, it was that service to his faith required periods of extended discomfort, like Allah was testing him each step of the way, daring him to fail, to quit, to show weakness.

But Felix was too far along for that. The blasphemer in the seat across from him was proof of Felix's newfound faith. The way he rationalized it was that if his faith wasn't strong, if he hadn't pushed himself and his men to the edge, then surely this prize would not be sitting there with blank eyes like he was looking through a haze.

When the bus stopped, he and his remaining four men got out with the Pope in between them. Their weapons were hidden but ready. It wasn't hard to break into the front door and disable the alarm. Apparently his new companions from Los Angeles had ample experience in such things.

Felix had studied the blueprints of the church and knew exactly where to go. When they got to the worship space, they marched straight to the altar. A wooden cross with a wreath hanging over the crosspiece greeted them. Felix tore down the wreath and threw it into the pews.

"Get him changed," Felix ordered, setting a pair of duffle bags on the floor. He unzipped one, grabbed a mass of white from inside and tossed it to one of the men. "Make sure he puts it all on. If he doesn't, do it for him."

The man nodded and took their prisoner to the side. There would be no bathroom privacy for the holy man. He would change right there in front of his enemies.

As the Pope stripped himself down and discarded his former disguise, Felix and the others set about organizing their own cargo. Tripods were erected and bulbs were screwed in. Once they were done, Felix checked the equipment. It all worked.

"Get him on the cross while I get ready," Felix said, grabbing a pile of neatly folded clothing out of one of the bags. He made his way to a side room to get changed. No need to expose himself to the man who would soon be burning in hell. That would be bad luck, Felix thought, going over the rehearsed lines in his head as he closed the door.

———

SOUTHWEST ARIZONA AIRSPACE
9:34PM

Travis took the call, listening intently as the Secret Service agent on the other end relayed the information.

"Got it. Thanks."

He ended the call and turned to Cal.

"We got a line on the last bus."

Cal made him a *give it to me* motion with his hand.

"The Archdiocese of Phoenix confirmed that a white bus dropped off nineteen kids and supplies just after eight-thirty. The kids are safe and another team is headed that way to secure the scene."

"I'm glad you suggested drifting into Arizona. How far do you think we are from its last confirmed location?" Cal asked.

Travis pulled up a map on his laptop and did some quick math.

"I'd say twenty minutes, thirty max. The pilots could tell us for sure."

Cal nodded.

"Give them the location and tell them to get us there as fast as we can."

Travis got up and made his way to the cockpit. Not for the first time, he wondered if they would get to the Pope in time.

CHAPTER 37

Felix checked himself in the mirror. Everything had to be perfect. Nothing could be visible just in case his identity was revealed. He was even wearing mirrored sunglasses over his balaclava. Not a sliver of skin was showing, just the way they'd trained him.

He made his way back into the chapel, strolling in as his compatriots gave him short nods of deference. This was his show and the others were just there to watch.

They had done as instructed and the Pope was now chained to the wooden crucifix, a fitting image for the camera. He smiled up at the leader of the Catholic Church, but then realized the man couldn't see the smile and he turned from the man's steady gaze. Something about it made him uneasy.

Felix pointed to the man behind the camera and the red light came on. It was time.

ARIZONA AIRSPACE

9:47PM

The Predators had been close before, but with the new intel, the net closed in. An alert flashed across Cal's screen and then the voice of someone in Yuma.

"Possible target acquired. Location, Carefree, Arizona."

Cal watched as the two Predator cameras zoomed in, recording different angles of the church's grounds.

"Target confirmed," came the voice again. Cal saw the lettering on the white bus parked close to the church.

"Thank you, Yuma. Please stand by," Cal said.

He pulled up their current location and measured the distance. Just under thirty miles.

OUR LADY OF JOY CATHOLIC CHURCH

CAREFREE, ARIZONA

9:55 PM

The red light switched off and Felix peeled off the balaclava. He felt energized, like he'd been plugged into a conduit that powered the universe. The words had flowed from his heart and he knew they would fly like daggers into the chests of the American infidels. They would pay for their sins.

Felix looked up at the Pope and said, "Now we leave you. Do you have any last words before I go?"

The Spaniard expected a spit in the face or a flurry of curses to rain down, the final heresy of a condemned man. Instead, the Pope looked down at him with sad eyes and said, "I pray that you find what it is you are looking for, my son."

Felix stared at the old man, words failing him. He turned to hide his embarrassment and barked, "Get your things. The helicopter will be here soon."

He made his final preparations without looking at the doomed man again. Felix would never admit to anyone that the look in the Pope's eyes haunted him, like someone seeing into his soul and finding his deepest fears. He shook the image away and headed for the door. It wouldn't matter soon. Felix was the one walking away, not the Pope.

———◆———

ARIZONA AIRSPACE
9:59PM

"Alpha, we have five possible tangos leaving the building," came the call from Yuma.

The report was unnecessary but part of the process. Cal and his team had been observing the feed and watched as the figures made their way out of the largest building, leaving one man behind.

"How long until we touch down?" Cal asked the pilot.

"Five minutes."

The men on the screen didn't go back to the bus. They crossed the road, running along the western boundary of the church, heading for the short runway. They'd been afraid of that. As soon as Cal had pulled up a map of the objective, the obvious outlines of the airstrip jumped out at him. When he pulled it up on Google and went down to the street view, he saw that the strip wasn't even surrounded by a wire fence, just one of those wooden railing numbers. The place was called *Skyranch at Carefree* and its website tagged it for what it was: a private lily pad for rich people. Minimal security and easy access. A perfect way for the bad guys to get away.

———

SKYRANCH AT CAREFREE
CAREFREE, ARIZONA
10:03PM

There was just enough room for the five men to squeeze into the helicopter. One more and they would've had to leave him behind. Felix only half-paid attention to the pilot, who was giving them a rundown of the trip out. They would fly low and transfer to a plane in fifteen minutes.

Felix heard what he was saying, but his eyes were glued to the tablet in his hands. He watched the live feed in the chapel, marveling at his mastery. In seven minutes, his people would have proof of their enemy's destruction. Once he arrived at his safe house, he would upload the footage to where some video expert would edit it, condense the timing, and send it out into the world. The part of him that still felt insecure about others' perception of him worried that maybe the videographer would edit his monologue. He hoped not. He'd meant every word and felt that they would carry much weight with the millions watching.

He smiled at the thought. Overnight he would be a celebrity, a shining example of what a holy warrior should be. He'd invaded the guarded lands of the enemy, piercing them and billions of Catholics in one fell swoop.

One of the others tapped him on the shoulder and he looked up in annoyance. He met the man's eyes and then saw him pointing. He followed the finger to where they'd just come from, the main church building. But now it wasn't just the outline of the top of the buildings, there was something else there, something Felix had never seen in person. It was one of those new aircraft, the ones the Americans were now using all over his ancestors' land. It took a moment for the name to come as he went for the door handle. *Osprey.* They'd named the aircraft after a bird.

"No, no, no," he said as he opened the hatch and stepped outside. "Get your weapons and follow me," he called to his men over the sound of the helicopters engines. They only hesitated for a second and then they were right there with him. It would be stupid to run right into the enemy, but if the timing was just right, Felix could watch their demise. It might even be possible to get more footage of the event. He pulled out his cell phone as he moved, clicking on the video camera feature as he eased himself back over the low wooden fence. It was a risk to stay, but the payoff would make it worth his time.

OUR LADY OF JOY CATHOLIC CHURCH
10:07PM

Cal listened to the voice from Yuma as he and half of the team burst into the church. They all knew where they were going and that the building was probably empty, but they still did it by the book, clearing as they moved.

They got to the chapel without incident, and then everyone froze when they beheld the scene in front of them.

"Mother of God," Gaucho said.

The Pope was secured to the upright cross on the altar, thick metal chains running around his torso and along the lengths of his arms and legs. To make matters worse, there was an assortment of contraptions on the ground below the Pope. They bleeped angrily, red lights counting down the minutes and seconds before the explosives detonated.

Cal didn't think, he just ran straight to the altar. The others followed him.

The largest digital display said two minutes when he got to the first step. He looked up at the Pope, who was thankfully conscious and fully aware of the peril.

"Get to safety," the Pope said. "They have my hands shackled and the cross is cemented to the ground. Save yourselves."

The Pope was right about the man-sized crucifix. Without a chainsaw, they weren't getting him out. By now Brother Hendrik and his fellow monks were surrounding the Pope, pulling at the chains in a futile effort to get their master free.

The explosives were chained to the bottom of the cross or else they would've just moved them. There wasn't time to disarm all of them. Cal was at a loss.

"You go," Brother Hendrik said to Cal. "His Holiness is our responsibility now."

It was a noble thing to say, but pretty fucking stupid in Cal's opinion. Hendrik was just gonna let those jihadis win. He knocked over the tripod with the video camera and stomped his boot on the lens until it filmed no more. There had to be another way.

MSgt Trent moved up to the altar.

"I think I can do it," he was saying to Gaucho.

Cal looked up in confusion.

"Do what?"

"Top thinks he can knock it over."

Cal looked at the cross and shook his head.

"Even if you do, you'll crush the Pope."

Trent met his gaze.

"I can do it, Cal."

There wasn't time to do anything else.

"Okay. Go for it."

Trent told everyone to move to the front. The rest of them would catch the cross, if and when it fell forward. The big Marine hustled around to the back and stepped far enough away to where he thought he'd have enough room to run.

"This might hurt a bit," Trent said to no one in particular.

To Cal's surprise, it was the Pope who answered. "I can take it if you can. May God give us strength."

Something in the man's words gave Cal a glimmer of hope, that maybe the idea of one man bulling over a six-by-six pole that was cemented into the ground wasn't so crazy. He found himself saying a prayer as he lined up with the others.

Marine Master Sergeant Willy Trent let out a war cry, and sprinted for the cross.

CHAPTER 38

He laughed when he watched the men rush into the chapel on the video feed. They had quickly seen the futility of the situation and that made him laugh inside even more. While it might have been nice to have a remote detonator, the countdown was good for the audience. Felix imagined that the video editor would probably piece together a few clips of the countdown, along with the doomed look on the pontiff's face. They'd gotten much better with their propaganda and this would set a new standard for decades to come.

Felix watched the operators as they tried to figure out what to do. And then he frowned when one of them knocked the camera over, and probably smashed it into pieces, because his feed went gray. It was a minor nuisance because he switched to the backup camera they'd installed high above the pews. It afforded Felix a nice view of the whole thing.

And then something strange happened. One man motioned for the others to move and he went deeper across the altar. The rest of the operators lined up in front of the

Pope. The backup camera did not have audio, so he couldn't hear what they were saying. He looked at the clock and saw there was one minute left. Whatever the enemy had in mind would never work, but the show might be nice. This part they'd surely have to edit out, unless someone saw the benefit of the last pitiful actions of the American weaklings.

Felix watched as the man who had been off camera a moment before sprinted back into the picture. The Spaniard pulled the tablet closer, his eyes widening at what he saw. He dropped the tablet on the ground, hoisted his weapon, and ran across the road.

———

10:10PM

They burst from the building with seconds to spare, yelling for the men outside to seek cover. The splintered crucifix, along with the chained Pope, was being carried by Trent and Brother Hendrik. Nobody stopped, their momentum taking them as far as they could get.

And then the explosion enveloped the church, shaking the ground and throwing them all to the desert floor. When he lifted his head, Cal saw that Trent and Brother Hendrik had somehow kept the Pope from smashing his face in the dirt.

Luckily the Osprey had taken to the air just after dropping them off. Now it was hovering somewhere nearby. Cal tried to radio the pilots to tell them to land, but something wasn't working with his headset. Maybe it was the explosion or just shitty luck, but it looked like they had to do it the old fashioned way.

"Gaucho, take some of the guys and see if you can signal the bird down. We need to get out of here."

Gaucho nodded and grabbed a handful of men, switching on his flashlight as he left.

"Does anyone have comms?" Cal asked.

"I'm down," Travis said.

"Me too," Daniel added.

There wasn't anything they could do about that for the time being. The priority was getting the Pope to safety. He wished he had confirmation about the bad guys. Having a bunch of jihadis running around in the middle of Arizona wasn't Cal's idea of a secure environment.

"Daniel, take some guys and make sure our friends aren't still hanging around at the airstrip."

"I'll come with you," Travis said.

Daniel nodded and told the others where he wanted them. As they went to leave, machine gun fire erupted from the road, followed by the thump of two grenade launchers. Everyone scattered and attempted to find cover. There wasn't much. The rounds landed and Cal heard grunts through the ruckus.

"I'm hit," said one of the TJG operators.

"Me too," said another.

Dammit, Cal fumed. Just when he thought everything was getting back on track.

He pushed himself off the ground and weaved his way toward the firing. Travis was a couple steps ahead of him, taking shots at targets Cal couldn't see. Daniel was even farther still, leading the small pack of warriors, four monks among them.

There was another barrage of heavy fire, and Travis spun around and fell to his knees. Cal pulled him to the side and immediately saw blood running from more than one wound.

"You okay?" Cal asked.

"I'll be fine. You keep going."

Cal hesitated, staring at the pained, yet determined look on his cousin's face.

"I'm serious, you go. I'll wait here," Travis said more forcibly.

There wasn't time. He couldn't even see Daniel anymore and the gunfire was picking up.

"Okay, but stay down," Cal said.

Travis gave him a wink, and then gritted his teeth.

"Get a couple for me."

———

10:13PM

Daniel felt it when he took the first man out. *Four to go*, he thought, slipping into his former self, the animal that he'd made peace with long ago, and now let out only when the situation warranted a higher level of awareness. Two more rounds downrange and he saw his target fall back.

Two down. Three to go.

———

10:14PM

Father Pietro looked around at the destruction. He'd been with the Americans when massive Mr. Trent somehow cracked the crucifix from its perch. The priest knew in that moment that God was with them, that He would see them through.

That feeling grew as they'd run past empty rooms and out into the night, crashing to the ground as the world exploded around them. Then he saw men go down, heard their steady voices announcing their injuries. Something in him changed. No, it didn't change, he went back, back to when he was not part of the Church, when he was an elite warrior sent in to do the impossible. When he was Gabriel Fusconi of the 9th Parachute Assault Regiment. The feeling enveloped him, like an invisible suit of armor had just descended from the heavens and sealed itself around his body and soul.

The monks were with His Holiness, so now he had to do what was necessary.

He ran, slowly at first, and then faster. He found Travis Haden, the president's chief of staff and Cal Stoke's cousin, and skidded to a halt. Haden was wounded, his face was pale, but he was still conscious.

"Hey, Padre," Haden said.

"How bad?"

"Bad, but I'll live."

Father Pietro nodded. "May I borrow your weapon?"

Haden looked at him in surprise, but reached for his rifle and a couple extra magazines. He kept the pistol at his side.

"You remember how to use one of these?"

The priest grinned.

"Always."

He checked the chamber out of habit and clicked the safety on then off.

"I must go," he said to Haden.

Haden grimaced, grabbing his stomach.

"Good luck," he offered.

PAPAL JUSTICE

Father Pietro nodded and ran toward the gunfire.

———•———

Felix hadn't expected the counterattack. He thought the explosion would take out most, if not all, of the enemy. Wrong again.

He fired an extended burst, then lobbed a grenade from the cover of the shallow ditch. His companions were still firing, so at least he had that. Maybe he still had time to finish things. He hadn't seen the American Osprey yet, so there was a chance that he could kill the Pope himself. It would involve martyrdom, but at least he had the chance to grab his tablet and upload the video he had. They could splice something together. The end result would be the same.

Felix said a silent prayer, gulped down his fear, and slipped across the road away from the firing.

———•———

It was two against two. Cal and Daniel leapfrogged from concealment to concealment, using what little of it there was, mostly scrub brush. Cal's trigger finger was ready when he saw target number one poke his head out. Two shots. Tango down.

Up and to his left, Daniel leapt over a short wall and into the street, no man's land. Cal watched as the sniper ran at a full sprint, obviously seeing something that Cal couldn't. Sure enough, a couple seconds later, the figure popped up, thinking he had the drop on Daniel. Bad move. Two shots from Daniel's automatic weapons, then two more.

Daniel kept running and Cal jumped up to follow. By the time they got to the other side, things were quiet. They found four dead guys.

"Where's the fifth one?" Cal asked.

———◆———

10:19PM

It was only a shadow that he saw. Instead of following the Americans, he went to the right, thinking that the enemy was trying to outflank them. His steps were steady as he stalked behind the creeping shadow. The weapon in his hands begged to be fired, but Father Pietro waited. He wanted to be sure.

———◆———

10:20PM

Felix got across the little side road without incident. He heard the firing stop from where he'd left his men and knew they were dead or soon would be. That was the price they'd agreed to. It looked like paradise would have more warriors to feed this night.

He pushed through the prickly bushes and stopped before he hit pavement again. Somewhere in the distance he heard the sound of the Osprey over the crackling of the fire that had now consumed three of the parish buildings. The light from the blaze illuminated the parking lot in a flickering glow, the smoke settling low in the windless night. The perfect cover.

Then he found what he was looking for: the cross surrounded by a handful of men. The smoke was closing in on them, and a few seconds later they were obscured from view. This was the best chance he had. He stood up and walked into the billowing darkness.

10:21PM

The shadow disappeared in the gathering smoke, but Father Pietro knew exactly where his target was headed. He didn't hesitate, fading into the fog, his heart pulling him forward.

10:23PM

MSgt Trent knew he'd dislocated his shoulder during the explosion. At least Brother Hendrik had popped it back in for him, but he was gonna have a helluva time carrying that cross again. Everyone was bloody and bruised. The Pope was good considering the situation. Somehow the guy kept his composure. Trent had to give it to him. Most civilians would've been crapping their pants.

The smoke was making it harder to see a damned thing. With the monks guarding their position, at least he didn't have to worry about protecting them anymore. As soon as they hopped on that bird again, he was going to take a deep breath of cool, clean, Marine Corps air.

He heard the Osprey as it bore in a minute later, the downdraft cleared some of the smoke in funny swirls that looked like little tornados.

"You ready to pick him up again?" Trent asked Brother Hendrik.

"I am, but perhaps you should have someone else carry your side."

"Nah, I'm good. Hell, we've come this far, right?"

Brother Hendrik didn't look convinced, but he nodded anyway. *Good dude, that Brother Hendrik,* Trent thought, mustering the strength to pick up his half of the cross again.

They got the cross upright as the Osprey settled to the ground, the crew chief stepping down the ramp.

"Okay, on three," Trent said, rolling his injured shoulder once. "One, two—"

The clatter of automatic fire cut through the night. All the weight of the cross was suddenly on his side. Trent looked over as the monks tried to find out who was firing, unwilling to level fire unless they had something they could see to shoot at. The smoke was still thick enough in each direction that even Trent couldn't see who'd shot at them.

Then he saw Brother Hendrik, lying flat on his back. There was a smear of blood on his throat, and when he moved his mouth, a gush of blood rushed out.

Trent almost dropped the cross to help, but then heard the Pope moan. He looked at the pontiff and noticed the dark stain on his right sleeve.

"Jesus," Trent said.

"He is here," the Pope nodded. A joke? "I am fine."

"Okay, this won't be easy, but I need to get you over to that aircraft. Do you think you can handle it?"

The Pope nodded.

Trent took two deep breaths and stood to his full height, the cross and Pope hoisted a foot off the ground. Ignoring the pain, the Marine Master Sergeant ran to the ramp.

10:24PM

Felix was fairly certain that he'd hit the Pope. There'd been a brief clearing through the smoke and he fired. Marksmanship was one of the surprising things he'd taken to during his initial training. He'd actually out-fired most of his peers on their final evaluation.

So as he moved around to take another shot, he knew he would hit something. But then he heard a shot from behind, and then another. He moved faster and then another shot followed by a searing pain in his leg. He screamed. He'd never felt such pain before. It felt like someone had taken a barbed blade and was thrusting it in and out of his leg. When he lifted his hand, it was covered in blood and he almost passed out. He didn't faint, but he did fall, his weapon clattering to the ground. How could a leg wound hurt so much? He'd always heard that chest or stomach wounds were the killers, the ones that took men out before they could be helped.

He saw the truth of the matter when he finally had the courage to look. Not only was his leg gushing blood, but there was something white sticking out of the side. It was his bone. For some reason he wanted to touch it, and when he did he screamed again. So this is how it would end, with a shot to the leg, a compound fracture, and his blood pouring out onto a church parking lot.

He'd taken a chance. In his head, Father Pietro pictured where the Osprey was, where the Pope and the monks were, and where his target could be. He took one shot at a time and then he'd heard the scream. When the recipient of the bullet hadn't returned fire, he quickened his step.

The man was propped up on his elbows, his right leg bent at the knee, and there was blood flooding out from his thigh. Father Pietro saw the bone and knew he'd somehow hit the femoral artery.

With no weapon in his hands, the man was not a threat. But when the priest's gaze settled on the man's face his eyes went wide, recognition stealing the breath from his lungs. It was the man from that night in Acapulco, the one who had ordered so many killed, the one who had killed Father Josef.

"You."

The man looked up at him. Instead of the stalwart conviction of a warrior, there was only fear in the jihadi's eyes.

"I'm dying," he said.

Father Pietro nodded.

"Yes."

The man retained a small measure of his dignity by not begging for help. Father Pietro could have put a bullet in the man's head and saved him from more misery. But instead he just watched, and he prayed that God would have mercy on the man's soul.

CHAPTER 39

Cal and Daniel made it all the way to the small airstrip before they realized the helo that was supposed to take the terrorists to safety was already gone. They turned back to the mess at the church and were careful to make sure the area was clear when they returned.

"Make sure the Pope is in the Osprey. I'll go check on Trav."

Daniel nodded and loped off to help the others.

Cal trotted through the smoke and tried to remember where he'd left his cousin. He called out, but Travis didn't answer back. Maybe they'd already taken him onto the aircraft.

He was just about to join the others when he saw a form a few feet away.

"Trav?" he said, walking closer.

It was Travis. He had his arms crossed over his chest and his eyes were closed. Cal bent down and nudged him.

"Hey, it's time to go."

Still nothing.

He shook Travis's shoulder and one of his cousin's arms flopped to the ground.

Cal put his ear to Travis's mouth. No breath sounds.

He put his fingers to Travis's neck, searching for a pulse. Nothing.

"Oh no you fucking don't," Cal said, setting his weapon on the ground and starting chest compressions. "Don't you die on me. Don't you fucking die on me!" He kept pressing until someone pulled him off. He punched whoever it was and went back to administering compressions.

"Don't die. Please don't die."

He pounded Travis's chest with his fist, once, then twice, and a third time.

Nothing.

His tears ran freely, splashing onto his cousin's placid face. His breath came in anguished gasps, his throat tightening like it was encircled by a hangman's noose.

And then, not for the first time in his life, Cal's heart broke.

EPILOGUE

The ceremony was simple, exactly the way Travis wanted. As per his instructions, everyone held a tumbler full of Jack Daniel's Tennessee Whiskey as Waylon Jennings sang in the background. The air was cool, but not uncomfortable, just one of those perfect Tennessee spring mornings that makes you want to grab a fishing pole and hit the water. Songbirds chortled back and forth as the tree branches creaked lazily overhead. It was a perfect setting for the somber sendoff.

Cal watched it all like he was in some crazy dream. He kept telling himself to wake up, but it didn't happen. It was all wrong. So fucking wrong.

The graveside service concluded, and Diane took his arm. "Are you okay?" she whispered.

He nodded even though he felt the exact opposite.

Cal and Diane led the way, followed by President Zimmer, MSgt Trent, Gaucho, Daniel and the rest of The Jefferson Group, and all of Stokes Security International. They came to pay their respects, to their friend, their former CEO, to a brother. They'd all lost friends and family before, but this was different. Travis was Travis. He was a SEAL who'd looked after them when Cal's dad died, who'd taken over the reins when everyone outside SSI said he was too young. He'd provided for them and cared for them. He was like a father to many of them.

They sipped their whiskey as they walked, some exchanging funny stories of things Travis had done or said, others retelling how Mr. Haden had saved their careers, given them a second chance.

It was a sad day for all of them, but at least he was resting at home on a private lot amongst fellow warriors, on a beautiful hill overlooking the day-to-day training of his men.

11:47AM

"How's he doing, Diane?" The President asked, sipping from his glass.

"He's not good," Diane Mayer answered truthfully. She knew she should probably sugarcoat it, make it look like things were going to get better, but that's not what she felt. Cal had barely touched her since getting back. He said as few words as possible to get through the day. She felt like she was losing him.

"Maybe I should have a talk with him."

"It couldn't hurt," she heard herself say.

"Okay," Zimmer said, patting her on the arm reassuringly. "We'll get through this, I promise."

She nodded a thank you and then excused herself to get some fresh air.

———◆———

11:53AM

President Zimmer watched his friend from across the room. Cal stood there and accepted the condolences, but Brandon could see that his mind was somewhere else. His heart ached for Cal just as it ached for Travis. He'd been the one to let Travis go despite the dangers. He'd recognized the risk, and also known the heart that beat in the SEAL's chest. He was a warrior first. They'd bonded and become something like best friends. They'd battled through the fiery streets of political careerists and built something they could both be proud of. A SEAL and a Democrat President. An unlikely pair who'd taken the world by the short hairs and turned it in the other direction.

He was going to miss Travis. He was going to miss their frank talks and their heated arguments. Most of all he was going to miss the man, the guy who would drop everything to come to the aid of a friend, like he'd done before getting killed. No one could have foreseen the tragedy, but this fact didn't make it any easier to rationalize the loss of this spirited man, a true leader.

At least they'd saved the Pope, minus some bruising and a minor gunshot wound. Relations with the Vatican were much improved. The pontiff had even suggested that maybe they could sit down and talk about The Zimmer Doctrine and how he could assist with bringing fellow religious leaders into the fold.

As for Father Pietro, the Pope had informed Brandon that the priest had taken his invitation to join the Brothers of St. Longinus. But he'd done one thing before doing so. With the blessing of the Pope, he changed his name back. Until he died, Father Pietro would now be known as Brother Gabriel.

And the mystery of the children's cargo had also been solved by an inquisitive CDC investigator. Embedded in each container of liquid soap was a clear plastic bag. The sack contained a biological agent that was still being laboratory tested. Initial results pegged it as a new highly contagious and fatal virus. As soon as the first unsuspecting person depressed the soap dispenser button, a needle would have punctured the clear plastic sack around the agent. The devilish soap-like concoction would have easily passed into the population, ultimately fulfilling the intent of the jihadi three headed dragon. As if America didn't have enough to worry about, now there were terrorists with mad scientists at their disposal, willing to cook up brews that could kill millions. Luckily they'd caught the bags in time.

The only unknown for now was Armando Ruiz. Gaucho and his uncle were trying to figure out a way to get him out of Mexico in one piece. Zimmer had offered anything he could provide, including protective services and immediate asylum, but Ruiz wanted to make sure the gains he'd made within the cartel world weren't wasted. Zimmer was confident that the man would find a solution.

Brandon moved across the room and cut through the crowd. They parted for him as he walked, most still in awe of his presence.

"Hey, you wanna take a walk?" he asked when he got to Cal.

Cal looked up and shook his head.

"Come on, Cal, a little fresh air will do us both some good."

Cal's eyes snapped back at him.

"You think a little fresh air will make this better?" The words came out slowly, like a sticky sweet syrup laced with poison.

"I just thought that—"

"You just thought that you would come over here and fix me, is that it?" Cal's voice was getting louder. Brandon grabbed his arm gently and tried to usher him toward the door.

Cal shook out of the grip.

"Cal, I really think we should—"

"You think we should what, go have a drink and talk about how much we miss Trav?" Cal slammed his glass against the stone wall behind him, and immediately Brandon saw blood on his friend's hand. If Cal felt it, he didn't acknowledge the wound or the fact that the entire room had gone quiet. He went on, his voice icy and sharp. "You never should have let him go. You NEVER should have let him go!"

Zimmer avoided the urge to look around.

"You're right I shouldn't have let him go, but that was his choice and you know that. He wanted to, so I let him."

Cal's chin hit his chest and Brandon saw fresh tears fall from his eyes. He said something under his breath that the president couldn't hear.

"What's that, Cal?" he asked in a half-whisper.

Cal's head lifted and he said, "It should have been me."

Zimmer didn't know what to say, so he just stood there.

"He was all the family I had left," Cal went on. "He was the best of us, better than me. He knew right from wrong. He knew what to do no matter the situation. It should have been ME."

And with that, Cal left the room, leaving only silence behind him.

———

Daniel followed at a respectful distance. President Zimmer and Diane were already outside, trying to get Cal to come back, but Cal wouldn't listen. Daniel knew why.

He joined Zimmer and Diane.

"Is he going to be okay?" Diane asked.

"It'll take time," Daniel answered.

"He said he was leaving," Diane sobbed. "He said I should forget about him."

Daniel nodded, his eyes watching as Cal took the dirt path that wound up to the private cemetery. Travis was now buried there. But it wasn't the first time Cal had lost someone special to him. He'd lost his parents on 9/11, the tragedy that had sent him running to the Marine Corps. Then he'd lost his fiancée. Jessica was also buried in the cemetery overlooking the 2,000 acre SSI campus. And now he'd lost Travis. As far as Cal could see, his world was gone. It didn't matter that he was surrounded by friends that loved him. For all intents and purposes, he was standing in a barren field bereft of love and companionship.

"I'll take care of him," Daniel said, stepping off the stairs and onto the dirt path below.

"You'll make sure he's okay?" Zimmer asked.

Daniel turned, looked at them both, and nodded. Then he picked his way up the path, ever Cal's faithful shadow.

I hope you've enjoyed this story.
If you did, please take a moment to write an honest review. Your reviews fuel this book's success and are much appreciated.

TO GET A FREE COPY OF ANY *CORPS JUSTICE* NOVEL AND HEAR ABOUT NEW RELEASES: >> http://CorpsJustice.com <<

TO SEE ALL BOOKS IN THE CORPS JUSTICE SERIES:
http://CorpsJustice.com

DID YOU FIND AN ERROR? REPORT
IT TO THE GRAMMAR POLICE!
http://www.corpsjustice.com/grammar-police.html

MORE THANKS TO MY BETA READERS:
Andy, Susan, Cheryl, Don, Karen, Wanda, Pam, Doug, Richard, Nancy, Kathy, Alex, Cary Lory, Marsha, Glenda, John and David: This novel wouldn't be what it is without your hard work. A million thanks.